Beloved and Unseemly

A Concordia Wells Mystery

K.B. OWEN

Beloved and Unseemly
A Concordia Wells Mystery

This is a work of fiction. Names, characters, places, and incidents are either the product of the author's imagination or used fictitiously. Any resemblance to actual events, locales, organizations or persons, living or dead, is entirely coincidental and beyond the intent of the author and publisher.

Cover design by Melinda VanLone, BookCoverCorner.com

Formatting by Debora Lewis
arenapublishing.org

ISBN-978-0-9912368-7-9

For my husband Paul,
always beloved.

Chapter 1

Hartford Women's College
Week 2, Instructor Calendar
September 1898

S ome might find it possible to sleep through twelve alarm clocks going off in succession in the middle of the night, but Professor Concordia Wells was not one of those fortunate few. She had no sooner pulled the covers over her head after the clamor of the first three clocks had stopped when two more went off.

Glancing at her own clock, perched on the washstand—two in the morning!—she groped for her robe and spectacles. There were bound to be more going off. Willow Cottage was uncomfortably close to Sycamore House, home to the male administrators. The sneering and cantankerous dean, Randolph Maynard, would not take kindly to his sleep being disturbed. Willow Cottage was already infamous for the number of disciplinary restrictions it had incurred last year.

Amidst the tinny bells came the sounds of shuffling feet and distraught freshmen voices directly over her faculty quarters. The hunt was on.

Mercy, what pranks would the sophomores dream up next? Better not ask.

In the dimly lit hall she all but collided with the resident matron, Ruby Hitchcock, also hurrying toward the source of the commotion.

"Oh! Beg pardon, miss." As if girding for battle, Ruby tied her threadbare sacque more securely around her short, squat waist and dug her feet into her homely felt slippers. "Barely back to school, and them girls start their carryings-on. We're in for a wild semester at this rate—" A fresh chorus of bells drowned out her next words.

Concordia took the stairs two at a time, no small feat for a lady of her short stature. She found Charlotte Crandall, bless her, already knocking on bedroom doors and rousting the sophomores. Miss Crandall was all too familiar with school hijinks, having graduated from Hartford Women's College only two years before. How her sophomore class managed to suspend two-dozen freshmen gloves from the rafters of Memorial Chapel was still a mystery to most.

Though radiating the composure bred from the rigid dictates of Miss Crandall's blueblood upbringing, the stubborn set of her jaw and narrowed brown eyes made clear her annoyance. As Concordia well knew, being a teacher charged with keeping pranksters in line is not nearly as fun as pulling the stunt.

The extra help was certainly welcome. Every female professor—except for a few senior faculty members—was obliged to live with the students in her charge, acting as surrogate mother and chaperone. The male teachers had no such responsibility.

"Why do *we* have to get up?" one sophomore complained, as she and her roommate shrugged on their wraps. "The freshies are the ones making all the noise." They exchanged a smirk.

Concordia folded her arms and glared as yet another bell went off. "I suppose you would prefer a cottage-wide restriction imposed by Mr. Maynard? That would undoubtedly make you popular among your fellow cottage-mates."

One of the girls made a face. "Can't have May-Not getting involved," she muttered to her friend. They hurried down the hall.

Concordia shook her head. The students had gleefully adopted the impertinent nickname coined by Miss Kimble, the school's new bursar. It was spreading quickly. Admittedly, it suited the dean. Many a *may not* had fallen from those lips.

At last, all fifteen clocks were retrieved. Most had been concealed in the four freshmen rooms, though Concordia and Ruby found one in the kitchen dustbin and another under the chaise cushion in the parlor.

Ruby shook her head as she switched off the last of them. "Right mischievous, these girls. At least Mr. Maynard didn' come stormin' down the hill."

Concordia twitched the parlor curtain aside. Sycamore House was dark. "We escaped notice this time."

Wait a minute. Was that movement?

A window in Sycamore House opened, and a man stuck his head out. Concordia squinted for a better look.

"Who is it?" Ruby leaned closer.

Concordia blew out a breath. "Never mind. It's Mr. Guryev, thank goodness. Not the dean."

"Whew!" Ruby said. "Well, g'night miss."

Concordia stayed by the window, curious. Guryev wasn't staring in the direction of Willow Cottage, but directly down, into the Sycamore House gardens. She watched him for several minutes as he peered into the dark. Finally, he withdrew and shut the window.

She went back to bed, too tired to remove her dressing gown. As she drifted off to sleep, she wondered how they were going to get up for chapel on time, since they had switched off all of the alarm clocks.

Chapter 2

Week 2, Instructor Calendar
September 1898

"Notebooks out, ladies," Concordia said, swiveling the blackboard toward the light from the long, leaded-glass windows. She could have switched on the electric lights retrofitted to the forty-year-old classroom building, but they had recently taken to emitting a high-pitched buzzing sound. Her head already ached from too little sleep. She smothered a yawn as she wrote out the writing theme due Monday:

Describe the three sources of persuasion
in Baker's Principles of Argumentation.

With a swish of skirts and the creaking of leather, the girls extracted their copybooks. Concordia frowned as she took a quick head count. Two juniors were missing. She checked the clock. Ten minutes into the class period. Both were Willow Cottage residents, and she knew they weren't ill. Sleepy, certainly. The entire cottage barely made it to chapel this morning.

Most of the students had finished copying and looked up expectantly.

"Has anyone seen Miss Lovelace and Miss Gage? No? Very well, we will proceed without them. Miss Smedley, come up with your theme from yesterday and read aloud to the class. Your clearest diction, please."

Alison Smedley, dressed smartly in a ruffled white shirtwaist and soft camel hair skirt, made her way to the instructor's podium.

As Concordia listened, she marveled at the young lady's progress since last semester, when her sulky lack of effort had nearly caused her dismissal. Charlotte Crandall had taken the young lady in hand, and Miss Smedley was applying herself at last. A change in room assignments had helped as well. Last year, Miss Smedley and Miss Lovelace had had the misfortune to be roommates. They were as opposite as two girls could be: Miss Smedley the product of an illustrious family, interested in literature, the arts, and the society pages; Miss Lovelace the daughter of a tradesman, here on scholarship, single-mindedly occupied in tinkering with all things mechanical. Each derided the pursuits of the other.

Concordia peeked at her watch again. Twenty minutes into the period. Where were they?

She saw the door open a crack as Miss Lovelace applied an eye to the opening. Concordia held up a hand for her to wait for Alison Smedley to finish.

"Nicely done, Miss Smedley," Concordia said, finally waving in the two girls. "I was particularly impressed by your explanation of Hibben's universality of consciousness as the primary postulate for inductive logic." Miss Smedley flushed a becoming pink.

Concordia watched as Maisie Lovelace pawed through her bag for a pencil and settled her skirts. "Do not get too comfortable, Miss Lovelace—"

"Oh, Miss Wells, we did not mean to be late," Maisie Lovelace interrupted. "Mr. Guryev was demonstrating Archimedes' screw, and we were building our—"

"Now is not the time for explanations, young lady," Concordia said sternly. "Pull out your theme and come to the front. And put your gloves back on, if you please." It was unsuitable for a young lady to give a class presentation barehanded, no matter how close to the new century they might be.

"Umm," Miss Lovelace said, her voice subdued as she tugged her gloves over smudged fingers, "I forgot...the theme was due today." A blush crept up her throat.

Miss Smedley smirked and several students tittered. Maisie turned a deeper red.

"I see," Concordia said. She turned to another student. "Miss Andrews, your turn."

The young lady stood and smoothed her skirts.

The rest of the period passed without incident, as successive students read their essays aloud. Concordia could not help but notice Miss Lovelace's distracted air.

Concordia had expected the girl to be ecstatic over the new engineering program at Hartford Women's College. Last year, she and her fellow mechanical enthusiasts had gone to great lengths to coax the college to start such a program, including disassembling and reassembling President Langdon's buggy in then-Bursar Isley's office.

It had seemed a lost cause. Finally, through a grant from the original foundress of the school back in its seminary days, the old gymnasium was refurbished, equipment brought in, and Mr. Sanbourne and his assistant, Ivan Guryev, were hired. Tonight's reception at Sycamore House would celebrate the new program.

Peter Sanbourne, the renowned inventor and engineer, was considered quite a catch. Concordia had not yet met the gentleman and only knew his assistant by sight. Sanbourne remained a recluse in his laboratory these first few weeks.

The appeal of Sanbourne's assistant was much easier to grasp. The girls chattered on about the fine form and dark good looks of Ivan Guryev. Concordia imagined his classes were well attended.

She glanced again at the pencil-fiddling Maisie Lovelace. Perhaps the girl was lovesick.

The dismissal bell interrupted her thoughts.

"Very promising so far," she said, with a nod to the student upon the platform. "You may finish tomorrow."

Concordia adjusted her spectacles and collected her books. She was not eager to meet with the lady principal, but their talk was overdue.

As the others filed out, Miss Lovelace and Miss Gage hurried up to her desk.

"We're so sorry, Miss Wells," Miss Gage said. "Cleaning up the laboratory took longer than we realized." She gestured to Miss Lovelace. "Maisie still hasn't gotten all the grease off her hands."

"Yes, I noticed," Concordia said. "Your laboratory sessions obviously need to be longer. I will speak to the dean about adjusting the schedule."

Maisie Lovelace's features softened in relief. "I *am* sorry about forgetting the assignment. This certificate program is more demanding than I thought."

Concordia slid her book bag strap over her shoulder. "I believe you are equal to the challenge. But I must have your essay by the weekend."

Miss Lovelace smiled. "I promise."

"Is there anything else you want us to do, to make up for our tardiness?" Miss Gage asked.

Concordia hesitated, her hand on the door. "Can anything be done about the electric lights? They make a terrible buzzing noise."

"We'll start on that right away," Miss Lovelace said enthusiastically, rummaging in her satchel for the pouch of tools Concordia knew she always carried.

Concordia smiled. "After the essay, Miss Lovelace. After."

Chapter 3

Week 2, Instructor Calendar
September 1898

David Bradley leaned against a pillar outside Moss Hall. The sight of his compact, muscular form beneath the rumpled houndstooth jacket and his lingering gaze made her heart pound in a disconcerting manner.

"Hello, Con-Miss Wells," he said, straightening.

Misses Lovelace and Gage giggled as they passed by. Concordia rolled her eyes at their retreating backs.

He drew her into the shadow of the deep doorway. After a quick glance to make sure no one was in sight, he placed a kiss on her inner wrist, just below the glove.

She shivered with both delight and alarm. "David! This is not the time or place, no matter how soon we are to be married."

He grinned. "Your satchel is slipping."

She made a grab for it, but he adjusted it on her shoulder, his hand lingering just a shade longer than necessary.

"You are not helping my composure in the least," she chided, stepping out of the shadows.

"That was my objective." His tone was teasing, but her expression sobered him. "Still anxious about your talk with the lady principal?"

They walked towards Founder's Hall, known simply as "The Hall" to everyone at the college. The library occupied the entire ground floor of the building, with the staff offices on the two upper floors. The solid gray stonework, set against the cloudless blue sky of this warm, early fall day, held the promise of permanence, of revered traditions. She sighed. She would miss it so.

"I should have told her when I returned in August. I put it off much too long."

"It is difficult to leave the job one loves."

She gave him a grateful glance. It was to his credit that he had come to understand her difficulty in giving up the teaching she loved in order to marry him. Although the twentieth century was nearly upon them, many refused to entertain the notion that a woman could derive her happiness from a vocation other than wife and mother.

However, her decision had been made, and the teaching had to go. She clasped her bag more firmly.

His brow furrowed in concern. "Do you want me to accompany you?"

"I'll be fine."

"Yes, of course."

The silence stretched between them as they approached the door to the Hall.

"Don't forget," he said finally, "we are dining at my parents' house tomorrow evening. Seven o'clock. You have yet to meet my Aunt Drusilla."

Her heart sank. *Mercy*, another relation. One gained an entire family, for good or ill, when one acquired a husband. She had not fully appreciated that fact before.

David pulled a slim book from a stack under his arm. "When she heard about our engagement, she asked me to give you this."

Concordia opened the book. *Manners & Social Usages,* by Mrs. John Sherwood. She frowned. "Your aunt believes I need *etiquette* instruction?"

He shrugged. "I am simply the book-deliverer. I am sure she means well."

She tucked it away. "Anything I should know about your aunt, besides her apparent fondness for self-help books?"

David hesitated. "I shouldn't keep you. Shall I call for you tomorrow at six-forty? We can talk on the way."

She was tempted to inquire further. Better not. One problem at a time. "See you then," she said, opening the door.

Lady Principal Pomeroy's office was next to Mr. Maynard's. Concordia heard voices through his partly open door. Perhaps when she finished with the lady principal, she could speak with him about adjusting the engineering students' schedule.

She smoothed a few unruly strands of red hair in her topknot, adjusted her lenses, and tapped on the door.

"Enter!" a high-pitched voice called.

When one first laid eyes upon Gertrude Pomeroy, it was difficult to envision the lady as an accomplished French literature translator and scholar. Her diminutive stature, fluffy gray-brown hair coming out of its pins, chubby cheeks, and bright blue eyes behind gold-rimmed glasses called to mind an aging china doll, albeit ink-stained and bespectacled.

Miss Pomeroy glanced at the clock as she gestured toward a chair. "Oh my, three o'clock already? Have a…a seat."

Easier said than done. Concordia gazed doubtfully around the room at the stacks of books and papers that rested on both furniture and floor. It was a wonder the woman managed to lay her hands on anything. She selected the chair with the smallest pile and held it in her lap.

Miss Pomeroy peered at her over glasses perilously balanced on the end of her nose. Her impatient attempt to push them back into place left them more crooked than before. "What did you wish to see me about?"

Resisting the impulse to straighten the spectacles herself, Concordia brought her attention back to the matter at hand. "I have come to give…notice." She choked out the words. "I will be leaving at the end of the semester."

Miss Pomeroy frowned briefly before her brow cleared. "Ah, so you have decided to marry that young man…what's his name?"

"Mr. Bradley. Yes. We are to be married in January."

"Well, then, I suppose congratulations are in order. We will miss you, dear."

Concordia gave a wan smile. "I thought Miss Crandall would be a suitable replacement. She already lives at the cottage, and her substitute post will be finished by then." She swallowed a lump in her throat. For a brief, selfish moment, she wished her absence would be felt more keenly.

Miss Pomeroy nodded in distraction, her eyes already straying to the stack in Concordia's lap.

"Miss Pomeroy?"

"Hmm?"

"Is there not a way...even though I am to be married...that I could teach here?" She clenched her hands, heart racing. *There must be a way. Please.*

Gertrude Pomeroy hesitated for a long moment. She sighed. "I do not see how. The board of trustees is very firm on that rule. Besides, there is no provision on campus for married couples."

"But the school has male professors who are married. They travel to campus daily from their own households in town. Why could I not do that?"

"I agree, but I have no authority to change the rules. Our women professors must be unmarried and live on campus in order to provide a nurturing environment for the students in their charge. The trustees feel that given the divided opinion our society already has regarding women's higher education—which you have no doubt encountered yourself—it is best that the school not undermine the traditional roles of married women."

"In other words, a woman's duties as wife and mother," Concordia said. Although she did not like it in the least, she had to concede Miss Pomeroy's point. More than once, she had met those in society, women and men alike, who considered women's colleges to be a hotbed for radicals, serving to glorify the unmarried state and create "unfeminine" women. Some considered academic study too strenuous for the female brain, even detrimental to a young lady's reproductive system. What nonsense. And yet, how does one change a belief?

Concordia stood and returned the papers to the chair. "I will let you get back to—" She broke off at the sound of angry voices in the corridor.

"One would think you had never kept accounts before." It was Maynard's deep growl.

"The method I propose is far more efficient. I am the bursar of this institution, Mr. Maynard. *Not you.*" Frances Kimble's voice was shrill in her agitation.

With a sigh, Miss Pomeroy got up and opened the door. "Not again," she muttered.

Concordia shook her head and reluctantly followed her out. If *she* had an office this close to Maynard's, she would rarely be in it.

The slightly built Miss Kimble stood in the hall, her long, thin nose flaring with indignation.

Maynard towered over her. "You are an intractable woman," he hissed through clenched teeth.

Neither of them noticed the staff and students poking their heads out of office doors along the corridor.

"You know that I am right," Miss Kimble said, hands on hips. She stood on tiptoe to meet Maynard's eye. "The old way is not going to work. We have too many vendors—"

"You may *not* experiment with our institution's accounting practices!" the red-faced Maynard bellowed.

"*May-Not,*" Miss Kimble muttered under her breath. "I did not ask your permission, you old—"

"Miss Kimble, Mr. Maynard," Miss Pomeroy interrupted. She gestured to the open-doored offices, whose occupants withdrew their heads in haste. "Perhaps a *quieter* discussion is in order."

Miss Kimble's dark eyes narrowed. "You may tell this…gentleman…that no amount of bullying is going to convince me to continue with antiquated accounting methods."

Concordia attempted to act as peacemaker. "I am sure that each of you has the same goal—the smooth operation of our school's finances. It is merely the approach that is under debate."

Maynard snorted. "The devil is in the details, Miss Wells."

"Can you not try Miss Kimble's method?" Concordia asked.

Maynard's brows lowered. "I am hardly inclined to take advice from a teacher who cannot keep her mischievous students in line. Or was that barrage of alarm clocks I heard in the early hours a figment of my imagination?" His lip curled.

Concordia bit back a retort. When would she ever learn? It served no purpose to step into the fray when Randolph Maynard was involved.

Miss Kimble jumped in. "If you had sufficient imagination, dean, you would agree to—"

"What in thunder is going on here?" President Langdon interrupted, climbing the last few stairs in quick strides that belied his bulk. "I could hear you down in the library."

Miss Pomeroy's shoulders sagged in relief. "There seems to be a...professional difference of opinion."

Langdon looked from Miss Kimble to Maynard and back again. "I see. Let us talk in my office."

Concordia left them to it. She had an etiquette book to peruse.

Chapter 4

A certain exclusiveness must mark all our matinees and soirees;
they would fail of the chief element of diversion if we invited everybody.
~Mrs. John Sherwood, *Social Manners and Usages*, 1897.

Week 2, Instructor Calendar
September 1898

The windows of Sycamore House lit up the evening dusk. Gaily colored Chinese lanterns greeted the reception guests in the entryway, along with strains from the student quartet playing in the parlor. A hand-painted banner with the greeting *Welcome Mr. Sanbourne and Mr. Guryev!* adorned the mezzanine railing. Within the ballroom, electric lights gleamed through sparkling leaded-glass wall sconces. It would be hot in here soon. Concordia left her wrap in the foyer.

A cluster of her girls had gathered around a man in the center of the ballroom. At first she could not see who it was, as he was only of a height with the taller students in the group. Then she caught a glimpse of longish, straight black hair, rakishly swept across his forehead. Ah, Ivan Guryev. He was attracting the ladies like flies to honey.

She went over to join them.

"Ooh, Miss Wells, have you met Mr. Guryev?" Maisie Lovelace asked.

Concordia inclined her head politely. "Not formally. A pleasure to meet you."

Guryev gave a deep bow. "The honor, it is mine." His speech was moderately accented. "You are a student here?"

Concordia suppressed an unladylike snort. "Hardly. I teach literature and rhetoric."

"She's also our teacher-in-residence at Willow Cottage," another girl chimed in.

"Ah." The man grinned. "But so young you look…." His voice trailed off.

Concordia knew perfectly well that, on the far side of twenty-nine, she was in no danger of being mistaken for one of her pupils. "One could say the same for you, sir," she countered.

The gentleman could not be much more than twenty-five years of age. His trim figure, smooth chin, and lively dark eyes set under heavy brows spoke of youth and vigor. He shrugged, a smile curving his full lips.

"How are you settling in?" she asked politely.

"The visitor quarters here are quite comfortable, thank you." He turned and smiled as a stooped, elderly lady approached.

Guryev smiled. "Ah, *Matushka.*" He solicitously adjusted the shawl over her shoulders and gestured to the group. "My mama, Nadya Guryev. She is here in Hartford this month." He leaned over and spoke quietly in what Concordia assumed to be Russian. She recognized *Wells* and realized she was being introduced.

The woman gave her a sharp-eyed appraisal before putting forward a delicate, bony hand. Concordia clasped it gently, afraid of crushing it.

"A pleasure to meet you, Mrs. Guryev." Concordia could see the resemblance, in the shrewd brown eyes and prominent brows, though her mouth had lost its fullness with age.

The lady nodded and answered in a torrent of Russian.

"What did she say?" Concordia asked Guryev in a low murmur.

"Sorry…it is difficult for her to speak English," he said. "She is confused by…a ladies' college. Does not understand the need for it." He gave a small laugh as Mrs. Guryev gave a nod and headed for the refreshment tables. "She thinks you should find a husband."

Concordia cleared her throat. A change of topic was in order. "Have you been working for Mr. Sanbourne very long?"

Guryev's face lit up in animation. "Eight years I know him, first as a student at Boston Tech when I come on scholarship. Then I become apprentice and decide not to return to St. Petersburg. Mama was not happy about that." His gaze strayed to the far side of the room, where Miss Kimble was helping the lady pour from the teapot. "After that, I was promoted to assistant for Mr. Sanbourne and Mr. Reeve, when they designed hydraulic pump."

"Hydraulic pump?" she asked, regretting the question as soon as she uttered it. More engineering talk was sure to follow.

"A mining tool. To more efficiently fracture shale," he said, gesturing in excitement. "Mr. Sanbourne, he is brilliant man. Unlike his competitors—they were working on same kind of device—he came up with a way to—"

"Where *is* our guest of honor?" a voice interrupted.

Her rescuer was Randolph Maynard, immaculately attired in a well-fitting black tailcoat and trousers, the white stand-up collar nearly to his chin. Instead of waiting for a reply, the dean peered down along his nose at her, his heavy brows drawn. "I did not expect you at such a gathering, Miss Wells. I thought your interests lay along the literary line." He dropped his voice for her ears alone. "When you are not sleuthing, of course."

She flushed. It was true she had become involved in some disagreeable matters in the past, and had even been helpful upon occasion. But really, Lieutenant Capshaw of the Hartford Police had done all of the hard work. She had been especially grateful for Capshaw's efforts this summer, when he tracked down the remaining Inner Circle members who had been monitoring her movements.

Still, she was in no mood to trade barbs with the dean, or to defend her sleuthing history within earshot of the present company.

Apparently Maynard had not expected a reply. He shook his head, gesturing to the banner and student decorations. "All this fuss for a *mechanic*. I fail to understand it."

Guryev bristled. "Mr. Sanbourne is no mere mechanic," he answered hotly. "He...he is a well-respected inventor. The Secretary of the Navy has commissioned a new project. That is why we need the extensive laboratory here."

Maynard raised a bushy eyebrow. "Indeed? Let us hope the board of trustees does not regret the expenditure. As I understand it, Sanbourne has only committed to being here for a year. The school's resources are stretched thinly enough as it is." He waved a hand toward the half-dozen students of the group. "All to suit the whim of young ladies bored with studying Milton and home economics."

The students in question watched the exchange in open-mouthed silence.

Concordia's own mouth hung open. She had never heard Maynard, in his eighteen months as dean, deride a student's area of study. To be sure, he was of a traditional mindset in terms of what constituted ladylike decorum, but this was something more.

"Mr. Maynard," a no-nonsense woman's voice broke in, "we are here to welcome Mr. Sanbourne and his assistant to the college, not heave pitchforks at them."

Concordia turned to see the white-haired Hannah Jenkins, who served as the school's infirmarian, basketball coach, and physical education instructor. Her plaid skirt and simple navy shirtwaist emphasized a trim figure that defied the relentless march of decades. Her ubiquitous coach's whistle was nowhere in sight. Perhaps on this occasion it would have been useful in keeping Maynard in line.

"The new program will be a boon to the college's reputation," Miss Jenkins went on. "Other students besides our own already benefit from Mr. Sanbourne's presence here."

Concordia nodded. She had heard that students at nearby Trinity College—an all-male institution—also attended Sanbourne's lectures here. Of course, the increased presence of the young men on campus necessitated additional protocols. One must not distress the young ladies' mommas, after all.

The dean grunted and stalked off.

Concordia drew Miss Jenkins away from the group. "What on earth is wrong with him?"

"Hard to tell with May-Not," Miss Jenkins said with a shrug.

Concordia grimaced. "Perhaps it's the friction with Miss Kimble. This afternoon they were both 'in a fine pucker,' as Ruby would say. Miss Pomeroy and Mr. Langdon had to step into the fray."

Hannah Jenkins grinned, emphasizing the deep lines of her face from hatless years in the sunshine. "So I heard. He does not like change, that one. Insists upon remaining in charge of the bursar's duties as well as his own until Miss Kimble does things his way."

"That may be a while." Concordia surveyed the room. No sign of Miss Kimble. Perhaps that was preferable. It would not do to have the dean and bursar sniping at each other at such a public event. *The better part of Valour is discretion*, as Shakespeare's Falstaff had put it, though she had difficulty picturing the tiny-but-feisty Miss Kimble as the plump and cowardly knight. The more appropriate Shakespearean reference might be *though she be but little, she is fierce*.

Perhaps she should have a chat with Miss Kimble. A bit of fierceness in dealing with May-Not might come in handy.

"They are a pair, I must say." Miss Jenkins broke into her thoughts. "I've wondered…could they have been acquainted before she was hired? The animosity between them strikes me as more personal—" She broke off, inclining her head toward the doorway. "The Sanbournes are here."

Concordia stood on tiptoe to see. After hearing about the famous inventor and his accomplishments for the last two weeks, Peter Sanbourne was disappointingly average in the flesh—a fortyish man of average height and a lean frame, with a thin, dark mustache and dark hair graying at the temples. A tall, blonde-haired woman stood beside him.

"Sanbourne is married? Surely they do not live here on campus?" Concordia asked.

"They have a place in town, though he keeps late hours in his laboratory, I hear. That cannot be congenial to his wife. Shall we go over and be introduced?"

As they made their way among the throng of well-wishers, Concordia got a better view of Mrs. Sanbourne. The lady was older than she had first supposed, most likely in her late thirties. Her delicately arched brows, thin patrician nose, and the elegant tilt of her head indicated a woman of quality and sensitivity. Concordia wondered if she would be lonely or bored this school year, a mere ornament to a famous inventor.

Miss Pomeroy stood beside Mrs. Sanbourne, making polite introductions, while President Langdon stood next to Peter Sanbourne and did the same. As Concordia waited to greet the couple, she noticed Margaret Banning attempting to engage Dean Maynard as he sulked beside the refreshments table. The elderly lady thumped her cane to get his attention. Concordia wondered if she would smack him with it next.

She grinned. Miss Banning had been teaching history at Hartford Women's College since its endowment more than twenty years ago. The faculty, having grown accustomed to her eccentricities and grumpy demeanor, usually let her have her own way. It was easier in the end. The lady had "retired" at least twice, only to return in some capacity or other. She was more than a match for Maynard.

After a ten-minute interval whereby Misses Lovelace and Gage monopolized the Sanbournes in conversation, with Miss Pomeroy ineffectually trying to redirect them—really, had the girls completely forgotten their manners?—Concordia and Miss Jenkins advanced to the head of the line.

"Mrs. Sanbourne," Miss Pomeroy said, "may I present our infirmarian, Miss Hannah Jenkins, and one of our literature teachers, Miss Concordia Wells?"

"Charmed, I am sure," Mrs. Sanbourne answered. Though refined, her voice possessed an appealing warmth.

"As am I," Concordia answered. "Have you been in Hartford long? Autumn in our area is quite beautiful."

Mrs. Sanbourne's light brown eyes crinkled as she smiled. "I am a landscape painter. I look forward to capturing your lovely scenery." She gestured toward the dark windows. "I have plans already for promising vistas to paint."

"A landscape painter? How impressive," Concordia said. *Not a mere ornament on her husband's arm, then. Interesting.*

"I should like to see your work," Miss Jenkins said. "Are any of your paintings on display in a local gallery?"

"Alas, I am too new at the endeavor for that," Mrs. Sanbourne said with a deprecating laugh.

"I have seen some of her pieces," Miss Pomeroy said. "They are quite wonderful. We have converted the old potting shed near the stables into a studio for her use."

"In return for your kindness, I have already told your lady principal that I shall be happy to work with students interested in perfecting their technique," Mrs. Sanbourne said.

Concordia, who could not paint the side of a barn much less a recognizable rendering of any kind, gave a polite nod and moved on.

President Langdon introduced her to Peter Sanbourne, who bowed with a half-distracted air, as if he wished to be elsewhere.

"A pleasure Miss...Wells, is it?" Sanbourne's hooded eyes assessed her with a glance, ready to move on.

Edward Langdon, who managed to rumple any suit he put on his large, pear-shaped body, smiled paternally at her. "So good of you to come, Miss Wells. I know engineering is not of general interest to you."

Concordia nodded. "True, but as all of the engineering students have been assigned to Willow Cottage, I considered it prudent to become acquainted with the man who will direct their work." She met Sanbourne's eye. "You have a wonderful group of young ladies, Mr. Sanbourne—eager and hard-working. I hope you appreciate, however, that they have other classes of equal importance?"

Sanbourne drew his brows together, puzzled. "Naturally—ah, you mean the students who were late to your class today? I heard about that. My apologies, Miss Wells. I shall speak to Ivan. He is the one who runs the experiments and oversees the young ladies' projects, along with those of the Trinity fellows."

Langdon frowned. "It was my understanding that *you* were in charge of their studies."

Sanbourne waved a dismissive hand. "Yes, yes, of course. I lead several seminars and will assess the young ladies' final projects. I am much too busy to involve myself in day-to-day teaching duties, however. My assistant is more than capable."

Before Langdon could respond, the maid approached. Two gentlemen followed at her heels and presented their cards to Langdon.

Sanbourne stiffened.

"Ah!" Langdon said, "Mr. Reeve, Mr. Oster, so glad you could come. I thought my surprise had gone astray."

A more disparate pair of men Concordia had not seen. Reeve was rail-thin and easily the tallest man in the room, with a dark, gypsy-like complexion. Oster, on the other hand, was light-eyed and fair-haired with a short, barrel-chested physique. Judging from his slightly crooked nose and the scar along his left eyebrow, he had spent time in the boxing ring during his youth.

"Our apologies for being late," Reeve said with a deep bow over Mrs. Sanbourne's hand, which she quickly withdrew. "Our train was delayed." He turned to Sanbourne. "Peter! It has been years, my good fellow. Congratulations on your new project."

Sanbourne reluctantly clasped the extended hand but said nothing.

Reeve's lip curled in what was either derision or amusement. "Where's your man, Guryev? I wish to congratulate him as well." He craned his neck to scan the room.

Oster inclined his head. "There."

"We will take our leave," Reeve said. "I, at least, am willing to let bygones be bygones. Good luck to you."

As they made their way across the room, Sanbourne turned to Langdon. "What are they doing here? Did you invite them?" His voice, though quiet, trembled in anger.

Concordia, meanwhile, was watching Reeve and Oster greet Ivan Guryev. As they shook hands, Reeve glanced back over his shoulder toward Sanbourne before pressing a slip of paper into Guryev's hand. Sanbourne saw none of it.

Langdon thrust his hands in his pockets and cleared his throat. "Ahem, well...I knew you had worked with Reeve and his assistant back in the day. Since the Boston Institute of Technology is only a train ride away, I thought it would be a welcome surprise." He hesitated. "I suppose I should have asked you first. I had no idea you and Reeve were on poor terms."

"Not poor terms, simply a misunderstanding," Sanbourne said. "Forgive my outburst. I was merely...surprised."

Mrs. Sanbourne waved an impatient hand at her husband and leaned in to whisper, "Of all the—!"

Sanbourne made a *shushing* gesture. "Later, Rachel. Later."

Concordia took this as her cue. "I believe I will get some tea. Excuse me."

The offerings at the refreshments table were sadly few—hardly a surprise, if the dean still controlled the expenditures. She hoped Miss Kimble would be more generous in that regard, once she managed to wrest the duties from Maynard's grasp.

After helping herself to a couple of ginger crisps and a cup of tea, she found a chair next to Miss Banning, now chatting animatedly with Charlotte Crandall. It was clear that Charlotte had remained Miss Banning's favorite.

The old lady squinted through her thick-lensed spectacles as Concordia took her seat. "*Hmph.* You have more freckles than ever, missy. You would do well to stay out of the sun, but if you insist upon riding around on that bicycle machine, at least wear a bonnet."

Concordia's lips twitched in a suppressed retort as her glance strayed to the lacy muslin cap perched upon the old lady's head. She would not be taking advice about headwear from Miss Banning any time soon. Nor any other piece of fashion attire, she thought, glancing at the silk shawl draped over the lady's shoulders, embroidered with a garish green dragon and trimmed with what appeared to be black ostrich feathers.

"Where is that beau of yours—Mr. Bradley?" Miss Banning inquired with a sly smile.

Concordia shifted in her seat, still uncomfortable with such terms as *beau*, *swain*, and *suitor*. They seemed more appropriate for a cotillion dance floor than a women's college. "He wanted to attend, but there is a time-sensitive experiment that bears watching." She gestured in the direction of the Chemistry Department chairman, now chatting with the Sanbournes. "The prerogatives of leadership, I suppose. Professor Grundy can assign his junior professor to mind the store while he attends the party."

Charlotte had turned aside, idly watching Dean Maynard as he made his way over to greet the Sanbournes. Concordia and Miss Banning followed her glance.

Maynard suddenly stopped short, eyes wide and the color leaving his face.

The moment passed. Taking a deep breath, he straightened his shoulders and approached Peter Sanbourne to be introduced.

"What is wrong with the man now?" Miss Banning complained.

"He spends too much time at his desk, I imagine," Charlotte said.

Concordia was not so sure. The expression on Maynard's face had been one of distress rather than fatigue. She took a bite of her ginger crisp as she mused. *Ugh*. Grimacing, she tucked the rest of it in her napkin. Perhaps he'd eaten too many of these stale cookies.

"I have coaxed him to resume our Saturday morning rides," Charlotte went on, "no matter how busy he claims to be. The fresh air and exercise are restorative." She smiled at Concordia. "Perhaps you would join us?"

Concordia suppressed a shudder. The last time she rode a horse—not an activity she relished—she had been holding on for dear life and had trouble sitting down for days afterward. Maynard for company hardly made it more appealing. "You have a mischievous sense of humor, Miss Crandall."

Chapter 5

The reception of an engaged girl by the family of her future husband should be most cordial.

~Mrs. John Sherwood

Week 2, Instructor Calendar
September 1898

Concordia had not been looking forward to the visit. David's family was pleasant enough and welcomed the upcoming marriage, but they would undoubtedly want to discuss wedding plans. Mother was coming, too, and was sure to fuss over details of flowers, invitations, and menus.

Concordia did not really care what she ate, or wore, or carried at her wedding, so long as David was waiting at the steps of the sanctuary. She could understand why some found elopement appealing.

And now there was a new family member to meet.

"Tell me about your aunt," she said to David, as the cab lurched away from the college gate.

He cleared his throat. "Not much to tell. Drusilla Fenmore is my father's older sister."

"Fenmore…is she related to the man who runs Fenmore Funeral Home?"

"*Ran* the funeral home," David corrected. "Edmund Fenmore, yes. He passed away a few months ago. Aunt Drusilla recently moved in with my parents."

Concordia refrained from wondering aloud: who takes care of the undertaker when it's his turn to shuffle off this mortal coil? "What is she like?" she asked instead.

Judging by the way he puckered his lips, she knew she was not going to like the answer. "Let us say that she is a...strong-minded woman of fixed opinions and does not hesitate to express them."

She made a face. *Strong-minded* did not trouble her—lively debates were commonplace within the collegiate setting, and she relished them—but a person of *fixed opinions* was exasperating. One might as well ask the mountain to fling itself into the sea. "Am I to assume that women's higher education and vocations outside the home are topics your aunt possesses fixed opinions about?"

He chuckled.

She raised an eyebrow. "Oh, you find it amusing, do you? Perhaps I should engage Mrs. Fenmore in conversation about the new engineering program at Hartford Women's College. I am sure the discussion would entertain you no end."

He held up his hands in mock surrender. "Let us make a pact to nod and grit our teeth together, shall we? Besides, who cares what the old lady thinks? We won't be seeing her all that often."

She sighed. Refraining from debate about an earnest subject was not her strong suit.

In the dimness of the cab, he moved closer and took her gloved hand in his. "In the meantime, let us consider more pleasant matters."

She suppressed a tremor as he rubbed his thumb along her gloved palm and gently massaged her fingers.

"I thought myself too old to require a chaperone in your company, Mr. Bradley," she managed finally, in a quavering voice.

David's eyes gleamed, though she could not tell if it was from amusement or amorous feeling. "You appear to have been mistaken," he murmured.

All too soon, they pulled up to the Bradley home, situated in the Asylum Hill neighborhood. Built thirty years ago in the lavish Italianate style, the house featured a deep, Corinthian-columned veranda, hipped roofs, and white-paneled bay windows. Topping the whole was a square cupola, whose curved windows took advantage of the sweep of russet-leaved trees in the distance.

She stiffened, and David patted her arm in reassurance. "I forgot to warn you about the house. Quite the relic, compared to the modern structures in the neighborhood."

"Rather…imposing."

"Well, you have already met my parents, so you know they do not match the house."

She nodded. The Bradleys came from self-made wealth rather than inherited money. While John Bradley's real estate investments downtown and his friendship with the mayor secured the family a prominent social position, they mercifully did not suffer from pretentious airs.

The maid ushered them in. The sight of the two-story entryway, with its marble floor and gilded moldings, made her glad she'd chosen the lace-trimmed Paris green satin her mother had coaxed her into having re-made last spring. Its wide side gores slimmed the waist and allowed for ease of movement. She had to admit the delicately embroidered elbow sleeves in contrasting ivory produced a charming effect. She tucked back a stray lock of hair and took David's arm.

His gaze was warm and lingering. "You look beautiful, my dear." She flushed with pleasure.

In the parlor, the plump Mrs. Bradley lounged against the sofa cushions. "Pardon me for not getting up, dears. I have had quite the fatiguing day." She nodded toward Concordia, brown ringlets bouncing beneath a satin-trimmed muslin cap. "What a charming gown. Come, sit next to me." She motioned with a be-ringed hand.

David frowned. "You should have sent word. We could have postponed our visit."

Concordia sat beside the lady. A cloud of liberally applied, white heliotrope perfume made her nose twitch in a threatened sneeze. Her own mother, along with her cronies, favored the scent as well. *Hmm*, perhaps it was a preferred fragrance of the matron set? She smiled at the thought of being handed a weighty glass atomizer of the stuff once she joined the ranks of staid matronhood.

"No, no, I will be fine." Mrs. Bradley sat up straighter and tugged at her cuffs. She turned a sharp eye toward the light-brown, pug-sized dog snoring on a mat beside the fireplace. "That wretched little beast of Drusilla's is what caused the problem. Dug up all my bulbs in the flowerbed beside the porch, then got into John's cigar box and chewed through several of his finest Havanas before I caught him. The first time, that is. Then he wriggled out of my grasp, ran into the dining room, and got sick as—well, sick as a dog, as they say—on our best Turkish carpet."

Concordia's eyes watered in her effort not to laugh. Or was it the perfume? She snorted into her handkerchief.

"Why didn't Aunt Drusilla or the servants take care of the mutt?" David asked, after a quick glance at his fiancée.

Mrs. Bradley grimaced, creasing the deep lines of her forehead. "We are short-staffed, and Drusilla is out with John. It had fallen upon me to keep Bandit out of trouble. I am sorry to say I was not equal to the task."

The dog's ears pricked in his sleep at the mention of his name. He rolled over with a contented sigh.

They heard the bell, and soon Letitia Wells joined them in the parlor.

"Mother!" Concordia stood and embraced her.

Mrs. Wells returned the embrace, then stepped back. "How nice to see you wearing one of Mary's gowns. The hue complements your coloring."

Concordia's smile stiffened. More than two years had passed since her younger sister's death. Apparently, the ache never quite goes away. Mother had grieved even more deeply for Mary. The two had been especially close. While Concordia had gravitated toward her father's company during childhood, reveling in a love of books and scholarly study, her sister and mother had pursued the whirl of social doings: who was marrying whom, what concerts and soirees were in the offing, who was attending the new exhibit at the Atheneum, and what they wore. Should one have opened the armoire of each sister, the differences between Mary's array of colorful gowns and Concordia's serviceable shirtwaists and walking skirts would have been readily apparent.

Concordia's fragile delight in being found presentable collapsed beneath the reminder that it was all due to what Mary had left behind.

"Speaking of dresses," Mrs. Wells went on, "we must make an appointment with Mrs. Feeney."

"I assume she is a dressmaker?" David inquired.

Mrs. Bradley and Mrs. Wells each gave him a pitying glance.

"Not simply a dressmaker, dear. One of the best in Hartford," Mrs. Bradley said.

Mrs. Wells made a face. "But do not repeat that—if she becomes too successful, it will take forever to have any clothing made!"

David's lips twitched. "Your secret is safe with me, madam."

"I told her of your upcoming wedding," Mrs. Wells said, turning to Concordia. "She said we should have you fitted for your gown soon, before the holiday rush."

Concordia shrugged. Why she could not walk down the aisle in her best blue silk was beyond her understanding. That shade was more flattering to her red hair and freckled complexion than white would ever be. But Mother was not to be denied.

"Sara and Gracie have been asking for you," Mrs. Wells added. "Will you be able to visit soon?"

"I don't know. I will try." In addition to her academic duties and the day-to-day needs of the young ladies in her charge at Willow Cottage, Concordia also led the Literature Club, the Bicycling Club, and the Debate Society. Then there were the mind-numbing faculty meetings that accomplished nothing but rehash the same rules and policies everyone knew by heart.

Mrs. Wells perched upon the settee across from David's mother. "What a lovely home you have here, Mrs. Bradley."

Mrs. Bradley inclined her head. "You must call me Georgeanna. We are to be family, after all."

Mrs. Wells smiled. "If you will call me Letitia."

"I am curious: who are Sarah and Gracie?" Mrs. Bradley asked.

"My young nieces, visiting from California."

Concordia wondered how her mother would explain the presence of the girls without their parents. It would not do for it to be generally known that their father was in prison. In the ensuing silence, it became apparent that Mother had decided upon not explaining at all.

"It must be difficult for them to be so far from home," Mrs. Bradley said.

If the lady was probing for more information, she was not about to get it from Concordia's mother, whose lips twitched at the ploy. "There is a bit of an adjustment, but we are—" She broke off as David's father walked in, accompanied by a middle-aged lady.

Even if Concordia had not already met John Bradley upon previous occasions, she would have known him to be David's father. The kinship was apparent in the compact, muscular build, the dark wavy hair—though peppered with gray—and the warm brown eyes, bright with ready humor.

"Ah, we are just in time," he said. "May I present my sister, Drusilla Fenmore? Drusilla, this is David's fiancée, Miss Concordia Wells." He smiled at Concordia as he escorted his sister to a chair. The pug stretched, tottered over, and jumped in the woman's lap.

Concordia would have liked to believe that widowhood was responsible for the lady's down-turned mouth and rigid carriage, but suspected not. Her hair was scraped back into a tight topknot that tugged at her forehead. She wore her copious widow's weeds like armor.

"Pleased to make your acquaintance, Mrs. Fenmore," Concordia said politely.

The widow's cool gray eyes, topped by arched brows of perpetual skepticism, lingered upon every detail of Concordia's appearance. "So, you are the woman my nephew is to marry. My, my, your hair is quite…red. Not a fashionable color these days, I'm afraid."

There seemed no good answer to this remark, as she doubted the lady was recommending she acquire a bottle of hair dye from the druggist.

"I have heard a great deal about you," Mrs. Fenmore went on.

The inflection of *a great deal* sounded none too favorable. She met the woman's sharp eye. "I have heard a great deal about you as well." She let the inflections fall where they may.

"Well, then, how nice that you two have finally met," David said briskly, pulling over a chair. "How are you, aunt? The weather has been exceptionally fine recently, has it not?"

Concordia and her mother exchanged amused glances.

Mrs. Fenmore's hooked nose quivered. "That is precisely the danger. Temperate weather in the autumn allows pestilence to breed, instead of killing it off. Then it lingers to plague us in the winter months." She turned to Concordia. "Every autumn I insisted that my dear Edmund increase his daily dose of cod liver oil. Then mustard plasters and flannel in winter, against catarrh." She sat back with a sigh. "Alas, I fear he was merely humoring me his last few months, and that is why he took ill and died. One will reap what one sows. You must take care that David does not meet the same end."

"Really, Drusilla," David's father objected, "Edmund died of an infection from a gouty leg, not some contagion."

"My poor Edmund, God rest his soul, had gout for years and was fine," Mrs. Fenmore retorted. "What made this time any different?"

"We really should be discussing the happy couple's wedding plans," Mrs. Bradley said smoothly, gesturing with a chubby hand. "Concordia, dear, have you and David settled upon a date?"

"We have decided upon January seventh, just after Twelfth Night," Concordia said. Her mother grimaced.

Concordia knew exactly what she was thinking. A winter wedding was not at all fashionable, and could not be carried off as elaborately as a June ceremony.

Which was exactly why she had decided upon it.

"What an odd time of year!" Mrs. Fenmore exclaimed. "Where is it to be?"

"Memorial Chapel." When the lady eyed at her blankly, Concordia added, "It is on the campus of Hartford Women's College."

Mrs. Fenmore's lips thinned in a disapproving line. "I heard that you teach at one of those girls' schools. Thank goodness you will soon lead a more respectable life."

Concordia stiffened, but before she could retort, her mother stepped into the fray. "It is a *women's college*, Mrs. Fenmore, not a female reformatory. It is eminently respectable. Young ladies from the best families in the area attend the institution."

Concordia suppressed a sigh. Here they were, on the brink of the twentieth century, still having the same argument about respectability and women using their brains.

As frustrating as the conversation had become, it was gratifying to hear her mother defend her vocation. It was also delightfully ironic. Mother had originally opposed her pursuit of higher education and the teaching life. Eventually, she had come to understand that Concordia was also her father's daughter, who embraced his love of scholarship. He had been the one to name her, after the Roman goddess of harmony. Had he lived long enough, he would have been proud to know she had become a teacher and scholar.

As Drusilla drew breath to reply, the butler came in to announce dinner.

David's father jumped up from his chair. "Splendid."

"Yes, let us go in," David chimed in, offering Concordia his arm. "That was close," he murmured.

The dining room table bespoke elegance without ostentation, laid with a smooth white damask cloth and heavy napkins at each place setting, folded in three-corner pyramids to hold a roll. The light from the chandelier reflected in the crystal goblets, silver cutlery, and tiny salt cellars of bone china.

As expected, wedding arrangements dominated the table conversation. Concordia had not imagined she would be as grateful for a discussion of such fripperies as she was now—anything to distract the opinionated old harpy seated across from her. Drusilla peered at her with hawkish eyes throughout the soup course, then mercifully turned to converse with David.

By the time the main course was brought out, Concordia knew her close-fitting bodice would not allow her to do more than sample the remaining dishes before breathing was impossible.

"Ah! David, Cook made your favorite, veal *rissoles*," Mrs. Bradley said.

David smiled as the platter was presented.

"Concordia, I am sure Cook can give you the recipe for your use," David's mother continued.

Concordia hid her grimace. "Thank you, Mrs. Bradley." She was not at all skilled in the kitchen and hoped they would have sufficient funds to hire a cook. She glanced at David, already digging in to a second *rissole*.

"Have you engaged any staff yet?" Drusilla asked. "You should not put it off much longer."

Concordia shook her head, trying not to panic. The prospect was overwhelming. "We must find a house first." Easier said than done. The ones they had seen thus far were either too small or too expensive.

David blotted his lips. "One in particular appears promising. Once we have it secured, we shall worry about staff."

Concordia frowned. "This is the first I have heard of it."

David flushed. "I planned to tell you about it later. Naturally, if after you see it you don't like it, we will resume our search."

Drusilla leaned toward Concordia with a pitying look. "No doubt your ladies' college has accustomed you to doing things all your own way, dear. Out here in the real world, it is the man's job to provide for his wife, and make these difficult decisions. It makes life much easier. You will see."

John Bradley, sitting beside Concordia, was the only one to notice her hands clenched around the napkin in her lap.

Drusilla went on. "Did David give you the book?" She gave him a quick glance. "Men can often be forgetful."

David kept his eyes on his plate, as if he had not heard.

Concordia nodded. "Yes, thank you, Mrs. Fenmore. I have been reading it most...attentively." She didn't volunteer the fact that she and Ruby had been hooting over several passages of the stuffy book last night.

Drusilla's face softened. "You must call me Aunt Drusilla, dear. We are to be family, after all."

"What book?" Mrs. Wells asked.

Drusilla's face became animated. "*Manners and Social Usages*, by Mrs. John Sherwood. It contains everything a new wife should know about proper etiquette."

Concordia's mother stiffened. "I have taught my daughter all about comportment in society. She needs no *handbook*, Mrs. Fenmore."

Drusilla waved a placating hand. "No doubt, no doubt. However, I am sure a friendly guide is welcome, after your daughter's time at such an...institution. I hear it is quite the hoydenish lifestyle in those places! We must set these young ladies on the right path in their married lives."

Concordia opened her mouth to utter a retort. David gave her a pleading look across the table.

Georgeanna Bradley, attending to only part of the conversation, said, "Speaking of donating little items to the bride, I have an aquamarine brooch for you to wear on your wedding day, Concordia dear." Her eyes became misty. "It was a gift from my own mother-in-law, God rest her soul—" her husband's lips twitched in either a grimace or an aborted laugh as he coughed into his napkin "—and it has great sentimental value to me. Besides, it is lucky, you know, for the bride to wear something blue. *Something old, something new, something borrowed, something blue, a silver sixpence in her shoe*, as the saying goes."

Concordia hid a brief smile of her own. "How kind." Given the smirk on her future father-in-law's face, she prayed the brooch in question was not too hideous.

By the time she and David had left the Bradleys, her mind was reeling with thoughts of flowers, ribbons, dressmakers, and the inevitable appointments to come. She was dreading the whole. She leaned back against the cushions. "Would you consider eloping?"

David chuckled. "We are through the worst of it, you will see."

They would shortly discover he was dead wrong.

Chapter 6

A woman who cannot make bread or cook a decent dinner is a fraud.
~Mrs. John Sherwood

Week 3, Instructor Calendar
October 1898

Concordia thumbed through Ruby's tattered copy of *Mrs. Beeton's Cookery Book and Household Guide* as she sat in the sunny white-and-yellow kitchen of Willow Cottage. The splatter stains on certain pages made clear which recipes the house matron favored.

With Ruby and the girls attending a matinee concert in town, she had the entire cottage to herself. It was the perfect opportunity to do a bit of cooking. She'd been tempted to try her hand at the veal croquettes David liked, but in the end decided upon apple pie. She had seen Ruby prepare it on several occasions. It should be simple enough.

As she flipped the pages, she browsed a section called *Kitchen Maxims*:

Salt or cold water makes scum to rise.
A stew boiled is a stew spoiled.
Water boils when it gallops; oil when it is still.

She frowned. What on earth did *galloping* water look like? Shaking her head, she skipped the rest and turned to the page she needed.

After an hour, she was ready to concede that *simple* and *tedious* were not mutually exclusive. She had flour in her hair, eyebrows, and nearly everywhere else, just from making the pastry. She skeptically eyed the dough she had rolled out and set in the pie dish. It was rather crumbly. It didn't resemble Ruby's at all.

She started to peel and chop the apples. *Ugh*, the paring knife was duller than Maynard's sense of humor.

At last, after much sawing and muttering under her breath, she had the apple-and-sugar mixture bubbling in a pot on the stove. She swiped at stray hairs that clung to her damp forehead. A bit of a rest was in order.

She pulled out a chair and sat at the kitchen table with *The Ring and the Book*, a recent gift from David. He knew she enjoyed Robert Browning, though perhaps it was a peace offering for putting up with Drusilla Fenmore last week.

Browning was a master of dramatic monologue, and Concordia soon found herself engrossed in Pope Innocent's weighty decision to condemn a man to death:

> *Once more on this earth of God's,*
> *While twilight lasts and time wherein to work,*
> *I take His staff with my uncertain hand,*
> *And stay my six and fourscore years....*
> *Once more appeal is made*
> *From man's assize to mine: I sit and see*
> *Another poor weak trembling human wretch....*

Abruptly, she lifted her head and sniffed. Something smelled like…burning sugar.

"Oh!" She ran to the stove. The sticky apple mixture was boiling over with great abandon. She frantically rummaged for a tea towel to wrap around the hot handle, picked up the smoking mess, and carried it outside to the back stoop.

The contents of the pot were blackened, irrecoverable. She glanced back toward the kitchen. The stove wasn't much better. Ruby would surely take her to task for making a mess of her pristine kitchen.

She straightened. If she was lucky, she could get things cleaned up and aired out before Ruby and the girls returned. No one need know.

"Miss Wells!" a voice called from the path. The slight figure of Frances Kimble came into view. The lady crossed the grassy yard with rapid, energetic strides. Concordia froze, pot still in hand. So much for that plan.

"Do you need help?" Miss Kimble peeked into the pot, then coughed and waved a hand in front of her face. "Oh dear. What was it *supposed* to be?"

Concordia felt her face flush as she set the pot on the step. "Apple pie filling."

The bursar had the grace not to laugh, though her long, thin nose twitched in amusement. "Once the pot is cool, you should give it a good soak." She turned toward the kitchen. "I'll help you get the stove cleaned up before everything hardens."

Concordia followed her in, propping the door ajar. Miss Kimble was already tugging open windows. The woman was a whirlwind of decisive energy.

As they scrubbed the stove, countertop, and floor—at least the walls and ceiling had been spared—Miss Kimble nodded toward the book on the table. "I take it you were distracted?"

Concordia grimaced. "I am not suited for cooking."

Miss Kimble laughed. "You are a teacher. You don't have to be a cook, too."

"I'm to be married in a few months."

Miss Kimble lifted an eyebrow before applying her sponge to one last stubborn spot. "Ah. Well, if you are truly set on cooking, I'm sure you will learn eventually." She smiled. "But next time, start with something simpler, and leave the poetry elsewhere."

Concordia waved her into a chair. "I appreciate you helping me. Do you have time? I'll make some tea. I can manage that, at least."

Miss Kimble blew out a breath and sat at the worn oak table. "Most kind of you. I could do with a cup." She drummed on the table with restless fingers.

"I hope I'm not keeping you from anything," Concordia said.

Miss Kimble rolled her eyes. "I have little enough to do these days, with May-Not appropriating my duties. I've not been able to convince Mr. Langdon to step in." She paused. "Neither of them trusts me."

There was a depth of hurt in that last sentence. "Surely President Langdon trusts you," Concordia said. "He hired you, after all. He is merely trying to pacify Mr. Maynard at the moment."

"But why does Maynard treat me so?" Miss Kimble protested.

"You must admit, you don't compromise, either."

A smile tugged at Miss Kimble's lips. "True enough."

"Maynard's quite protective of this institution. The last woman bursar we had two years ago did not work out well." That was putting it mildly, as Ruth Lyman had embezzled funds from the college over the course of years before discovery. "He was not dean at the time, but it took some time for the scandal to die down." Concordia frowned. The last male bursar, Mr. Isley, didn't work out well, either. *Mercy*, they seemed profoundly unlucky when it came to bursars. She certainly hoped the streak had ended with Miss Kimble.

Miss Kimble pressed her lips together. "I heard about that. Unfortunate, to be sure, but not my doing."

They sat in silence after that, sipping their tea and eating shortbread straight out of the tin. Frances Kimble's glance strayed to the window. Although her posture appeared relaxed, the set of her chin and the tight muscles of her neck suggested otherwise. Concordia remembered Mrs. Jenkins' notion that there was more behind the conflict between the bursar and dean. *Could those two have been acquainted before she was hired? The animosity between them strikes me as more personal….*

Was that the reason for the friction, rather than a mistrust generated by a string of corrupt bursars? Concordia decided to take a chance. "Had Mr. Maynard been like this before?"

Miss Kimble turned to her with narrowed eyes. "Before?" she echoed. "Before when?"

"Before you came to Hartford Women's College. Miss Jenkins had the impression you two already knew each other."

Her eyes widened. "Indeed? Whatever gave her that idea?"

Concordia tugged at her lip. "I...I do not know. I am sorry to intrude."

Miss Kimble waved a dismissive hand, though the tension in her face did not ease. "No matter, Miss Wells. My issue with Dean Maynard is very much current." She tapped a finger to her chin, lost in thought. "Although we are each a product of our past lives, aren't we?"

Concordia shrugged. It was a truism with an obvious answer.

The lady stood. "I must be going. Thank you for the tea."

After she left, Concordia was so preoccupied with the puzzle of Miss Kimble and May-Not that she forgot to soak the pot.

Chapter 7

As for the conduct of the betrothed pair during their engagement, our American mommas are apt to be somewhat more lenient in their views of liberty to be allowed than are the English.

~Mrs. John Sherwood

Week 3, Instructor Calendar
October 1898

Founder's Day started out cool and dry, but one glance at the dark clouds in the distance told Concordia they had better finish with the outdoor part of the festivities soon.

They had already attended chapel, where the school's anthem, "Forward, Woman, to Thy Calling," was sung, and this year's student benediction poem was read aloud. Alison Smedley beamed proudly during President Langdon's recitation. He had transposed the last two lines, but no one besides Concordia and Miss Smedley noticed. After a hurried recessional, the girls tossed their gloves in a communal heap beside the fountain and started working on the chrysanthemum chain that would adorn the balusters of the dining hall. Miss Kimble, Miss Jenkins, and Miss Pomeroy formed them into groups and divided the flowers among them.

Concordia watched the girls cavort in delight. Freshman or sophomore, junior or senior—today, the pranks and rivalries did not matter. She breathed in the distinctive sharpness of bruised chrysanthemum stems, mingled with the scent of impending rain. Her chest tightened. How she would miss these traditions.

A few drops of water landed on her nose. *Uh oh*. It would be an unholy mess to move the operation indoors. The young ladies did not care if they got wet, of course, but it would not do for them to take a chill.

Concordia smiled to herself. *Mercy*, now she was thinking like Aunt Drusilla. Would she be wrapping David in mustard plasters after they married?

Where *was* David? He'd had ample time to check on his experiment and return. She stood on tiptoe to check the crowd. More drops fell.

Latecomers approached the periphery of the group, the Sanbournes among them. Peter Sanbourne was immaculate as usual—hair neatly combed and parted down the middle, tie knotted precisely and shoes carefully polished—but his smothered yawns and shadowed eyes revealed his exhaustion. Rachel Sanbourne watched her husband, a worried frown tugging her brow. Concordia could imagine her distress. How long could the man maintain such a rigorous work schedule?

"Concordia," a low voice murmured behind her.

She turned. "David! What kept you?"

He held up a wooden box. "Guryev asked me yesterday for these tools, but he's not in his workshop. I thought he may be here."

She shook her head. "I haven't seen him." She gestured toward Sanbourne. "Perhaps he sent him on an errand?"

"I may as well give them to Sanbourne. Be right back."

She watched as David navigated the crowd. She saw him shake hands with Sanbourne, pass over the box, and lean in to converse.

Soon he returned, eyes narrowed. "Sanbourne has not seen Guryev since they locked up the laboratory last night."

"Someone must know where he is."

"Sanbourne says he has a few ideas. He is none too happy about any of them." He nodded toward the man, box tucked under his arm, now rapidly making his way out of the quadrangle toward the front gate.

Concordia frowned. "He said nothing else?"

David shook his head.

She took off her spectacles and polished off the drops. The drizzle had become impossible to ignore. Miss Kimble and Miss Jenkins were hustling the girls and their barely-completed chrysanthemum chain into the dining hall.

David and Concordia followed.

"After lunch, I have something to show you," he said.

"What is it?"

He shook his head with a smile. "It's a surprise."

The rain stopped just after the midday meal. "The young ladies will have their bonfire tonight after all," Concordia said, nodding toward the dining hall windows.

President Langdon brushed crumbs from his chest and tucked the napkin back in his lap, where it all but disappeared under his large belly. "I doubt anything is dry enough to burn."

She smiled, recalling the firewood and kindling the girls from Willow Cottage had been squirreling away in the tool shed for the past week. "I am sure they will find a way." A movement across the room caught her eye, and she saw David push back his chair.

Concordia did likewise. "If you will excuse me."

She hurried to meet him outside the dining hall. "What is your surprise?"

He merely grinned and patted his jacket pocket. "I am in the mood for a walk. Shall we?"

Although the path was muddy in places, especially along the old sheep tracks at the bottom of Rook's Hill, the rain had refreshed the air and brought a colorful carpet of leaves to their feet. A breeze rippled the branches nearby.

They had walked ten minutes in companionable silence and had nearly crested the hill when Concordia finally spoke. "Where is it we're going? There's nothing here but the old Armstrong place." She gestured toward the farmhouse ahead of them. No one had lived here since George Armstrong's death the year before. The place was sadly neglected: the barn was missing its door, the paddock and fields were overgrown with nettles, and farm implements had been left out to rust.

"His relations are selling the house and property." He helped her navigate a splintered wood step on the porch.

She stopped short. "You want to live *here*? Isn't it rather...large?" *Land sakes*, how many children did he expect them to have?

"Who can predict how much room we might need?"

She swallowed. He did want a large family. Well, she would disabuse him of *that* notion.

"Armstrong's family dropped the price. It is just within our range," he continued. "And it is so close to campus that I could walk to my classes."

He could walk to his classes.

Concordia drew in a breath, choking back tears. Why would he torment her so, and propose setting up their home within view of the life she was giving up?

David sighed and enfolded her in his arms. "Oh, my dear. You misunderstand me. This can be beneficial for you, too."

"I do not see how," she sniffed.

He held her at arm's length so he could meet her eyes. "Think of the possibilities! We are *walking distance* from the school."

She frowned, at first not seeing his point.

Then it came to her.

The property was practically part of the campus. In fact, the trustees of Hartford Women's College had tried to purchase a portion of the Armstrong land a couple of years ago. If she and David lived here, she could easily host students for teas and poetry readings, attend events at the school, perhaps even volunteer to head the Literature Club or direct the student play. If the college needed a last-minute substitute teacher, which happened upon occasion, she might persuade Miss Pomeroy of the expediency of pressing her into service. Surely, the trustees could not object to that.

"Ah, you see!" he said triumphantly, watching her expression change. "There is more than one way to skin a cat, you know."

She smiled. The tightness in her chest eased. "You, Mr. Bradley, are a devious man. Let us take a look." She put a hand to the door, praying it was not a mice-infested heap.

"Just a minute," he said, digging in his pocket. "We need the key."

"It's open already," she said, stepping into the gloom.

He frowned. "Strange. The caretaker said it would be locked."

She groped her way through the dark room. "No electricity, I suppose." Funny how one could become accustomed to such luxuries as electric lights and steam heat. Would it be terribly expensive to convert the old farmhouse to such amenities?

"Gas lighting, and it has been shut off," he said. "The caretaker said he left some lanterns on the kitchen table." He glanced around. "I had hoped for a sunny day to show you the place."

"No matter." She found a lantern and struck a match. "What an enormous kitchen!" Unfortunately, that appeared to be its only positive attribute. The cast-iron cook stove was absolutely ancient, and the deep sink still had a hand pump. She could only imagine the state of the pipes. The place needed a lot of work.

"All the easier for you to cook elaborate meals for me," he said with a grin.

She wrinkled her nose at him. "It could be the size of the Taj Mahal and be equipped with the most modern amenities and it still would not help. You know I cannot prepare anything more complicated than tea and toast. I do not suppose we will have the funds to hire a cook?"

"Not right away. I can always bring back leftovers from the dining hall." He ducked before she could find something to throw at him.

There was no help for it, she supposed. She would have to learn to cook, or burn the house down trying.

He smiled and drew her close. "I do not care if you char the toast every day of our married lives, my dear." He bent down and breathed in her ear, sending tingles along her spine. "Kiss me."

She slid her hands up behind his neck, pulse quickening. "How improper, sir," she murmured. "We are not yet married. What would Aunt Drusilla say?"

He chuckled as his mouth brushed her cheek. "Aunt Drusilla be—" Concordia's lips stopped the rest of his sentence.

After a time, he took a lantern and headed toward the parlor. "The house definitely has potential. Come and see the deep stone fireplace!" he called.

She joined him, holding up her own lamp. "There is plenty of room here to host students for gatherings. Now I understand why you thought a larger home would be advantageous." Her excitement grew. "David, I do think this may work—" A loud bang stopped her.

"That sounded like the back door." He put a hand to her arm. "Probably just the breeze rattling it loose, but best that you stay here." He headed down the narrow hallway.

She glanced around at the gloomy shadows of the parlor, and shivered. "Oh, no...I am coming with you." She hurried up behind him.

As if by tacit agreement, they moved carefully and noiselessly back through the kitchen to the rear screened-in porch. David's shone his light toward the screen door. His shoulders relaxed. "Ah, see? It was not latched properly." He shifted the lantern in his hands to secure the hook.

Concordia idly cast her light around the dim perimeter, piled with stacked furniture, a long workbench, and other detritus. What a mess. And who would leave a heap of cast-off clothing behind the bench? She moved closer. Her heart leapt in her chest and she let out a gasp.

More than clothing. A man.

"D-David...." Her voice quavered.

He hurried over and sucked in a breath. He crouched beside the body.

"Is he...dead?"

"I need more light."

She brought her lamp closer as he turned the man over.

"I do not recognize him," he said.

Suppressing a shudder at the sightless eyes, she leaned in. The man's otherwise fair hair was matted at the back of his head with something dark. Blood. She swallowed. He seemed familiar...that slightly crooked nose, the scar along the eyebrow.

Then she remembered.

"I know who he is," she said in a small voice. "Mr. Oster."

Chapter 8

There is, no doubt, a great pleasure in the added freedom of life which comes to an elderly girl.

~Mrs. John Sherwood

Week 3, Instructor Calendar
October 1898

Concordia rushed over to the college's gatehouse for help while David stayed with the body.

"There has been a death at the old Armstrong place. We need the police right away," she told Clyde, the gatekeeper. "Find out if Lieutenant Capshaw can come." She prayed he could. Although the policeman often rolled his eyes at the peccadilloes of *college people*, there was no denying he had experience in dealing with campus-related cases. To be sure, this was not *quite* on campus—a fact she hoped would keep the school out of the newspapers this time—but the fact that teachers at Hartford Women's College had discovered the body was bound to attract unwelcome publicity. "And fetch Mr. Sanbourne."

"That inventor fella? Why?" Clyde asked.

"He knows the man who has died. An old acquaintance."

Clyde grunted. "What happened? The fella have a fit or somethin'?"

She shook her head. She did not want to provide more fodder for rumor mongering. "The police will figure it out. Once we *call them.*"

"Right away, miss."

Lieutenant Capshaw arrived a short time later, accompanied by a patrolman. There was no mistaking his tall, gaunt form, or his habit of walking with a slight stoop, as if continually checking for a clue he may have missed.

He gave Concordia a melancholy look of disapproval beneath bushy red-haired brows. "Another body, miss? I thought once you married, we'd be finished with such things."

"I am not married yet, lieutenant," she retorted. Not that finding bodies was an occupation of hers, though to be fair it had happened with some frequency over the past couple of years.

Did Capshaw's lips twitch beneath his capacious mustache, or was it her imagination?

Sanbourne arrived, flushed and out of breath. "Clyde just told me."

"Who are you, sir?" Capshaw asked.

The man gave Capshaw a disdainful glance, though his usual haughty air was difficult to achieve, as the policeman towered over him by nearly a foot. "Peter Sanbourne, head of the college's engineering program."

"I sent for him, lieutenant," Concordia said. "He knew Mr. Oster."

Sanbourne frowned. "Though not at all well. Frankly, I doubt that I can help." He turned to Capshaw. "You are in charge of this case? What exactly has happened?"

"Can't say, yet." Capshaw gestured to Concordia to lead the way. "Haven't seen the victim or the place he was found. But tell me, sir, what you know about him."

Sanbourne paused, huffing a little as they climbed the hill. "Oster is—was—John Reeve's laboratory assistant at Boston Tech."

"Reeve? The name sounds familiar," Capshaw said.

"Probably because he and I patented a mining pump while we were both working at that institution. It received some attention in the newspapers."

Capshaw clung to his hat in the breeze. "I'll say. I remember reading there was a bidding war over it. And Oster worked on that project?"

Sanbourne nodded. "In a small capacity, as did Ivan."

"Ivan?"

"My assistant. Ivan Guryev. Brilliant young man."

"Are you still collaborating with Reeve?" Capshaw asked.

Sanbourne shook his head. "We parted ways after that. I had not seen them in years."

"Until the reception last week," Concordia interjected. "Mr. Langdon invited them, knowing they were old associates of Mr. Sanbourne."

Sanbourne scowled.

"Indeed?" Capshaw said. "Had you made arrangements to meet with them again, Mr. Sanbourne? I'm trying to understand what Oster was doing in an abandoned farmhouse near the campus where you work. Can you think of a connection?"

"At the reception," Concordia interrupted again, "I noticed Mr. Oster and Mr. Reeve were quite eager to renew their acquaintance with Mr. Guryev."

"You notice a great deal, young lady," Sanbourne said tartly.

Capshaw's mustache twitched again.

Sanbourne shrugged. "Their interaction seemed cordial. I did not attend to it closely."

They were within view of the farmhouse. Sanbourne's lip curled. "I cannot conceive how the poor man wound up in this desolate place."

Concordia took in the sight of the crooked shutters, rusting farm implements, and overgrown climbing roses obscuring nearly half of the lower windows beside the front porch. Where most people saw a wreck of a house, she had begun to recognize its potential.

Disappointment gripped her abdomen. Now that a man had been murdered here, that prospect was gone.

Capshaw pointed to a bench beside a tumbled-down arbor. "Wait out here. Oh, and Mr. Sanbourne," he added, pulling out his oft-folded wad of paper and a lead pencil, "I will want to speak with Mr. Guryev. What time is he usually at your campus laboratory?"

Sanbourne hesitated. "All day long, nearly every day of the week. However, I have not seen him yet today."

"Really?" He turned his head as a grim-lipped David Bradley came out of the house. "Never mind. We'll talk about it later. Miss Wells, wait out here with Mr. Sanbourne." Capshaw beckoned to the patrolman, and they followed David inside.

As Concordia sat on the porch bench and watched the day turn to dusk—the students would be building their bonfire soon—she thought back to the last time she had seen Mr. Oster alive. He and Mr. Reeve had spoken briefly with Sanbourne at the reception before seeking out Guryev. She had attributed that to Sanbourne's rancor—even his wife has been cold to them—but perhaps it was Guryev they wanted to speak with all along. She remembered Reeve checking over his shoulder in Sanbourne's direction as he slipped something into Guryev's hand. She must be sure to tell Capshaw about that.

The creak of rusty hinges brought her back to the present as David emerged from the house. She stood and brushed off her skirt. "Well?"

He shook his head. "It is definitely murder. Oster was bludgeoned to death."

She shivered. The body had been there the entire time, while they were...well, no matter. They would never buy the house now.

David shrugged off his jacket and put it over her shoulders. "I am sorry. We will get you home as soon as Capshaw is finished."

Sanbourne shifted impatiently. "I hope that is soon. I am behind in my work, and I expect Ivan has returned to the laboratory by now."

The old hinges groaned again, and Capshaw stepped onto the porch. He passed a weary hand over his head, making his hair, redder than Concordia's own, stand on end. "No doubt Mr. Bradley has told you that Oster was struck repeatedly in back of the head with a fireplace poker."

Concordia swallowed as she glanced at David. "Not that…specifically. When?"

The lieutenant shrugged. "Long before you two found him, I know that. Last night, most likely. The doc should be here soon. He can tell us." He pointed a thumb behind him. "The patrolman is waiting with the body until then. Mr. Sanbourne?" Sanbourne looked up but made no move to stand.

Capshaw dug in his pocket and pulled out a torn strip of paper, blue on one side. "I found this in Oster's clenched hand. Do you recognize it?"

Sanbourne paled as he held it closer. "It looks to be a fragment from a blueprint."

"That's what I thought. But a blueprint of what?"

Sanbourne squinted at it. "This isn't a big enough piece to be sure. I have several blueprints in my laboratory. Including one of—" he hesitated.

"Yes?" Capshaw prompted.

"—of my prototype, for the Navy."

"Do you typically store it in a cardboard tube? We found an empty one nearby."

"Only when I travel with it."

"Do you have additional blueprint copies of this project?" Capshaw asked.

Sanbourne's jaw clenched. "Only the one. I did not want to risk another copy falling into the hands of a competitor."

Capshaw's eyes narrowed. "Would you now consider Mr. Reeve a competitor, sir?"

"Not a competitor *per se*—the Navy contract is mine alone—but who knows what he could do with a diagram of mine? It is Reeve's penchant to build upon the work of others and take credit. "

"Everyone in pursuit of higher knowledge builds upon the work of others," David interjected. "Sir Isaac Newton once said: *If I have seen further, it is by standing on the shoulders of giants.*"

Sanbourne shrugged.

Capshaw brought them back to the subject at hand. "When did you last see this blueprint, Mr. Sanbourne?"

"Last night, when I locked it in the safe."

"Do you keep the original locked in there as well?"

Sanbourne sighed. "The Assistant Secretary of the Navy still has my original. I had submitted my latest modifications to Mr. Roosevelt in May. They kept it when Mr. Allen took over so that he could examine it."

"I see. So the blueprint is the only copy you have to work from at the moment?"

"Yes. In fact, I had scribbled new notations on the back."

"Would Mr. Oster have been able to open the safe and take it?"

Sanbourne's lip curled in derision. "I am not a stupid man, Lieutenant. Give Reeve's assistant access to my safe? Of course not."

"Naturally," Capshaw said, not giving the slightest hint of having been offended. "However, you say you have seen neither your diagram nor your assistant Guryev since last night, and here we find a ripped piece of what may be the blueprint of your latest invention in a dead man's hand. Your composure is a wonder, sir. If it were me, I would be quite alarmed."

Sanbourne paled. "You mean—dear God." He abruptly stood. "I must return to my laboratory."

Capshaw put out a hand. "We'll go together to check, after you've answered a few more questions." He pulled out his pencil and pad, doodling on the edge to test its point. "Tell me about your assistant, Guryev. When did you see him last?"

"It was early last night, around six, when we locked up the laboratory."

Capshaw raised an eyebrow. "Six o'clock is early?"

"We keep long hours in this business, lieutenant." Sanbourne shifted restlessly. "There is much to do before the prototype is ready for testing. We also have our obligations to the college." He nodded in Concordia's direction.

Capshaw scribbled a note. "And why did you stop work early last night?"

"My wife and I had a social function to attend."

"And the function?"

"The Dunwicks' charity reception."

"That would be Sir Anthony and Lady Dunwick, correct?" Capshaw made a notation. "But Mr. Guryev was not invited?"

Sanbourne snorted. "Hardly."

"Where was Mr. Guryev going after that?"

Sanbourne shook his head. "He did not say."

"Anyone he associates with regularly? Preferred entertainments?" Capshaw asked.

"As far as associations, I am aware of none besides people on campus whom he sees day to day," Sanbourne said. "In terms of his personal entertainments, well, I…I would rather not to go into that. Believe me, I have searched all of his usual haunts today when I realized he had not been seen. There is no sign of him. For all we know, he may be back at the laboratory by now."

"Still, we need the information, sir."

Sanbourne frowned. "Very well, but I would appreciate you keeping this confidential. His poor mother is visiting. If Ivan has in fact disappeared, she will be distraught enough."

Capshaw's eyes narrowed. "I cannot promise. I will try."

"Ivan has a predilection for…gaming. Cards, mostly. I have long tried to dissuade him from the practice, as it has gotten him into trouble more than once. I know of two establishments he frequents in town."

Concordia's eyes widened. The clever and handsome Mr. Guryev, a gambler? And Sanbourne knew of this. Why would he keep him on?

Capshaw passed over his pad. "Would you write them down, please?"

After glancing at what Sanbourne had written, he gave a satisfied nod. "That's a start, but there are probably more you know nothing about."

"Can we head back to my laboratory now?" Sanbourne asked. "I am anxious to make sure my blueprint is safe."

"What about finding Mr. Guryev?" Concordia asked.

Capshaw raised an eyebrow. She could almost hear the phrase: *meddlesome females*. "One thing at a time, miss. As Mr.

Sanbourne pointed out, perhaps he has returned. For now, I need you to inform President Langdon of what has happened, and tell him to expect a visit from me later."

"Of course," Concordia said. "I was wondering...Miss Lovelace or Miss Gage might know where Mr. Guryev was going last night. Do you wish me to inquire?"

Capshaw might have been rolling his eyes, though it was difficult to tell in the deepening dusk. "Could I stop you if I wanted to? Very well, but do not speak of Oster's death if you can avoid it. We do not want to distress the young ladies."

The bonfire beside the pond was burning merrily when they reached campus. The girls fed the flames with their wood cache from the tool shed, old school papers, and sticks and leaf litter that had escaped the afternoon rain. Concordia answered their cheerful greetings in as cordial a voice as she could muster. Fortunately, news of Oster's death had not yet circulated.

Anxious to check for his blueprint, Sanbourne headed for his laboratory, along with Lieutenant Capshaw and David. She wished she could have gone too, but the clever Capshaw had found a way to keep her out from underfoot. She went in search of Edward Langdon.

She finally found him, along with the lady principal, watching the bonfire festivities from the dining hall balcony.

Langdon's frown deepened as she recounted the discovery. "Most unfortunate. Why am I only now learning of this?"

Concordia plucked at her skirt. "I am sorry. I did not think of it. Mr. Oster was not found on campus, and he's not connected with the school." Not yet, anyway.

Langdon grunted. "Thank heaven for that, but what in Sam Hill was he doing at the old Armstrong place?"

Up to no good, she was sure, but she kept that to herself. She looked over at the lady principal, still staring at the bonfire. Was she paying attention? Gertrude Pomeroy was an enigma, ever fixed upon the joys of translating medieval French literature rather than heeding the world around her.

"That is not all, I am afraid," Concordia went on. "Have you seen Mr. Guryev on campus today?"

Langdon shook his head.

"Well, no one has seen him since last night. Lieutenant Capshaw believes there may be a connection."

Langdon shifted uneasily. "Surely not!"

"No doubt the lieutenant will explain his reasoning when he calls upon you later. He and Mr. Bradley are with Mr. Sanbourne in his laboratory. A blueprint may be missing."

Langdon passed a hand across his forehead. "And this is connected to Mr. Oster's death?"

She nodded. "A torn piece was found in his hand."

Langdon groaned.

"It is urgent that Mr. Guryev be found," Concordia went on. "I have Capshaw's permission to ask the engineering students if they know where he was going last night. Is that all right with you, sir?"

"Must you tell them about the murder?" Langdon asked.

She shrugged. "I do not know if I can avoid it. They will find out sooner or later."

"Most of them are participating in the bonfire at the moment. Don't spoil it for them."

"I will start with Maisie Lovelace," she said. "She wasn't by the pond. She may be back at the cottage."

"Better take Miss Jenkins with you," he said. "Miss Lovelace and the others are quite attached to Guryev. We don't want any fainting or hysterics."

Concordia grimaced.

"I will accompany you as well," Miss Pomeroy said suddenly, turning her head. Her thick spectacles reflected the light of the fire and obscured her eyes in an oddly disturbing way.

"Of course," Concordia said.

Hannah Jenkins was busy overseeing the bonfire. "Just toss it on there. Don't get too close!" she called out. "Miss Smedley, stop adding damp leaves, if you please. You are creating too much smoke."

Concordia drew closer, breathing in the acrid scent and rubbing her hands towards its welcome heat. "Can you be spared for a bit?" She gestured over her shoulder, toward Miss Pomeroy. "We'll explain along the way."

Miss Jenkins passed the stout branch she had been using as a poker to a senior girl and brushed off her hands. "I'll be back. Don't let the freshies get too close. We cannot have anyone's skirts catching."

When they reached Willow Cottage, Concordia sent Ruby to fetch Miss Lovelace.

Concordia felt a twinge of guilt when Ruby returned with the tousle-headed girl.

Concordia patted the seat beside her on the divan. "Come, sit here. We are sorry to disturb you, dear."

"That's all right," Miss Lovelace said, smothering a yawn, "my headache is gone now...." Her voice trailed off as she glanced around uncertainly. "Miss Pomeroy? Miss Jenkins? What are you doing here? Have I done something wrong?"

"No, no," Concordia said hastily. "But I am afraid we bring bad news. Mr. Guryev is missing, and we hoped you might be able to help us find him."

Miss Lovelace frowned. "Mr. Sanbourne doesn't know where he is?"

Concordia shook her head. "He has not seen him since yesterday evening, when they locked up the laboratory. We are trying to determine where he would have gone last night." She decided to refrain from mention of the murder. Miss Lovelace's face had grown rather pale. "You work with him regularly. Did he say anything about his plans?"

Miss Lovelace bit her lip as she thought. "No, nothing. But he doesn't usually speak of his personal life with us. Even though he's not much older than we are, he is very professional."

"Mr. Sanbourne said they locked up the laboratory at six o'clock. Is that right?"

"Hmm, probably. I went over after supper to check on my own experiment, but the lights were out and I couldn't get in. I even knocked."

"You knocked, when the lights were out? Why?" Concordia asked.

Miss Lovelace made a face. "Silly, I know…I had the impression someone was still in there. I thought I heard footsteps." She shrugged. "I was wrong."

"What time was this?"

"I don't know." Maisie yawned again. "Seven? Something like that."

"This young lady needs to go back to bed," Hannah Jenkins said firmly, putting a hand under the girl's elbow and helping her to her feet.

"Even when I'm tired, I have trouble sleeping," Miss Lovelace said, rubbing her dark-circled eyes.

Ruby got up. "I'll bring you some chamomile tea. Up with you, now!"

Only Miss Pomeroy and Concordia remained in the parlor. The lady principal made no move to leave. Concordia sat, hands in her lap, and waited.

"So, Concordia," Miss Pomeroy began, "we have another body."

"Yes." Concordia shifted in her seat. She was grateful the lady principal had not said, *You have found another body.* Perhaps she was thinking that.

The quiet was disturbed by a light rapping on the front door. Concordia got up to answer it.

"David! Come in." She led him into the parlor and gestured to a chair. "Any news? Has Mr. Guryev turned up?"

"No sign of him. There are several blueprints in the safe, but the one for Sanbourne's current project is missing. There are no signs that the safe has been broken into. Only Sanbourne and Guryev know the combination."

"Could the plans have been misplaced?" Concordia asked. "Oh wait, no…that wouldn't make sense. I forgot about the scrap in Oster's hand."

"We searched the laboratory thoroughly, nonetheless. No luck," he said.

Concordia shook her head. "I feel so sorry for Mr. Sanbourne."

"It's a double blow," David said. "To lose the work of months and to be betrayed by the man one considered a son."

"Are we sure Mr. Guryev stole the blueprint?" Miss Pomeroy asked, blue eyes wide behind her spectacles. "Not that man—Mr. Oster, was it?"

"It had to be Guryev," David said. "The blueprint was in the safe when they closed up for the night, and the laboratory was locked tight."

Concordia nodded. "Miss Lovelace went there after supper—something about checking on an experiment—and said all of the doors were locked."

"Only Sanbourne, Guryev, and our custodial staff have keys," he said. "Capshaw will double-check that, of course."

"What is Capshaw's opinion?" Concordia asked.

David shook his head. "He's keeping it to himself. If I were to guess, based upon his questions of Sanbourne, I would say Capshaw's working on the theory that Guryev stole the plans to sell to Oster, Reeve's intermediary."

"But why? Guryev was dedicated to Sanbourne," Concordia said, remembering Guryev's glowing praise at the reception.

"You remember what Sanbourne said of his gambling problem. Perhaps Guryev was desperate for funds."

"If Guryev sold the plans to Oster, why kill him?"

David shrugged. "A falling out?"

Miss Pomeroy stood with a sigh. "I believe we have done everything we can." She gave Concordia a meaningful look. "We must leave this to the police to investigate."

Chapter 9

*Never before were women so utterly regardless of the unbecoming
as they are when on a bicycle.*
~Mrs. John Sherwood

Week 4, Instructor Calendar
October 1898

Concordia awoke early on her day off, opening the
curtains to a beautiful fall morning. Many of the trees
had already shed their leaves, but the sun felt warm and the sky
was a boundless blue. There was just enough time for a bicycle
ride before she was to meet her mother and Sophia in town.

She heard a few students stirring overhead as she put on her
cycling attire. The shortened skirt, bloomers, and fitted leggings
allowed for greater freedom of movement, though it revealed a
fair amount of limb. Fortunately, no one on campus batted an
eye anymore at such an outfit. President Langdon had at last
caught up with modern times: the young ladies' new physical
fitness uniforms included bloomers, to Miss Jenkins's delight.

With a final tuck of her hair beneath her cycling cap, she
was ready. She extricated her machine from the shed—an easier
task now that the bonfire wood was gone—and set out for the
sheep tracks.

The ride was pure delight: the breeze upon her face, the blur
of color, the speedy lurch of the downhill slopes, the scent of
crisp fall air. After a while, between the warmth of the sun upon
her back and the heat of her exertions, she stopped to remove
her jacket and stow it in the basket.

Others were out early. Charlotte Crandall and Randolph Maynard stood in the stable yard, preparing for a ride. Charlotte had persuaded the dean to join her after all. Concordia was too far away to hear their words, but Charlotte was laughing at something Maynard said as he helped her in the stirrup. He was smiling, too.

Concordia's eyes widened. Will wonders never cease?

She climbed back on her bicycle and headed for the path around the pond. Charlotte Crandall and Mr. Maynard...the start of a possible romance? She supposed they were no less likely than any other pair, but the dean as a wooing suitor...he must be a good twenty years older. It certainly required a mental adjustment.

If it had a softening effect on the man, she was all in favor of it.

As she passed the front gate, she noticed Mr. and Mrs. Sanbourne parting ways, she with her paint box and easel heading toward Rook's Hill, he turning toward his laboratory building. The poor man walked with a defeated slump to his shoulders.

Concordia could only assume no significant progress had been made in finding Guryev, Sanbourne's blueprint, or Oster's murderer over the past week and a half. Lieutenant Capshaw did not confide in her, of course. He passed her with barely a nod the last time she had seen him on campus.

To the discomfiture of President Langdon and the board of trustees, the newspaper accounts placed Hartford Women's College squarely in the midst of the intrigue. It hardly mattered that the Armstrong farmhouse was the scene of the crime. The scandal revolved around Ivan Guryev. Reporters quickly learned of his staggering gambling debts and the threats upon his life by collectors. It was not a great stretch to conclude that Guryev had double-crossed Oster, killing him and fleeing with both money and blueprint to sell again. Many of the news stories had him back in Russia already.

After rounding the pond loop, Concordia stopped to catch her breath and check her watch. She should head back to change if she was to make it to the dressmaker's on time.

Mrs. Feeney's dress shop on Alden Street had the misfortune to be situated directly above a bakery. Perhaps the alterations that ensued after the ladies indulged in such treats provided a boon to the dressmaker. It required a stern effort of will for Concordia to pass by the delectable odors of gingerbread, cinnamon scones, and lemon curd tarts, her favorite. Her stomach rumbled.

Mrs. Wells and Sophia Capshaw waited inside. The shop had the smell of new lumber shelving and flooring. A wide, brightly lit countertop spanned nearly the width of the back wall. Racks lined both sides of the shop, stretching from chair rail to head height, though they were not even half-full with fabric. Mrs. Feeney apparently had an eye for future inventory and brisk business.

Sophia extended her hands in greeting. "Concordia! It has been weeks."

The two had been close friends since childhood, though their paths had diverged since then, with Concordia pursuing a teaching vocation and Sophia working with the poor and indigent at Hartford Settlement House.

Concordia tilted her head up—Sophia was a good bit taller—for a close look at her friend. Her walking suit of hunter green velvet softened the angles of her slim figure, and the toque bonnet was trimmed with the same amber braid that adorned the cuffs and hem, flattering the blond hair tucked smoothly beneath. Only the most discerning eye would see that the dress was several seasons old and the toque had been refurbished at the milliner's. Though Sophia had been raised in the wealthy Adams household, she had left that life behind for one of public service. And now that she was married to Lieutenant Capshaw, living within modest means was a necessity.

Concordia smiled. The one consolation of this dress excursion was Sophia's company. Doubly so, since she might be privy to details about Capshaw's investigation. Concordia had to admit she was hoping to find out more about the case.

If Mother would permit talk of a murder during a wedding-dress fitting. She glanced across the shop. Mother and Mrs. Feeney were huddled over an array of *Harper's Bazaar* issues scattered across the counter. "Here are the fashion plates we like," she heard her say.

Concordia leaned close to Sophia, her voice low. "Has the lieutenant made any progress in finding Guryev, or the man who murdered Oster?"

"He has been working on little else." Sophia's light eyes gleamed with suppressed excitement. "To start, Guryev's mother is not as innocent or as ignorant of her son's scheme as she originally claimed."

Concordia frowned, remembering the frail, stooped woman at the reception. "That sweet old lady?"

Sophia nodded. "Aaron finally coaxed the story out of her, through an interpreter. Apparently she knew her son was going to steal the blueprint and sell it to Reeve, with Oster as the intermediary."

Concordia's eyes widened. "A week before Oster's death, we had a reception to welcome Sanbourne and Guryev. Langdon invited Reeve and Oster. I noticed Reeve slipping a piece of paper into Guryev's hand." She hesitated. "I may have neglected to tell Capshaw about that."

"I'll pass that along. It confirms what Guryev's mother said. According to her, it was originally Reeve's idea to steal the plans. She staunchly maintains that her son did not want to betray his mentor, but the debt collectors had been relentless. She said they followed him everywhere."

Concordia's breath caught. *They followed him everywhere.* The night of the alarm-clock prank, she had seen Guryev leaning out the window of Sycamore House, eyeing the garden below. Had the debt collectors kept a covert watch on him even at the college? She shivered at the idea of strange men prowling about the grounds at night.

"Mrs. Guryev said she pleaded with him to return with her to Russia, and escape the debt collectors once and for all." Sophia added.

"Why did he not do that? Why steal the blueprint and cause so much trouble?"

"Money," Sophia said simply. "He needed to sell it for passage back."

"Concordia!" Mrs. Wells called, gesturing to the bolt of white satin overlaid in Brussels lace that the dressmaker had spread on the counter. "You two can chat later. This is to be *your* dress. Should you not be the one to make decisions about it? Mrs. Feeney and I cannot do everything."

"Just a minute." Concordia leaned closer to Sophia. "Does Capshaw think Guryev killed Oster?"

Sophia's eyes narrowed in a troubled expression. "Mrs. Guryev says she saw him that evening before he was to meet Oster. The plan was for him to give Oster the blueprint, take the money, and buy his steamer ticket. He was to meet her back at her hotel the next day. But she says she never saw or heard from him again."

"She could be lying."

Sophia shook her head. "Aaron believes her. That's why he allowed her to return to Russia. After a thorough search of her belongings, of course. I trust his instincts. He thinks the debt collectors may have killed Oster and kidnapped Guryev, along with taking the money and blueprint."

Concordia felt a chill at the base of her spine. "Kidnapped? Then what happened to Guryev after that?"

Sophia bit her lip. "Nothing good, I am sure."

"Perhaps he escaped when they killed Oster?" Concordia mused aloud. She frowned. "But that would mean he is still in hiding."

"Concordia!" Mrs. Wells called again.

With a sigh, Concordia went over to the counter, her mind teeming with questions.

They sifted through reams of fabric, spools of ribbon, and cards of lace. Concordia grimaced at the fabric heaped upon the counter. Why was white the standard for wedding gowns? It was the most unflattering color, if it could be called a color at all. Perhaps it would suffice for someone not as pale and freckled as she. Or as redheaded. Very few shades suited her.

Mrs. Feeney crouched over another bin. "We have this lovely antique ivory." She held it up to Concordia in front of the mirror. "And if we add a bit of chiffon, so the tint has depth and is not so flat…yes, yes, you see?"

Mrs. Wells nodded. "That is just the thing. Excellent."

Concordia peered over her spectacles. "I suppose…very well."

Over the next hour she was prodded, pinned, and nagged into standing up taller. A futile task, as she was as tall as she was ever going to be. Finally, they were done. She groaned and flexed her back. "I'd forgotten how exhausting dress fittings can be." On a teacher's salary, ready-made clothing suited her well enough.

Sophia smiled. "You are more fortunate than you realize. I was standing for nearly two hours during my fitting. Then the dress had to be taken in twice before the wedding." She grimaced.

Concordia doubted she would have *that* problem.

"I for one would have preferred a grander style gown," Mrs. Wells said to Sophia, "with a much longer train. But she wants a simple wedding."

Concordia choked back a laugh. "This is simple?"

Sophia smiled at Mrs. Wells. "Careful, she may elope…or join the gypsies."

Letitia Wells chuckled. "Well, at least she is getting married. I had despaired of that for quite some time."

Concordia cleared her throat in mock sternness. "I am still standing here, you know. I suggest it is time to feed the bride-to-be."

"Ah, yes!" Mrs. Wells checked her watch. "We are just in time."

"In time?" Concordia asked, following her mother and Sophia down the stairs. Mmm...that aroma. Pastries, fresh from the oven. Perhaps just one lemon tart—?

Her mother pulled her away. "None of that, now. You will eat something sensible. We must ensure you fit into that gown."

"Where are we going?" Concordia asked as they headed up Wethersfield Avenue, toward Main Street and the heart of the downtown district. The pavements bustled with office workers eager for lunch. The women dodged a line forming beside a sidewalk vendor selling sandwiches and ginger beer.

"*Dillon's*," Mrs. Wells said.

"Wonderful. I haven't been there in ages." Dillon's started as a bakery and over the decades had expanded to a dine-in tearoom. It was a popular spot, now serving hearty fare in addition to its renowned desserts.

"You had better tell her the rest," Sophia said.

Mrs. Wells gave an exasperated sigh. "You are right, of course."

The bell tinkled as they opened the door. "The rest of what?" Concordia asked. She hoped a table was free. Her stomach rumbled as she glanced down the crowded aisle.

Georgeanna Bradley and Drusilla Fenmore, seated in a corner booth, gave a little wave.

Concordia's stomach did more than rumble.

"Sorry," Mrs. Wells whispered, pasting on a smile as they made their way over.

"Indeed," Sophia murmured, "it was all your mother could do to keep them from coming with us to the dressmaker's."

Concordia grimaced.

After greetings were exchanged and they were seated, Mrs. Bradley rummaged in her reticule. "Concordia, dear, here is the memento I told you about." She passed over an ecru satin pouch. "Wear it in good health."

Concordia pulled out a gold brooch as large as a child's fist, thickly crusted with aquamarines. It appeared to be a peacock, though the crown of the bird's head had broken off. Perhaps Mrs. Bradley, in her younger days, had thrown it against a wall in a fit of pique? She hefted it. Or used it as a weapon. How could something covered in such lovely stones be so…ugly?

She made a move to hand it back. "It is most generous of you, Mrs. Bradley, but I cannot accept something so—so valuable."

Mrs. Bradley held up a hand. "Nonsense, my dear. As I mentioned before, it seems fitting to pass it down to you. My mother-in-law had given it to me, so I am continuing the tradition. I have no daughter of my own. Is it not extraordinary?"

As Mrs. Bradley looked at her expectantly, Concordia realized she would have to be polite about the hideous thing. "Indeed, I have never seen anything quite like it." She glanced at Sophia, who was biting her lip to hold back a laugh. "Would you not agree?" she added, holding up the monstrosity.

Sophia shot her a look. "Words fail me."

"Try it on," Mrs. Bradley coaxed.

Concordia was afraid she was going to say that. She glanced down at her linen shirtwaist. The stout pin would put holes in everything she owned.

"I am afraid that Concordia's attire at the moment is not suitable for such a…distinctive piece," Mrs. Wells said smoothly.

Concordia quickly tucked it back into the pouch and out of sight.

"I had hoped you would wear it on your wedding day," Mrs. Bradley said, voice rising in her distress. "After all, it is blue, and it is both old and new to you. It will be good luck."

The only good luck would be losing it. However, she did not want to offend her future mother-in-law. "Of course." After all, it was only one day.

"I believe I will have the sole," Sophia said, in a change of subject.

Concordia buried her face in the menu.

Drusilla frowned. "One cannot trust it to be properly cooked in a place like this."

"What do you mean, a place like this?" Mrs. Wells said. "*Dillon's* is one of the finest lunch establishments in Hartford."

"I was not going to say anything," Drusilla said in a low voice, leaning forward with the self-importance of one with exclusive knowledge, "but as we were passing the kitchen, I distinctly heard what sounded like—oh, I don't know, Russian? But not quite...I cannot tell those foreign languages apart."

Mrs. Wells nodded. "Portuguese, I believe. I heard that two Portuguese cooks were hired. The restaurant had been short-staffed for quite some time."

Drusilla waved a dismissive hand. "Russian, Portuguese, whatever." She nodded toward Sophia. "I would keep to simple fare, Mrs. Capshaw. Perhaps a soft-boiled egg."

Concordia rolled her eyes. "Just because they are foreigners does not mean they are half-witted."

"You cannot convince me that those of us born and raised in this country are not superior to foreigners in every respect," Drusilla declared.

"If we are talking about pedigree," Concordia said, "the Portuguese have a long history as accomplished navigators and cartographers, stretching back centuries. I am sure the new cooks are up to the task of preparing a piece of fish."

"Suit yourselves," Drusilla retorted, mouth turned downward in a sulk.

Soon the waiter poured the tea and took their orders.

"Have you and David resumed your house hunting since that dreadful business at the Armstrong farmhouse?" her mother asked, when he had left.

Mrs. Bradley set down her teacup with a clatter. "Angels preserve us, I heard about that. A sordid discovery!"

Drusilla sniffed. "At least David had not yet purchased the house. Quite a near escape."

"I pity the Armstrong relations," Mrs. Bradley said. "Who will buy the house, now that a man has been found—" she dropped her voice "—murdered in it?" She shuddered.

"I hear they have dropped the price again," Sophia said.

"No doubt," Drusilla said with a satisfied grunt. "It will not help them any."

Mrs. Wells set aside her menu. "Fortunately, that does not concern Concordia and David. But you must find a house soon," she added, glancing in her direction.

Concordia sighed. The Armstrong place had been ideal. If only Mr. Oster had not died there.

Her cheeks flushed. What was she thinking? The man should not have died *anywhere*.

Bu what if the murder was solved? Would the shadow over the house lift? Of course, discovering the murderer was a big *if* to begin with. A number of other *if*s stood in the way: *if* Guryev was the killer and had fled to Russia, there was no way of catching him. If a debt collector had killed them both, then where was Guryev's body? *If* Guryev had escaped Oster's fate, where was he now? *If* a debt collector had been keeping an eye on Guryev on campus, how did he go unnoticed? An unknown man would stand out a mile on a women's college. *If* she asked the engineering students whether they had observed a man trailing Guryev, would she be putting them at risk?

She squared her shoulders. Only one thing was certain. She had to try.

Chapter 10

Too much haste in making new acquaintances, however—"
pushing," as it is called—cannot be too much deprecated.
~Mrs. John Sherwood

Week 4, Instructor Calendar
October 1898

L ong shadows stretched across the gardens beside
Sycamore House as Concordia made her way to Willow
Cottage. A movement in the shadows caught her eye.

"Oh!" She let out a breath. Rachel Sanbourne emerged,
juggling easel, canvas, and a box of paints as she fumbled with
the latch of the garden's wicket gate. Concordia hurried over to
hold it open.

Mrs. Sanbourne, a smudge of paint alongside her thin,
patrician nose, blonde hair escaping her painter's beret, let out a
breath. "Thank you, Miss Wells."

"Do you need a hand carrying your supplies back to the
studio?"

Mrs. Sanbourne looked over her shoulder as Maynard
approached from Sycamore House. "The dean has offered to
do so."

Judging by Maynard's wrinkled brow and narrowed eyes, he
was none too pleased at the prospect.

"Touch only the edges," Mrs. Sanbourne instructed, passing
over the canvas. "It is still wet."

He complied with an aggrieved sigh and gave Concordia
barely a nod. "Miss Wells."

"I saw you this morning, heading toward Rook's Hill," Concordia said to Mrs. Sanbourne as they walked the path. Maynard trailed behind.

Mrs. Sanbourne shrugged. "I started there, but the light changed. The gardens are a congenial spot. Your president, I believe, tends to them?" She glanced back at a bed of chrysanthemums against the house, only now starting to die off before winter. "He has quite the green thumb."

Concordia nodded. It was propitious that she had run into Mrs. Sanbourne. The lady may know something of the debt collectors who had trailed Guryev. But there was little time. They had nearly reached the path to Willow Cottage.

Concordia kept her voice low, hoping the dean would not overhear. "Tell me, has Lieutenant Capshaw asked you about anyone who may have threatened Mr. Guryev, or was following him?" She hoped the question was not too abrupt. How does one broach such a subject delicately?

Mrs. Sanbourne stopped short and arched an eyebrow. "I would not have believed it of you, Miss Wells. Although I suppose a spinster living an unexciting, sheltered life would find something as unseemly as murder titillating. The rest of us, however, do *not*."

Concordia felt the flush creep up her neck and heat her cheeks. "I am merely interested in seeing justice done. My students are fond of Mr. Guryev and are distressed by his disappearance and the implication that he is a murderer."

Mrs. Sanbourne gave an unbecoming snort. "Ivan is not the victim here. He betrayed my husband and stole his work. Then he tricked Oster, killing him and taking the money. I am sure he is in Russia by now, selling my husband's blueprint yet again. For all the good it does him. He will probably gamble away the money within a month."

The lines on the lady's face were sharp and harsh in her bitterness. Concordia opened her mouth to try to undo the damage, but could think of nothing that would not make it worse.

"My husband is the one to be pitied," Rachel Sanbourne continued. "He has responsibilities at the college and deadlines to meet, all while reconstructing his design from memory."

"From memory?" Concordia repeated. "He does not yet have the original back from the Navy?"

Mrs. Sanbourne let out an exasperated sigh. "It has been misplaced. Mr. Roosevelt first had possession of it, but claims he turned it over to his successor months ago. No one can find it."

"I am sorry," Concordia said. Maynard, standing behind them, shifted the bulky canvas with barely concealed impatience. "I imagine it is a painstaking task for him."

"Save your pity," she snapped. "You have no idea what you are talking about. Your kind occupies itself with mooning over the scribblings of dead poets, while men like my husband do the real work of this nation." She turned on her heel and stalked off without a backward glance.

Concordia gaped after Rachel Sanbourne's retreating figure as Maynard approached. His upper lip curled. "You never learn, Miss Wells. Sleuthing is unsuitable for a lady. No one cares for an amateur poking her nose into weighty matters." He shifted his grip again. "Though she *was* unkind."

That was uncharacteristic of him. She glanced up in surprise. "Thank you for that."

He chuckled. "After all, you are not a *spinster.*" He walked away before she could think of a suitable retort.

As she turned down the path to Willow Cottage, she noticed Charlotte Crandall sitting on one of the porch rockers. "You heard?"

Charlotte grimaced. "I was taking in the sunset. I must say, Mrs. Sanbourne's attitude surprises me. For someone who is a painter, she does not have a favorable view of the arts and letters."

Concordia sat on the bench next to her. The sunset was indeed striking, foregrounded by the sun-tinged oranges and reds from the sugar maples that lined the path. "I was not exactly delicate with my question. She has a right to be angry."

"I wonder how she managed to get Ran—Mr. Maynard—to carry her things."

Concordia gave Charlotte a long look. "You and Mr. Maynard—there is something between you?"

Charlotte blushed to the roots of her dark brown hair. "Whatever gave you that idea?"

Concordia smirked. "I am an engaged woman, you know. There are signs."

Charlotte put her head in her hands. "I am so embarrassed."

"What have you to be embarrassed about? You have not behaved in an inappropriate manner, have you?" Not that she really thought so, though there was a certain young man's attentions during Charlotte's senior year at the school. The less said on that subject the better.

Charlotte sat up, indignant. "Certainly not!"

"Well then, you are fine. Does Mr. Maynard return the feeling?"

Charlotte plucked at her skirt. "I am not sure. Some days, he is warm and open. We laugh and talk about all sorts of things. But on other occasions, he is distant. On his guard."

Concordia remembered when Maynard and Charlotte had rescued her from a very dangerous predicament last May. He had seemed approachable then. It did not last long.

"If you could only see how he is, when we ride on Saturday mornings."

Concordia did not mention the fact that she had seen them today, from a distance. "A common interest is helpful."

"Riding is wonderful exercise. You should try it."

Concordia laughed. "You know how I feel about horses. No doubt the beasts feel the same way about me."

"Nonsense! We have the perfect horse for you—a gelding. His name is Joseph and he's very placid. Come join us next Saturday."

Concordia snorted. "*Joseph*? What sort of name is that for a horse?"

"He has a dappled coat, so he was named for Joseph in the Bible. You know—a coat of many colors. He is not terribly good-looking, but a child could ride him."

"I will confine my exercise to the bicycle, thanks. Is Miss Lovelace inside? I need to speak with her."

Charlotte nodded. "She is dressing for supper."

Concordia put a hand to the door. "I'm going in. Enjoy your quiet while you can."

She found Miss Lovelace with Miss Gage in the parlor, dressed and waiting to walk over to the dining hall. Miss Gage turned an excited face toward Concordia. "Miss Wells, have you heard? Maisie's uncle is to be Mr. Sanbourne's new assistant!"

"Really? Can he manage the time away?" Concordia asked. George Lovelace was a clockmaker with a shop along Kinsley Street. Over the years, he had allowed his niece and her like-minded friends to borrow tools and tinker with spare parts.

"He has an employee who can take over for a couple of months, at least until the Christmas season," Miss Lovelace said. "It will be nice to see more of him."

"That should give Mr. Sanbourne time to find a permanent replacement," Concordia said.

"Mrs. Sanbourne will be relieved, too," Miss Gage said. "She and Miss Kimble have been helping Mr. Sanbourne in the laboratory in the meanwhile."

"Really?" Concordia raised an eyebrow. "I did not know we had so many mechanically minded ladies here on campus."

"Miss Kimble's grandfather was a clockmaker, just like my uncle," Miss Lovelace said. "She said she has a lot of time on her hands."

Concordia frowned. "Mr. Maynard is still keeping the accounting books from Miss Kimble's clutches?"

Miss Gage made a face. "Apparently Mr. Langdon has intervened and given her *limited* bookkeeping tasks. But she sounded none too happy about it."

Setting aside Miss Kimble's woes, Concordia closed the door and gestured the girls into chairs. "I want to talk about Mr. Guryev's disappearance."

Miss Lovelace slumped in her chair. "I still cannot believe he has done what they say."

"What sort of questions did Lieutenant Capshaw ask?"

"He wanted to know about Mr. Guryev's associates and how he spent his free time," Miss Lovelace said. "We couldn't tell him much."

Miss Gage nodded. "Then he asked about the night before Founder's Day. We couldn't help him with that, either. Once our class was over at four o'clock, we went our separate ways."

Concordia nodded toward Maisie Lovelace. "You knocked on the laboratory door after supper and heard someone inside, isn't that right?"

Maisie Lovelace shifted uneasily. "The lieutenant asked me about that, but I'm not sure now. It could have been my imagination."

Concordia tried a different tack. "You know that Mr. Sanbourne's blueprint is missing?"

Miss Gage nodded. "Mrs. Sanbourne told us. She's very upset about it."

"Mrs. Sanbourne told you?" Concordia asked in confusion.

"I attend her lessons in oil painting."

"Ah. Quite generous of the lady."

"Then Jane told *me*," Miss Lovelace said.

"You don't take painting lessons?" Concordia asked.

"I might, if Alison Smedley weren't there," the girl muttered.

Miss Gage shrugged. "I do not understand the animosity between you two."

Miss Lovelace clenched her hands in her lap. "Miss Wells, do you really think Mr. Guryev stole the blueprint and then…killed Mr. Oster?"

Concordia did not want to lie to them. They were no longer children. "That appears to be the case, but there may be other possibilities." *None of them good.* "Tell me, did Mr. Guryev seem nervous or preoccupied?"

Miss Gage and Miss Lovelace exchanged a look.

"Well?" Concordia said impatiently.

"Sometimes," Miss Gage said. "In one class, he jumped a mile when a student came through the back door, just behind him."

"When was this?"

"The week of Founder's Day."

Miss Lovelace nodded. "It was also right around then that I asked him for help with a stuck bolt. His hands were shaking so much he could barely hold the tool." She made an impatient gesture. "We told all this to the policeman."

"I'm just trying to clarify things in my own mind," Concordia said. "Have there been any strangers lingering on campus, or someone who kept a particular eye on Mr. Guryev?"

"Lieutenant Capshaw already asked us about outsiders. We saw no one who wasn't supposed to be here," Miss Gage said.

Miss Lovelace tapped her chin in thought. "*Hmm,* I wonder…would the Trinity College boys count as strangers? Now that I think about it, I really only know a few of the fellows who come each week."

Concordia leaned forward, pulse quickening. "How many students from Trinity attend the engineering workshops and lectures?"

Miss Gage shrugged. "It varies. Sometimes as many as two dozen. Not always the same ones."

She felt a surge of excitement. Could Guryev's debt collector have posed as a college student and slipped in with the group? If Capshaw questioned the Trinity boys who attended the engineering classes here, someone might have noticed something.

Of course, Capshaw would not appreciate her *meddling,* but she would merely be supplying him with a piece of information. Surely he could not object to that.

Miss Lovelace sighed. "The program is not turning out the way we had hoped. Mr. Sanbourne has become withdrawn. We hardly get any time in the laboratory anymore. We attend lectures in another building instead of working with the equipment. It is all textbook study these days."

"Perhaps when your uncle comes, things will improve," Concordia said.

"I hope so."

They heard voices in the hall and Ruby opened the door. "Shall we go?"

As they walked over to the dining hall in the fall dusk, the girls chattering and laughing, Concordia's mind was awhirl with the puzzle. If Capshaw took her idea seriously and it helped to solve the case, perhaps she and David could buy the farmhouse, after all. Was it possible? The notoriety would subside over time.

"You are a million miles away," Ruby complained, as she caught Concordia's elbow to keep her from stumbling into a pile of raked leaves. "Dreaming of your beau?" she teased.

Concordia gave a wan smile. "In a way."

Chapter 11

But everyone, from the tired washer-woman to the student,
the wrestler, the fine lady, and the strong man, demands a cup of tea.
~Mrs. John Sherwood

Week 4, Instructor Calendar
October 1898

Concordia and Hannah Jenkins sipped their tea in the
staff lounge, relishing the cozy quiet of having the
space to themselves. Afternoon classes would soon let out and
the lounge would fill with faculty ready for a break.

Concordia gazed out upon the quadrangle. Leaves scuttled
in the brisk wind. She gave a shiver and settled more
comfortably into her shawl. "How are the plans coming for the
Halloween Ball?" Miss Jenkins had volunteered to organize it
this year. Customarily it was the lady principal's job, but
everyone knew that organization was not Miss Pomeroy's forte.

"I have plenty of volunteers for the decorating," Miss
Jenkins said, "although I wish they were not so eager to use
natural materials. Bittersweet vines, cornstalks, any number of
gourds—if it ripens in the fall, they'll gather it."

"Oh, I don't know. Those could make for charming
arrangements," Concordia said.

Miss Jenkins snorted. "Until last night, we hadn't had a
good frost to kill off the insects. One young lady had the
misfortune to discover an ants' nest in the last batch of vines
she gathered. I'm surprised you did not hear the shrieks across
the quadrangle yesterday."

Concordia chuckled. "Perhaps ribbons *would* be best."

Miss Jenkins raised her teacup in salute. "Amen to that."

"I take it we will have the usual entertainments?"

"The nut-burning, certainly. You know how the girls love to go on about suitors and marriage."

Concordia smiled. Burning the nuts—or *nits*, as the Scots referred to them—was a time-honored Halloween activity. A young lady threw two nuts in the fire, one to represent a specific young man she admired, the other for herself. If the nuts popped or jumped apart, the union was not to be. However, if the nuts burned brightly side by side, their love was purported to be strong and their future together promising. She had never subscribed to such foolishness, but the students enjoyed it. So long as they did not singe their skirts in their eagerness to approach the fire.

"There are other activities in the works," Miss Jenkins went on. "Mrs. Sanbourne has volunteered to sketch caricatures, and of course we will have dancing in the ballroom. I wish we could forgo the apple ducking. It makes an awful mess. But the hue and cry when I proposed *that* was not to be believed."

"I can help with that, if you'd like," Concordia said.

Miss Jenkins shrugged. "I had not asked because I thought you were busy with wedding arrangements. Fittings and trousseau shopping and so on."

Concordia grimaced. As she had feared, once word spread about her resignation many of her colleagues would treat her as if she were already gone. "I would be happy to help. I am trying to keep the wedding preparations as simple as possible, although that is a challenge when one has a mother."

Miss Jenkins nodded as she set down her empty teacup. "What are your plans after the wedding? Where will you live?"

Concordia hesitated. She dearly wished she had an answer to the question *where will you live?* She had tried contacting Capshaw to share what she had learned, only to be told he was out of town on a case. Or perhaps he was avoiding her and had ordered such a message be given? She should check with Sophia.

Concordia was spared a reply when the door opened and Miss Banning ambled in. The lady leaned heavily on her cane and trailed one of several shawls in her wake. Dean Maynard, close behind, stooped to pick up the end. Miss Banning adjusted it with barely a *humph* or a glance in his direction. Charlotte Crandall and Miss Kimble followed soon after.

Concordia smiled as she listened to the chatter. She loved the collegiality of such times, when the faculty gathered at their ease and shared their day. She knew she wanted to marry David, but at the moment her heavy heart whispered that it was too much to give up.

She slid over to make room for Charlotte and Miss Banning. "How are you today?" she asked the old lady, as Charlotte went to the sideboard to fetch the tea. "Our weather has turned cold quite suddenly, has it not?" She imagined the chill was especially difficult on that lady's rheumatism, though of course it would be impolite to bring up the subject.

Margaret Banning looked Concordia up and down through her thick lenses, which distorted her blue eyes into owl-like size. "A little cold weather is not enough to deter me, my good miss." Her eyes brightened as Charlotte passed over a teacup. "Ah, thank you, dear."

"How are your classes going? Any promising students this year?" Concordia asked.

Miss Banning scowled and gripped her cup with knobby hands. "Girls these days are preoccupied with chasing novelty: the latest style, club, and whatnot. The study of history is not nearly so glamorous, though it reveals more about the human condition than they will find in fashion magazines. 'Man is explicable by nothing less than all his history.' Emerson."

As further talk along that line would prompt more quotes from dead philosophers, Concordia turned to Miss Kimble, who had taken a seat across from her. "I hear Miss Lovelace's uncle has been hired as Mr. Sanbourne's assistant."

Frances Kimble dropped a sugar cube into her cup before looking up. "The engineering students have been sadly neglected. Since Mr. Sanbourne is much too occupied to conduct a search for a permanent replacement, I had a word with Mr. Lovelace. He is more than qualified to run the basic workshops and oversee the young ladies' projects."

Maynard, seated in the rocking chair a few feet away, turned abruptly. "You took it upon yourself to hire Lovelace, without consulting me first? I am dean of faculty here. I decide upon new hires, not you. Your job is to keep an accurate ledger. If you can manage it," he added under his breath.

"I would not be doing even that, had not President Langdon finally stepped in," Miss Kimble said sharply, setting her cup aside. Her slim shoulders stiffened as if braced for battle. "As to the new hire, the engineering program is uniquely funded through Theodora Blake's grant. It is technically not part of the faculty budget and therefore not within your purview. *I* decide how to allocate those monies. You do not have to be consulted, and you do not have to *like it.*"

Concordia watched with a sort of morbid fascination as the veins stood out on Maynard's neck and his face turned a dusky red. She almost felt sorry for the dean, especially when she glimpsed the distress on Charlotte's face. Maynard abruptly stood and stalked out of the room.

With a sigh, Miss Kimble sat back and sipped her tea.

Well, perhaps she would not miss some aspects of college life when she married. Concordia rose to refill her cup.

As if summoned by her thoughts, David stepped into the lounge. He wore his customary dark wool trousers and brown hounds-tooth jacket, worn at the elbows. His reading glasses were tucked into the breast pocket.

She self-consciously settled her own spectacles more firmly upon her nose as he met her eyes. *Mercy,* his smile still made her knees weak.

He crossed the room in quick strides, nodding to those he passed. "Allow me," he said, reaching for the pot.

"Thank you," she murmured.

Miss Jenkins got up to leave, depositing her cup on the sideboard. "Ah, Mr. Bradley! Concordia and I were discussing where you would be living once you are married. Have you found anything promising?"

Concordia frowned. Miss Jenkins was terribly nosy about the subject.

"In fact," David began, "we had been thinking of—" he winced as Concordia's well-heeled boot came down upon the arch of his foot.

"Oh, I beg your pardon! How clumsy of me," she said, taking a hasty step backward.

Miss Jenkins regarded the couple with a skeptical eye. "Well, I suppose I must be going."

David grimaced as he watched her leave. "So we are no longer considering the Armstrong house?" He discreetly flexed his ankle. "I didn't realize Oster being found there bothered you so."

"It does." She dropped her voice. "How can we live there without knowing who is responsible and seeing justice done?"

"So you have absolutely ruled it out?"

She hesitated. "If Lieutenant Capshaw can solve the case, I would feel better about it. In fact, I have some information that I hope might help."

David leaned closer. "Really? What is it?"

Concordia caught Miss Kimble glancing in their direction, her dark eyes narrowed attentively. "I'll explain later. But for now, I would rather keep the idea of buying the Armstrong place to ourselves. Everyone will have an opinion on the subject." She gestured at his foot in concern. "I hope I did not hurt you?"

He grimaced. "We shall have to determine a less painful signal in the future, or my feet will not survive it."

She smiled. "I promise."

Chapter 12

Nothing could be simpler than the riding-habit,
and yet is there any dress so becoming?
~Mrs. John Sherwood

Week 5, Instructor Calendar
October 1898

Concordia walked with Charlotte to the stables in the early-dawn light, wearing Charlotte's second-best riding habit. It was tight in the waist and long in the skirt. She had to take care not to trip over the hem.

"I cannot believe I let you talk me into this."

"Nonsense, the fresh air will be good for you," Charlotte said, tugging on her black kid riding gloves. "It is still too muddy for cycling, and we have been confined indoors for nearly a week, grading papers and refereeing student squabbles."

Concordia sighed. Charlotte was right about the squabbling. Two factions had formed once again at Willow Cottage: Miss Lovelace and her fellow engineering students, and Miss Smedley and her cohorts. The rainy weather this week had kept everyone inside and in a fine pucker.

At last the sun was out, and she was grateful to be away from the cottage. Even if she was to be atop an ugly horse and in the company of the dean, it was preferable to the past few days.

"There's Mr. Maynard now," Charlotte said, nodding.

Maynard bowed politely to Concordia, though he could not keep the sardonic glint from his eye. "Miss Crandall's powers of persuasion must be considerable. Shall we?" He tugged at the stable door.

A loud *crack* echoed in their ears. Concordia took a startled leap backward and tripped on her hem. Charlotte had fallen to her hands and knees.

The horses whinnied in panic. The largest of them, a large Frisian, thrashed in his stall, wood splintering under his hooves.

"Ransom!" Charlotte cried, scrambling to get her feet under her.

Maynard ran toward the horse to restrain him, but he was too late. With a final mighty kick and a leap over the debris, Ransom cleared the stall and sped past Maynard, heading for the only exit. Toward Charlotte and Concordia.

"Charlotte!" Maynard yelled, a look of horror on his face as the horse bore down upon them.

Charlotte froze.

Concordia lunged for her, yanking a handful of her jacket and swinging them both toward the hay bales in the corner. The hooves thundered past as Concordia's head struck the handle of a pitchfork.

The last thing she remembered before she lost consciousness was the barrel of a pistol, kicked by the horse and skittering in the dirt.

Chapter 13

The world is full of traps.
~Mrs. John Sherwood

Week 5, Instructor Calendar
October 1898

The blackness faded and she opened her eyes. Where—? The infirmary. She blinked a few times, the memory flooding back. The horse. Hitting her head. She put a hand to her aching temple. It felt so unreal.

Hannah Jenkins came over to her bed. "How do you feel?"

Concordia winced as Miss Jenkins helped prop her up. "My head aches. And I'm a little sore. Otherwise I seem whole." She surveyed the long, narrow aisle of empty beds. "Where are Charlotte and Mr. Maynard? Are they all right?"

Miss Jenkins pointed to a screened-in bed at the other end of the room. "The doctor is with Miss Crandall now. Mr. Maynard only had a few scrapes. He's resting back at Sycamore House."

"Why was I brought to the infirmary?"

"It's closer to the stables than Willow Cottage. Besides, you were unconscious for a good ten minutes. We were worried." Miss Jenkins gently probed the right side of Concordia's scalp. "I was able to get the bleeding to stop. I do not think you will need any stitches. No broken bones that I can tell, but the doctor will want to conduct his own examination."

"What about Charlotte?"

"She will be fine, thanks to you. The dean told us how you pulled her out of the way before the horse could trample you both."

Concordia put a hand to her head. "I am never going near a stable or a horse again."

Miss Jenkins patted her arm. "Let me get you a headache powder."

Concordia leaned back and closed her eyes.

When she opened them again, she realized she must have dozed for a time. The sun was shining brightly in the upper windows. Her mother perched in a nearby chair, placidly knitting.

Was she hallucinating? Concordia squeezed her eyes shut and opened them again. There she was, a slim-figured lady with the heart-shaped face and graying blond hair. "Mother?"

"Ah, you're awake," her mother said. "Would you like some water?" She reached a blue-veined hand for the pitcher.

"How did you...?" Concordia's voice trailed off in confusion.

Her mother smiled. "Ever since your escapade last spring, I made Miss Jenkins promise that she would inform me whenever you were injured."

"How...enterprising of you," Concordia said weakly. She sipped from the glass. "Were you told what happened?"

Mrs. Wells' lips thinned to a somber line. "Those girls have much to answer for. I still believe the police should be involved."

Concordia gingerly shook her aching head. Police? "I believe I've missed something. Tell me what you know."

Her mother hesitated. "I understand the young ladies are favorites of yours. I would rather not distress you."

Concordia pushed herself to sit up. "It would distress me more to be left in the dark. Please, Mother."

"You are right, I suppose." She set her knitting in her lap. "A mechanism was discovered, affixed to the top frame of the stable door. I am unaware of the specifics, but somehow the door being pulled open caused a gun to fire. Miss Lovelace and her friends from the engineering department are suspected of having staged the stunt."

Concordia's eyes widened as it came back to her. The loud bang and the ringing in her ears. The gun on the floor.

"There must be another explanation. Miss Lovelace would never do such a thing," Concordia declared, struggling to swing her legs over the side of the bed.

Miss Jenkins hurried over. "Where do you think you are going?"

"She insisted that I tell her about Miss Lovelace," Mrs. Wells said apologetically.

Miss Jenkins settled Concordia back in bed and smoothed the covers. "President Langdon is questioning the students now. I am sure it will take time to get the whole story. Besides, you have another visitor." She pointed.

Hovering in the doorway was David Bradley. The familiar sight of his trim form, dark curly hair and bright brown eyes made her chest feel lighter. "David," she whispered, reaching out her hands as he crossed the room.

He clasped them warmly. "Thank heaven you are safe. I could not believe it when I heard." His eyes narrowed with worry. "You are all right?"

Miss Jenkins made a notation on her clipboard and stuck the pencil back in her topknot. "She'll be fine. The doctor checked in while she was sleeping. I'll leave you now, but talk softly. I finally got Miss Crandall quieted down to sleep. She's still quite upset about Ransom."

"Ransom?" Mrs. Wells asked, as Miss Jenkins headed for her office.

"The school's black Frisian," David said.

"What about him?" Concordia asked. "What is going on, David?"

He hesitated. "In the animal's panic to break free of the stall, he was grievously injured. He had to be put down."

Concordia sucked in a breath. "How horrible. Mr. Maynard must be taking it especially hard. Ransom was a favorite of his."

"Well, he is certainly calling for the heads of Miss Lovelace and her fellows," David said grimly.

"But we do not know they are responsible," Concordia protested. "What possible motive could they have? It sounds like a fraternity prank to me. What about the Trinity boys? A number of them have been auditing the engineering classes." She felt a guilty pang. She'd been blaming Trinity College students for a great many things lately.

David pursed his lips. "Good point. I will mention that to Langdon."

"Are we to assume the dean was the target of the prank?" Concordia asked. "He's customarily the first one at the stables on a Saturday morning."

"A rather deadly prank, if you ask me," her mother said.

"A blank cartridge was used, surely?" Concordia asked. "I am sure no real harm was intended." Although the death of the poor horse was harm enough.

"It was a bullet, not a blank," David said. "Langdon found it embedded in the paddock post."

Concordia sat up straighter. "Someone tried to *kill* the dean?"

"Or Miss Crandall, perhaps," David said, glancing uneasily toward Charlotte's bed. "She has been the more regular Saturday morning rider, though I've noticed lately that she and the dean often ride together."

Concordia, knowing Charlotte's feelings for the dean, made no comment.

"If that is the case, why have the police not been called?" Mrs. Wells asked with a frown.

"I think we already know the answer to that," David said.

Concordia nodded. They did, indeed.

Mrs. Wells' brow cleared in understanding. "Ah. Notoriety."

"Heaven knows we have had enough of that these past few years," David said. "It would not do for the college to be embroiled in further scandal. Oster's death and Guryev's disappearance have kept the newspapers busy enough as it is."

"Where on earth did the gun come from in the first place?" Mrs. Wells asked.

David nodded toward the infirmarian, now stacking folded sheets in the closet. "It's Miss Jenkins' starter pistol. Someone must have taken it from the gymnasium equipment locker last night. She told Langdon she saw it in its case as recently as yesterday afternoon."

"I still don't understand who would do such a vindictive thing," Concordia said. Certainly not Miss Lovelace or her friends. She must speak with Edward Langdon, before a grievous injustice was done.

Chapter 14

The duties of a chaperon are very hard and unremitting,
and sometimes very disagreeable.

~Mrs. John Sherwood

Week 5, Instructor Calendar
October 1898

"I told you yesterday, Mr. Langdon, we had nothing to do with it!" Miss Lovelace cried.

They were all in the president's office: Miss Lovelace and her friend Miss Gage, Randolph Maynard, Lady Principal Pomeroy, Charlotte, and Concordia. Although it was the largest staff office in Founder's Hall, they were still crammed cheek-by-jowl in the space.

Concordia glanced over at Charlotte. Her weariness was evident in the dark circles under her eyes and the hollows in her cheeks. The high collar of her shirtwaist could not quite conceal the scrapes along her neck from her tumble.

Randolph Maynard held up a pouch that Concordia recognized all too well. "I believe this toolkit is yours, Miss Lovelace?"

Maisie Lovelace's mouth gaped. "I've been missing that for two days. Where did you find it?"

"So you admit it belongs to you?" Maynard asked.

Miss Gage shifted impatiently in her seat. "Of course it is hers. Everyone has seen her carrying that pouch. She always keeps it with her."

Concordia was familiar with the pouch, too. The tools within it, in fact, had been the saving of them last May. An uneasy grip in the pit of her stomach told her where Maynard was going with this.

"Not always," Maynard said between gritted teeth. "You have become careless with your tools, Miss Lovelace. I found the pouch behind a hay bale in the stable."

Concordia sighed. So much for the Trinity student theory. No college boy knew Miss Lovelace well enough to consider implicating her. It had to be someone closer to home. She clasped the girl's icy hand. "Someone must have put it there."

Maynard gave her a steely-eyed glare. "And what possible motive would anyone have for doing that, Miss Wells?"

Concordia returned the glare. "And what possible motive would Miss Lovelace have for attempted murder, Mr. Maynard?"

President Langdon cleared his throat. "Now, now, let us not talk of *murder*. This is not a penny-dreadful, Miss Wells." He folded his garden-roughened hands across his capacious middle as he leaned back in his chair. "Tell me, Miss Lovelace, is it possible that you merely intended to play a prank you thought to be harmless and startle poor Mr. Maynard and Miss Crandall? Could you have confused a blank cartridge for a live bullet, my dear? It was still a reckless trick, considering how it caused the death of our best horse. I do not like to think you or anyone on this campus capable of malice."

Miss Lovelace's voice quavered. "The difference between a bullet and a blank cartridge is quite obvious. A blank has a crimped end. I did not do this. Someone must have taken my kit and put it there." She turned to Concordia and whispered. "And I think I know who."

Concordia gave Miss Lovelace's hand a warning squeeze. "Not now," she murmured.

She knew whom Miss Lovelace meant.

Alison Smedley.

Could it be? There was no denying the animosity between them. But it would not do to accuse the girl in her absence. They needed time to investigate.

Concordia turned to President Langdon, purposely avoiding Maynard's eye. "The toolkit is poor proof for such a serious charge against her."

Maynard glowered. "It is sufficient for me. Particularly considering her past behavior—have you forgotten the episode of the buggy in the bursar's office?"

Langdon winced.

"It is time to expel Miss Lovelace," Maynard went on. "There is no proof against Miss Gage here—" he glanced at that young lady, who gave a defiant toss of her head "—though I am sure this was not accomplished alone. We should also dismantle the engineering program. Otherwise, we will continue to encourage this bold, dangerous, unwomanly behavior." He glared at Langdon. "You do not want that, do you, Edward?"

Concordia's hands grew as cold as Miss Lovelace's, and her chest constricted. She could not let this happen.

Finally, she summoned the breath to speak. "If you decide to expel Miss Lovelace and end the engineering program on the basis of such flimsy evidence, I shall call the police about the incident. It will need to be investigated properly to justify such drastic action."

Everyone in the room stared at her, open-mouthed. Miss Pomeroy's eyes widened, her wandering attention engaged at last.

"You would not dare." Maynard's voice was cold.

"Try me." Concordia hoped the tremor in her voice would be taken for anger rather than fear. She had never threatened an administrator. "You are blaming a student without sufficient proof and are about to ruin her future, along with the future of other students if you end the program. It is inexcusable. I will go to Lieutenant Capshaw if I have to."

Maynard crossed his arms and gave her a scathing look. "It is obvious you care nothing for the well-being of this institution. Is it because you will no longer be a part of it after this semester? Why not go home now, and knit booties for your impending domestic bliss?"

Concordia felt the air leave her lungs. She stood on rubbery legs, motioning for Miss Lovelace and Miss Gage to accompany her. Finally, at the door, she managed a few words. "Consider who wishes you harm, Mr. Maynard. Then you may find the true culprit."

She caught a glimpse of Charlotte's pale face as she closed the door.

"At least *you* believe us," Miss Lovelace said, as they walked back to Willow Cottage in the dying light. "Thank you for coming to our defense."

Concordia nodded, her heart too full to speak. She loved this school, and would never wish harm upon it. She knew the death of Ransom was a blow to Maynard, but to sacrifice Miss Lovelace for the sake of revenge was beyond the pale. She thought of the words she had flung at him when leaving. Who would wish Maynard harm? As disagreeable as he was, she could not imagine someone setting out to kill him.

There was the possibility that Miss Lovelace had raised. "We need to talk," she said to Miss Lovelace and Miss Gage. "We'll have tea in my sitting room."

Once they were settled and the door was closed, Concordia wasted no time. "You believe Miss Smedley had a hand in this?"

Miss Gage and Miss Lovelace exchanged a glance.

"Even I find it hard to believe," Miss Lovelace said slowly, "and you know I do not hold her in high regard."

"If she did it, she had to have help," Miss Gage said. "She is not very mechanically minded."

Concordia was not concerned about the practicality of the prank. Not yet. "Does Miss Smedley hate you so much?"

Miss Lovelace shrugged. "I know she resents the new program. She sees it as special treatment."

"And if Mr. Langdon follows Mr. Maynard's recommendation, the program will be over, and Alison will have what she wants," Miss Gage said miserably.

"I will explore the possibility," Concordia said. "In the meantime, do not make any accusations. After all, you know firsthand how it feels to be blamed for something you did not do."

"But that will take time," Miss Lovelace protested. "What if I'm expelled in the meanwhile?"

"President Langdon is a fair-minded man," Concordia said. "He will want more proof before doing that, no matter what Mr. Maynard says. However, you must admit last semester's stunt with his buggy has not endeared you to him."

Both girls dropped their heads.

"What will happen next?" Miss Lovelace asked.

"I do not know," Concordia said. "But be prepared for unpleasantness."

Chapter 15

No doubt a vivacious American girl, with all her inherited hatred of authority, is a troublesome charge. All young people are rebels.
~Mrs. John Sherwood

Week 6, Instructor Calendar
October 1898

Concordia was right about the unpleasant aftermath of the gun prank. Miss Lovelace was placed on restriction for an indefinite period. That meant she could attend classes and chapel services but nothing else. She ate her meals in the kitchen of Willow Cottage instead of the dining hall with the other girls. Concordia and Ruby kept her company as much as they could, and tried to boost her spirits.

It also meant that Miss Lovelace would not attend the Halloween ball. As the girls chattered excitedly and made their plans for the upcoming event, the girl became quiet and left more food on her plate.

Alison Smedley's exuberance, on the other hand, grew with each passing day. She often lingered in the hallway outside Miss Lovelace's door, discussing costume plans and the decisions of the decorating committee. Concordia had shooed her and her friends out of earshot more than once.

The factions within the cottage had become further entrenched. The engineering students expressed outrage over Miss Lovelace's restriction, while Miss Smedley and her cohorts blamed Maisie and her friends for the heinous prank. The other young ladies—neutral up to this point—were horrified that a beloved horse had died. They too turned accusing eyes to Miss Lovelace.

Even Charlotte Crandall, supposedly above the fray as a faculty member, kept her distance from Miss Lovelace.

"She thinks I did it," Maisie said to Concordia, sobbing on her shoulder.

Concordia sighed. There was no denying that Charlotte had been fond of the horse. "Miss Crandall simply has a lot on her mind lately," she lied, gently prying the girl off her shoulder and passing her a handkerchief. Miss Lovelace was getting herself terribly worked up about this business. She was sure to make herself sick.

Over the next few days, Concordia waited for an opportunity to speak with Charlotte alone. Her chance came when they both left their offices to dress for supper.

Charlotte had not been looking like herself since the incident. Her clothes hung upon her loosely, her cheeks were pale, her expression distant.

"Could I have a word?" Concordia asked.

Charlotte nodded, and they fell into step together.

Concordia got right to the point. "You believe Miss Lovelace is responsible for rigging the gun, don't you?"

Charlotte stopped abruptly, and a student hurrying by bumped into her. "I beg your pardon," she said absently, to the girl's retreating back. She met Concordia's eyes. "I do." She gestured toward the path to the stable. "Come, I will show you."

Curiosity aroused, Concordia followed her. "It has been a week since the incident. Everything has been cleaned up, surely?"

"I had the chance to see it all beforehand," Charlotte said. "I want to show you how complex—" She broke off as they saw an unfamiliar workman of middle age, standing on a wooden crate and running his hand along the top of the stable doorway.

"Excuse me, sir. May I help you?" Concordia called out.

The man stepped off the crate and brushed his hands on his faded overalls. "Not at all, ladies. Though if ye're looking to ride, I daresay ye've not enough time afore the supper bell." He squinted. "An' not dressed for it, neither."

"Who are you?" Charlotte asked.

"Ah! Where are my manners?" the man exclaimed. He swept off his cap and gave a little bow. "George Lovelace, at yer service."

"Maisie Lovelace's uncle? And Mr. Sanbourne's new assistant?" Concordia asked.

"Yes to both questions, little lady." He smoothed his shaggy iron-gray mustache with tobacco-stained fingers, stuck his cap in his back pocket, and returned to his examination of the lintel. "An' who might you be?" he said over his shoulder.

"We are both instructors here," Concordia said. "This is Miss Crandall, and I am Miss Wells. Your niece lives with us at Willow Cottage. She is also in my Rhetoric class."

The man turned. "Miss Wells, ye say? My niece speaks often of ye. Ride a bicycle machine, I hear. My Maisie helped ye fix the chain when it broke."

Concordia nodded. "Your niece is quite skilled." She watched as he tugged at something with a grunt. "What is it you are doing?"

"Looking for proof that Maisie didn' do what they say. The girl's a spirited one, but she don' have a mean bone in her body."

Charlotte Crandall watched him with a skeptical eye as he jumped off the crate. "Her tools were found here. Not many students on campus have the ability to contrive the counter-weight mechanism. I saw it all before they took it down."

Lovelace held out a screw between a grubby thumb and forefinger. "True enough. I figured I'd take a look, anyhow. Good thing I did, too. The anchors were left in. There's still things ye can tell." He gestured to the screw. "See how the wire's wrapped? That's not how my Maisie wraps her wire when she's securing it to a nail or a screw. The girl is left-handed. If she'd twined it around the screw head, it'd be wrapped counter-clockwise. The twist to secure the end would be counter-clockwise, too. And she leaves her ends nowt like this. A lot of wire wasted here. Her work is a sight more neat, I can tell ye."

Concordia felt her chest lighten. Miss Lovelace could be proved innocent! She was sure Mr. Langdon would reverse the restriction. The Halloween ball was tomorrow. Perfect.

She glanced over at Charlotte. "Are you convinced now?"

Charlotte nodded, a flush creeping up her cheeks. "I feel terrible at how cold-hearted I have been to the poor girl."

Concordia turned back to Mr. Lovelace. "Could you retrieve the other anchors, and bring them to President Langdon's office after supper?"

Lovelace's face creased in a wide smile. "It'll be a pleasure."

Chapter 16

Women of the world are not always worldly women... brilliancy in society may be accompanied by the best heart and the sternest principle.
~Mrs. John Sherwood

Week 6, Instructor Calendar
October 1898

Concordia could hardly contain her excitement. "Do not say anything to Miss Lovelace," she cautioned Charlotte, as they hurried in to change into their dinner dresses. "I don't want to raise her hopes."

In spite of herself, her own hopes were riding high. Certainly they were no nearer to finding the person responsible, but at least an innocent girl would no longer be suffering for it. And perhaps the rift within Willow Cottage would be mended.

She wondered how Miss Smedley would react, once she learned that Miss Lovelace had been vindicated. That young lady would bear watching. Concordia still did not know how Miss Smedley could have pulled off such a stunt—Miss Gage was correct in her assessment that the young lady was not mechanically minded. At least no additional pranks had occurred in the past week.

When the meal was over, Concordia and Charlotte went over to the Hall.

They found Mr. Lovelace waiting patiently outside President Langdon's darkened office.

"That's odd," Concordia said. "He usually works for an hour or two in the evening. Come to think of it, he wasn't at supper." She pointed to Miss Pomeroy's open door, light spilling out at the far end of the hall. "The lady principal may know where we can find him."

Charlotte motioned toward the dean's lighted office next door. "We would have better luck asking Mr. Maynard. Miss Pomeroy pays little attention to the comings and goings of her *confrères*."

Concordia had hoped to avoid that contingency, but Charlotte and Mr. Lovelace were already heading toward his door. She had no choice but to follow.

Maynard scowled at the disruption, but his expression visibly softened at the sight of Miss Crandall. "Yes?"

"Do you know where we would find Mr. Langdon?" Charlotte asked.

"He had an unexpected emergency that called him out of town."

Concordia's heart sank. The president could be gone for days.

Maynard set down his pen when he caught sight of Concordia and Mr. Lovelace hovering in the doorway. "He put me in charge until he returns. What is it?"

Concordia was ready to give up the entire business until Langdon's return when Charlotte sprang forward eagerly. "Oh, if you would. It concerns Miss Lovelace."

There it was. The return of the scowl. Concordia had never before noticed what agile eyebrows the man had. They seemed to go up and down along his forehead of their own accord.

Charlotte paid little heed to the eyebrows, however, and promptly seated herself, patting a space on the bench beside her for Concordia.

With a sigh of resignation, Maynard waved Lovelace into the other chair. He gave the man a penetrating look. "Who might you be?"

If the man was intimidated by the dean's brusque manner, he did not show it. "George Lovelace. Mr. Sanbourne's temporary assistant."

"And Miss Lovelace's uncle," Charlotte put in.

Concordia doubted that bit of information was necessary, and certainly not helpful. She remembered how upset Maynard had been at Miss Kimble hiring Lovelace without his permission. One strike against the man already.

"Mr. Lovelace was at the stables examining the scene," Charlotte continued. "He has discovered something important which clears Miss Lovelace of wrongdoing."

Maynard sat back and crossed his arms over his chest, dark brows hard at work again. "Indeed?"

Charlotte nodded to Lovelace, who pulled the three anchor screws from his jacket pocket and explained the manner in which the wires had been wrapped, and what he knew of his niece's methods.

To give him credit, Maynard listened attentively, though he did not bother to examine the screws closely. When Lovelace had finished, the dean pulled out a crisp envelope from his desk drawer and held it out. "Put those bits in here. I will show them to Mr. Langdon when he returns."

After Maynard had stowed away the envelope for safekeeping, he stood to usher them out.

"What about Miss Lovelace? Are you going to lift the restriction?" Charlotte asked.

Maynard's lip curled. "Absolutely not."

Concordia rolled her eyes. She knew it.

"Ye have the evidence of yer own eyes," growled Lovelace. "What more do ye want? My girl is innocent."

"That is precisely the problem," Maynard snapped. "She is your blood relation. You might say anything to clear her. Oh yes, I have observed that she is left-handed, but anyone setting up such a contraption in the chill air, with dim light and an awkward overhead angle, might do things a bit more sloppily and not at all typical of her usual work. This proves nothing."

"The Halloween ball is tomorrow," Charlotte said. "Can you not give her the benefit of the doubt?"

Maynard stiffened. "I cannot. If you will excuse me, I must get back to work."

He closed the door in their faces.

"Well, that's that," Charlotte said dispiritedly, as they headed for the stairwell. "I suppose we shall have to wait for President Langdon to return. We are grateful for your discovery, Mr. Lovelace. I still believe it will make a difference."

"Thank ye for trying," Lovelace said, with a shake of his head. "I don't understand why that man is so fixed on Maisie being to blame."

Concordia hesitated. "You go on ahead," she said to Charlotte. "I will catch up."

Charlotte nodded. Concordia hurried back to Dean Maynard's office.

"The discussion is closed, Miss Wells," Maynard snarled, after she had knocked and let herself in.

"Oh, I am not here to persuade you to reconsider, Mr. Maynard."

His brows went up again.

"I am here to repeat my warning of last week. Consider carefully who may wish you harm. You see, now I know for certain that Miss Lovelace is innocent. I admit that even I had my doubts about her until today. You may deny the significance of what Mr. Lovelace has brought you, but not because the proof is as flimsy as you say. I think it is because you do not want to consider the alternative. Someone tried to kill you. And that person could try again."

Maynard's face paled.

Concordia gentled her voice. "Who is it, Mr. Maynard? Who is trying to kill you?"

Maynard stood so abruptly, his chair crashed to the floor behind him. "Get...out," he hissed between clenched teeth.

Concordia made a hasty exit. As she did so, she heard footsteps, light and quick, upon the nearby stairs. Someone had been eavesdropping. She ran to the stairwell, but whoever it was had gone.

Chapter 17

Week 6, Instructor Calendar
Halloween 1898

"Don't you worry, now," Ruby said, as she anchored the black-and-orange feather comb more firmly in Concordia's hair. "Miss Lovelace and I will be cozy as church mice here."

Concordia glanced at the matron in the mirror. Despite Ruby's bright voice, a frown puckered her brow as she finished the last of the buttons at the back of the gown. "Miss Gage has decided to stay behind, too."

Ruby's frown softened. "A kind-hearted girl, that one. Well, we'll be glad to have her. I've made plenty of treats, an' we'll tell ghost stories and whatnot. So! Let's have a look at you."

Concordia stood, adjusting her glasses for a better view of her reflection. She had decided against a costume this year, instead selecting a black velvet evening gown with a touch of cream gauze at the bosom, so as not to wash out her freckled complexion. The bodice nipped in more tightly than she was accustomed to, but the effect made the discomfort worthwhile.

Ruby grinned. "You're right pretty, miss. Mr. Bradley won't be able to keep his eyes off you."

Concordia flushed. "Never you mind about Mr. Bradley," she chided, although if she were honest with herself, that was just what she was hoping for.

Ruby chuckled.

"I had better be going." Concordia gathered her shawl. "Oh, I nearly forgot: Miss Gage wants to burn nuts in the parlor fireplace. Be sure to keep an eye on that." The last thing they needed was their new rug to go up in flames.

Ruby clucked her tongue in disapproval. "Such foolishness. If the circumstances were any different, I wouldn't allow it. But it may cheer them up a bit." She grunted. "How I wish that sour-puss Maynard had lifted her restriction! A stubborn one, he is."

Concordia abruptly turned to face Ruby. "How do you know about that?"

Ruby packed the combs back in their case. "Charlotte told me. Came through the door last night, mad as a hatter and breathing fire."

"That was supposed to be confidential. No harm done, I suppose, as long as it didn't reach Miss Lovelace's ears. The girl is miserable enough as it is."

Ruby tugged nervously on her lower lip. "Um, well, about that...."

Concordia put her hands on her hips and blew out a sigh. "She knows?"

"It's mighty hard to keep a secret around here," Ruby said, rolling her eyes. "Miss Smedley overheard us talking and wasted no time taunting Miss Lovelace about it."

Concordia groaned.

"But you know something," Ruby said, dropping her voice and leaning forward conspiratorially, "I think the talk of proof being found has made Miss Smedley a little nervous. She hasn't been walking around with her usual bravado today."

Hmm. Concordia wondered if she could make use of that. An idea was beginning to form, but it would have to wait until later. "You are sure you'll be all right here? I would stay if I could—"

"—but you have to help chaperone them hoydens," Ruby finished. "I know. We'll be fine. Go on, now."

Chapter 18

A ballroom should be very well lighted, exceedingly well ventilated, and very gayly dressed.

~Mrs. John Sherwood

Week 6, Instructor Calendar
Halloween 1898

Sycamore House was awash in the glow of luminarias and hurricane lamps lining the stone steps. The young ladies had certainly outdone themselves this year, Concordia thought, noting the massive bows atop the columns wrapped in bittersweet vines. Free of ants' nests, one hoped. Clusters of chrysanthemums, pumpkins and autumnal gourds flanked the sides of the double doors, opened to let in a cooling breeze.

Concordia left her wrap in the foyer and went in search of David. She found him chatting with the clipboard-wielding Miss Jenkins. That lady was formidably dressed tonight as Artemis the huntress, wearing a simple white tunic, sandals, and gold belt. A quiver of arrows was strapped to her back.

Miss Jenkins' eyes brightened. "Ah, now our chaperone list is complete."

"Sorry I'm late. Do you still want me at the apple ducking?" Concordia asked, flushing, but whether it was from her brisk walk to make up time or David's lingering gaze of approval, she could not decide. His evening attire, with its high-necked white shirt, well-tailored black tails and smooth pleated trousers, was a decided improvement over his usual wrinkled suit.

"Yes. Mr. Bradley will assist." Miss Jenkins paused, giving them each an inscrutable squint over the rim of her spectacles.

"The cook tells me she left washtubs and aprons on the back porch for your use. I hope you do not mind getting a wetting," she added.

Concordia shrugged. "I'll manage. What other events are we having tonight?"

"There is the nut-burning in the library. I have put Mr. Maynard in charge of that, so we are assured of no monkeyshines. Miss Banning and Miss Crandall are reading tea leaves in the kitchen, Miss Kimble is telling ghost stories in the butler's pantry, and—" she checked her clipboard "—ah, yes. Mrs. Sanbourne is sketching caricatures in the side parlor." She rolled her eyes. "It was a fight to get that space, I can tell you. Apparently the room has become Mr. Maynard's private study, and he was none too happy to give it up—"

The sound of high-pitched chatter interrupted them. The students were arriving. Concordia glanced at David. "We should get ready."

David gave a little bow. "After you."

As they made their way through the growing throng in the ballroom to reach the kitchen and back porch beyond, Concordia asked, "Did you request that we be assigned together? Miss Jenkins gave me the strangest look." Heaven only knew what the woman assumed David had in mind. Her cheeks flamed at the thought.

David grinned. "Guilty."

"I wish you would be more discreet. You know better. Although we are engaged to be married—*especially* because of that—we have to ensure our comportment is above reproach."

David did not quite achieve the crestfallen air she was hoping to see. "We have both been so busy. I wanted the chance to talk during any quiet times tonight. Is that so wrong?"

"Well, not really," she admitted. "But you know how gossipy people can be. I don't think this is the best time and place for wedding talk, anyway."

"Actually, I wanted to ask you again about the Armstrong place."

She fussed with her sleeve before answering. "You want to know if I have changed my mind?"

"The manager of the property approached me with a lower offer. And he has had the entire place cleaned out. Scoured top to bottom. No debris. No sign that anything...happened there. We would have very little to do to get it ready."

They had reached the porch. She shivered in the chill air.

He stepped closer and clasped her hands, warming them. "We could afford a cook, at that price."

She pulled her hands away. "A man was murdered there. And we may never know who is responsible, or why." She pulled an apron from the hook and tied it around her waist.

"Did you speak to Capshaw?"

Drat, this business with the gun in the stables had completely occupied her this past week. She had forgotten to check if Capshaw had returned from his trip. "Not yet."

"You never told me what sort of information you had for him."

"The debt collectors who had been threatening Guryev may have managed to keep an eye on him here on campus." She told him of the time she had seen Guryev peering anxiously out his window in the middle of the night, and the nervous behavior that Miss Lovelace and Miss Gage had observed just before he disappeared.

David's eyes widened. "That's an interesting possibility, but I haven't noticed anyone suspicious hanging around campus."

"Keep in mind that we have a number of male students from Trinity who visit regularly. Not even the girls recognize all of them. Who is to say that someone, in the guise of a college youth, was not covertly watching Guryev?"

"Why haven't you told Capshaw yet?"

"He was out of town when I first thought of it. I've had my hands full since then." She grimaced. "I'm not even sure he would listen to me. After that business last spring, I know he doesn't want me involved in any more cases." She had to admit, despite her efforts to the contrary, trouble seemed to find her.

Even last summer, when she had traveled across the country to evade the Inner Circle.

David set the washtub on a stool. "Well, I am certainly in agreement with him, though I'd say we are already involved. We are simply trying to extricate ourselves from this mess and get on with our lives. What if I went with you?"

She fought back the pride-filled refusal that threatened to bubble out of her. After all, what did it matter how they arrived at the truth? The important thing was to clear the specter that stood between them and the home that could make them happy. "Yes. Perhaps he would listen then."

After a quick glance over his shoulder, he reached for her hand and drew her close. "I love you."

She rested her head on his chest, feeling the steady beat of his heart and his strong arms encircling her. She was content.

David reluctantly let her go, listening. "We had better start dunking those apples. It sounds as if we are about to be bombarded."

Over the babble of approaching students, she heard the distinctive *thump, bump* of Miss Banning's cane and Charlotte's voice in the kitchen. "Perhaps some are heading for the tea-leaf reading rather than the dunking."

He shrugged. "One can only hope."

The apple dunking proved a popular pastime. Young ladies in every sort of costume imaginable—from Alibaba to Zulu chieftain—lined up to be blindfolded, hands behind backs, in order to plunge their faces in the chilly water and grope for the slippery, floating apples. Much squealing ensued.

Concordia's apron kept most of her gown dry, but her hem was soon sopping. "I should get more kitchen towels," she said, after failed attempts to wring it out.

The kitchen was blessedly warm. Charlotte and Miss Banning sat alone at the rough-wood table, drinking tea. Saucers of wet tea leaves littered the surface.

"The two of you have the more congenial assignment," Concordia said, rummaging in the drawers.

Charlotte smiled. "We were busy for a while." She gestured toward the old lady, slurping her tea and ignoring them.

"How are you this evening, Miss Banning?" Concordia asked. Whether it was out of politeness or because she wanted a few more moments in the warmth of the kitchen, she could not say.

"*Humph,*" was all she got in reply. She appeared to be nodding off.

"It is a tiring evening for her," Charlotte said, adjusting the shawl over the old lady's shoulders. The corners of Miss Banning's thin lips turned up just a bit. Concordia wondered if a wide smile would crack the woman's face.

When Concordia returned to the porch, the students were gone and David was putting away the equipment.

She grimaced. "Oh dear, I was gone much longer than I planned. I am sorry to have abandoned you."

"You needed a bit of warming up." He smiled and checked his watch. "It is nearly time for supper." He held out his arm. "Shall we look in on the nut-burning along the way?"

"An excellent idea," Concordia said, taking his arm.

Furniture in the library had been pushed back to make room for the eager young ladies. Concordia noticed a pair of large wicker picnic hampers behind the wingback chairs, a blanket thrown over them. The girls must have raided an entire forest. They would not need *that* many nuts.

A perspiring, red-faced, and exceedingly grumpy Randolph Maynard stood by the fire, wearily scooping nuts from the bowl beside him and handing them out to the girls. Like David, he was in evening dress attire rather than a costume. Concordia wondered what costume such a man would adopt, should he be possessed of sudden whimsicality. Robespierre? The Marquis de Sade? The corners of her mouth twitched.

"Not too close!" Maynard roared, startling a tentative freshman into nearly doing that very thing, as she stumbled toward the hearth. Another girl caught her in time.

Concordia stepped forward. "Shall I take over, Mr. Maynard?" She reached out a hand for the bowl, which he wordlessly relinquished.

After he left, David helped her keep the girls in order. "He could have thanked you," he murmured.

She shrugged. "Our conversation yesterday was not a cordial one." At his frown, she added, "I'll tell you later." She glanced at the clock. "We only have time for a few more students," she called. "The supper bell will ring soon."

Chapter 19

Nothing should be said which can hurt anyone's feelings...
nor should one talk about that which everybody knows,
for such small-talk is impertinent and irritating.
~Mrs. John Sherwood

Week 6, Instructor Calendar
Halloween 1898

The bell came even sooner than expected, to Concordia's immense relief. It had grown quite warm by the fire. Strands of damp hair clung to her neck, but at least her hem was dry.

"Come on," David urged, as she straightened chairs. "I am starving."

"You are always starving," she teased. "It may be worse after we marry."

He grinned. "If you make it, I will eat it."

The buffet in the dining hall ran the entire back length of the room. The offerings were so numerous it was hard to decide where to start. She felt a surge of gratitude that Frances Kimble, rather than Randolph Maynard, was now in charge of such expenditures.

"Here." David took her plate. "Allow me."

Concordia pointed, and David filled her plate: cold salmon *mayonnaise*, garlic mashed turnips, and crab puffs, one of her favorites. Concordia eyed the dessert end of the table. She would have to save room for the pumpkin *crème brûlée*. Such luscious sweets did not come her way often.

They found seats at a large table with the Sanbournes, Miss Pomeroy, Mr. Maynard, Miss Kimble, Charlotte Crandall, and Miss Banning. Concordia sat between Mrs. Sanbourne and Charlotte, with Miss Banning on the girl's other side.

"The cooks have outdone themselves," David said between mouthfuls.

"It is a shame that Mr. Langdon had to miss all this," Concordia said. She nodded across the table at Maynard. "Any word from him?"

"He returns tomorrow," Maynard said gruffly.

The lady principal roused herself. "Oh? Mr. Langdon has been out of town? Whatever for?"

"I told you yesterday, Miss Pomeroy," Maynard said, barely concealing his impatience. "He went to visit his niece, who just lost her baby and nearly died herself."

Concordia felt a jolt to her abdomen. Such a tragedy was no longer so remote. Mrs. Sanbourne and Charlotte on each side of her shifted uneasily.

"How awful," Charlotte whispered.

Maynard flushed a mottled red as he glanced at the women. "I apologize. I should not have mentioned it."

Groping for a change of subject, Concordia turned to Mrs. Sanbourne. "I hear you were sketching caricatures in the side parlor this evening. Your talents were undoubtedly in high demand."

Mrs. Sanbourne had been gazing into her water glass. "Hmm? Oh yes, the drawings. I am quite pleased with them." She swept a hand in the direction of the far windows. "I have lined them up over there, should anyone care to see. The young ladies may take them home tonight. I also sketched from memory several subjects who did not sit for me. I thought it would be amusing."

"We shall certainly take a look," David said. "So, Mr. Sanbourne, how goes your work? Have you been able to reconstruct your missing blueprint?"

Peter Sanbourne grimaced. "I have not had time to finish. I am at work on a knotty problem with the depth sensors.

Fluctuations in temperature keep throwing them off. Once I have resolved that issue, I will return to the diagram."

David leaned forward in interest. "I take it you are working on an improved torpedo guidance system?"

Maynard leaned forward, gray eyes glittering with interest. "Ah yes. *Blue Arrow.*"

Sanbourne dropped his fork with a clatter. "How did you learn of it?" He turned accusing eyes from one gentleman to the other.

"My dear fellow," Maynard said scathingly, "you cannot expect to labor in obscurity when your blueprint is stolen, your assistant is missing, your rival's assistant is murdered, and the dead man's employer has resigned from Boston Tech in disgrace. There has been a break in the case. I just read about it in this evening's late edition."

Marynard had everyone's attention now, including Miss Banning and Miss Pomeroy.

"Well?" Sanbourne said impatiently, holding his fork in a white-knuckled grip. "What has happened?"

"The body of Ivan Guryev has been found."

"What?" Concordia exclaimed. "Where?"

"In the river. Not far from the State Street dock."

Sanbourne's lips grew pale. "Ivan's…body."

Rachel Sanbourne reached for the water pitcher and quickly poured him a glass.

"We assumed he'd fled to Russia," she said, her voice subdued.

"Well, he never made it there," Maynard said grimly.

"Was it suicide?" Miss Kimble asked. "After he killed Mr. Oster, perhaps he could not live with what he had done."

"The police don't yet know, at least according to the *Courant.*"

Some of the color had returned to Sanbourne's face. He shook his head. "What a waste. Ivan was so talented, so full of life." He turned to his wife. "He was practically a son to us. How could he have betrayed us so?" The agony in his voice was painful to hear.

Mrs. Sanbourne patted his arm. "We must be more vigilant." Her voice hardened. "Betrayal can come from anywhere, even one's own doorstep."

Miss Kimble clenched her jaw and glanced at Maynard. "It can indeed."

Maynard abruptly stood. "If you will excuse me."

Concordia glanced at David, who shrugged. He obviously didn't understand the interchange, either.

Charlotte also stood. "I believe Miss Jenkins needs me."

Margaret Banning started to get up.

"No, no, Miss Banning, you stay here," Charlotte said. "I will not be long. Shall I bring you a slice of pound cake when I return?"

Miss Banning nodded. "Thank you, dear."

It was David who fetched the cake for Miss Banning, as Charlotte did not return. Curious, Concordia excused herself. The band was starting up and the tables cleared in preparation for the dancing.

David helped her out of her chair. He leaned in to murmur, "Will you be back soon? I want at least one dance with you."

Concordia smiled. "My good sir, more than two dances in one evening with the same partner would be scandalous. But you may count upon one."

Concordia noticed the caricature boards lined up along the chair rail and decided to take a quick look on her way out. She smiled as she surveyed them, recognizing Miss Smedley, Miss Gage, and Lady Principal Pomeroy. Mrs. Sanbourne had skillfully captured a single distinctive feature, playfully distorting it so that one could not help but laugh. Concordia lingered over the sketch of Miss Pomeroy, noting how perfectly Mrs. Sanbourne had portrayed the lady's look of wide-eyed distraction behind the spectacles dangling from her skinny nose.

Another board was turned to the wall. Curious, she flipped it over. It was a caricature of Maynard, Charlotte, and Miss Kimble. She knew they had not posed for it. Mrs. Sanbourne must have sketched them from memory. Unlike the others, these faces had been distorted in an unflattering manner.

Maynard's scowl dominated his features, making him appear predatory, and Charlotte's broad forehead and strong jaw were exaggerated to the point of masculinity. Miss Kimble's face seemed terrier-like as she stood behind the pair, clutching a fist full of dollar bills and shaking it at Maynard.

She turned it back to the wall. Mrs. Sanbourne had obviously observed the budding courtship between Charlotte and Maynard. Somewhat poor taste to call attention to it. And what was Miss Kimble doing in the sketch?

Students were beginning to crowd the ballroom floor as the band struck up a merry polka. She saw Miss Jenkins near the door, clipboard in hand, directing staff to remove additional furniture to make room. Miss Kimble was pitching in to help. No sign of Charlotte.

Concordia passed Alison Smedley, regally dressed as Marie Antoinette, and stopped to greet her. "Are you enjoying the party?"

Miss Smedley started in surprise. "Indeed, yes, Miss Wells." She smiled. "It is a shame that Miss Lovelace was not able to come."

Concordia wanted dearly to wipe that smug expression from the girl's face. Her idea was beginning to solidify. "Have you heard of the evidence found that might clear her? Miss Pomeroy has it safely in her office."

Miss Smedley bit her lip. "I heard Mr. Maynard had it."

"Oh, he did at first, but the lady principal asked to see it. I do not believe she has given the envelope back to the dean yet. When Mr. Langdon returns tomorrow he will resolve the matter, and Miss Lovelace's ordeal will be at an end. Perhaps the items in question will indicate who the real prankster is." Concordia shook her head. "I would not want to be in that person's shoes."

She walked away from the pale-faced Alison Smedley.

There would be work to do about that tonight. Perhaps she could recruit David to help.

In the meantime, where was Charlotte? Had she stepped out for a breath of air...or to speak privately with a certain person?

Concordia peeked in the library. Empty. She cocked her head at a soft whisper of sound. She waited, but didn't hear it again. Impossible, she decided. There was nowhere in here for a person to hide.

She was sure of the voices coming from the nearby side parlor, however. The door was closed. She quietly leaned close to the keyhole.

Drat, the music from the ballroom made it difficult to hear. Concordia covered her other ear.

"…didn't you tell me before?" It was the anguished voice of Charlotte Crandall.

"It was so long ago. That's where I want the matter to stay. In the past." Maynard's voice was rough with emotion.

Concordia expelled a breath. As she had suspected. Charlotte had sought out the dean for a private word.

What was Maynard trying to keep quiet?

In her preoccupation, she had taken her hand away from her ear. The next words were inaudible. She quickly put her hand back.

"…she will try again? Bitterness of that sort does not subside." Concordia could hear the anxiety in Charlotte's voice.

"Not to worry," Maynard said. "A week has gone by, and nothing untoward has happened."

"Thank heaven for that, but you cannot allow Maisie to be punished unjustly," Charlotte said, her voice stronger.

"I regret that," Maynard said. "I wanted to believe it was a foolish student prank rather than something…else. I still think a student is involved. We will clear Miss Lovelace tomorrow, when Langdon returns."

Concordia nodded to herself as she listened. She too suspected a student was involved, and hoped to catch her tonight. But who was this woman from Maynard's past? Was she trying to kill him or simply frighten him? And why?

She was so preoccupied that she nearly missed Charlotte's next words.

"…should say something. No one can blame you for what happened. It was not your fault. Expose this woman for who she is."

"No!" came Maynard's sharp answer. "It cannot be made public. I cannot bear to tell even *you* the entire story. To have newspapermen peering into my past private life and hers? Writing about it in the scandal sheets? We would bring ignominy upon the school as well. The college has had enough of that. Look at what has appeared in the papers after the death of Oster. And now Guryev is dead."

Charlotte's sobs were muffled, as if Maynard had pulled her close. Concordia strained to hear her next words. "I do not care about any of that. I could not bear it if you came to harm."

The sound of brisk heels on the parquet made Concordia spring back from the door. She ducked into the library.

She startled four sophomores, dragging the pair of wicker baskets she had noticed earlier. Given how the girls dropped them as if touching live coals, something was up.

"Whatever are you doing here?" she demanded, hands on hips. She heard the soft sounds again. Rustling. Coming from the hampers clearly now. "What is inside those?"

The girls merely gaped at something behind her. Dean Maynard stood in the doorway, his expression black as thunder. No sign of Charlotte.

"Yes, ladies," Maynard said, crossing the room in quick strides, "what is inside the baskets?"

"No, wait!" one of the girls said frantically, putting her hand to the lid, but Maynard impatiently brushed her aside.

Perhaps if he had not flung back both hamper lids at once, Concordia thought later, they would not have had the degree of pandemonium that ensued. For, freed at long last, four-dozen birds of varying species—sparrows, swallows, wrens, and it appeared the girls had raided the dovecote above the stables as well—flapped and flew around the room in a panic. The girls shrieked, covering their heads.

"Get those doors closed!" Concordia yelled, as she grabbed an afghan from the back of a chair to trap some of them. Maynard struggled to open the window to shoo out others.

Before the girls could tug on the double doors that stood wide, the birds, drawn by the brighter light of the hall that led to the ballroom, had swooped out of the room. A few of the more sedate doves remained, settling themselves on bookshelves and other perches in the library. Guano and floating feathers littered the room.

"I blame your lax discipline, Miss Wells," Maynard said through gritted teeth, dashing out of the room toward the sounds of fresh shrieking. Concordia closed the library doors and reluctantly followed. She suspected that David would not get his dance tonight.

Chapter 20

It is impossible to be too careful of the reputation
of a young lady.

~Mrs. John Sherwood

Week 6, Instructor Calendar
November 1898

Lady Principal Pomeroy and Dean Maynard supervised the tricksters' rounding up of the birds, much to the entertainment of the onlookers.

As the miscreants dragged out ladders and tried to catch the last contrary birds that roosted on the beams of the ballroom's high ceiling, Concordia drew David aside. "Do you know where I might find a toolkit?"

David grinned. "Are you planning to build a bird-catcher?"

"More of a prankster-catcher."

David raised an eyebrow. "Now, *that* I have to see. Langdon's garden shed should suit. What in particular do you need?"

"A few screws and a bit of wire."

"All right then, let's go."

They slipped out through the back porch to the shed. David lit the lantern hanging by the door. "It's too cramped in there for both of us." He eyed her attire. "I don't want you to snag that lovely gown on anything. Wait here."

She was happy enough to comply. It *was* a pretty gown, and the shed was exceedingly cobwebby.

A few minutes later, he was back. "You may also need a pair of pliers." He stuffed them in his pocket.

"Good thinking."

"Where to next?"

"My office," she said. "We have to prepare an envelope. I will explain on the way."

As they headed for Founder's Hall, Concordia told him of her suspicion that Alison Smedley was responsible for the gun above the stable door, her motive being to discredit Miss Lovelace and raise doubts about the suitability of the new engineering program. For the time being, Concordia kept to herself the conversation she had overheard between Maynard and Charlotte.

"What are we doing with screws and wire?" David asked.

"I told Miss Smedley that an envelope containing evidence about the gun prank was in Miss Pomeroy's desk for safekeeping, until Mr. Langdon has a chance to examine it."

"Evidence? What evidence?"

She described what George Lovelace had found over the stable door.

David frowned. "That doesn't sound like particularly damning evidence."

Concordia smiled. "Alison Smedley doesn't know that."

"So you wish to create a spurious envelope and place it in Miss Pomeroy's office?"

She nodded. "Everyone knows President Langdon returns tomorrow. If Miss Smedley is the perpetrator, she will want to secure it before he sees it."

"And you selected Miss Pomeroy's office because the lady never locks her door."

"Exactly."

"Who has the real envelope?"

"Maynard."

They reached Founder's Hall, and she paused at the door. "You don't have to stay with me."

"What, and miss an event nearly as exciting as dozens of birds swooping down upon my head?"

She grinned. "Your sense of adventure is irresistible, Mr. Bradley."

With David's help, the envelope was prepared and placed in Miss Pomeroy's desk drawer. It was a challenge to navigate the lady principal's office in the dark. They stepped upon and toppled stacks of papers on both floor and furniture.

"I fear we are making a terrible mess," she said ruefully.

"I doubt she will notice." He leaned against the desk, sending another stack of papers sliding to the floor. He bent to retrieve them. "How does the woman get any work done?"

Concordia came over to help, brushing past his shoulder.

He dropped the remaining papers and took her hands in his.

She did not pull away, though it was difficult to suppress a tremble. She affected a jesting tone. "It would not do for us to be huddled together in the dark in the lady principal's office."

He kissed her wrist. "Anywhere I am stuck with you is heaven to me."

Just as she recovered breath enough to answer, they heard light steps echo in the stairwell. "I left my office door unlocked," she whispered. "Keep watch from there with the light off. I will join you afterward."

He frowned.

She prodded him toward the door. "Don't worry, I will be perfectly safe."

After he left, she slipped behind the coat rack, Miss Pomeroy's large woolen cloak concealing her quite effectively. She waited, her breaths quiet and shallow. She must keep a cool head when she caught out Miss Smedley. It would be all too easy to heap aspersions upon the girl. Sneaking around, causing the death of a beloved horse, and putting people at risk of serious harm, all in order to place blame on someone whom one envied—abominable, yes, but such behavior also pointed to a troubled soul.

She could hear the footsteps along the hallway, getting closer.

With a faint click of the latch, the door swung open. Miss Smedley carried a shuttered lantern that cast her hooded face in shadow. Concordia strained to see as the girl set the light down upon the desk. Something was not quite right.

The pool of light illuminated only the edge of the desk as Miss Smedley rummaged through the drawers, quietly sliding open each one and easing it shut again before moving on. Concordia heard the catch of breath and the crackle of paper as the envelope was discovered. With a sigh of satisfaction, the young lady pushed back her hood, leaning closer to examine her find in the light. Concordia saw her face at last.

It was not Miss Smedley.

Only by sheer effort of will did she refrain from crying out in surprise. Her heart thumped wildly in her chest as she kept a hard grip on Miss Pomeroy's cloak.

Though similar in build to Alison, this lady was dark-haired and dark-eyed, with a nervous energy in her movements that Concordia knew all too well.

Frances Kimble.

The bursar looked through the envelope with a frown, then re-folded the flap and placed the envelope back in the desk drawer. She left quickly. Concordia listened to the lady's light footsteps in the stairwell. It had a familiar sound. Her eyes widened in recognition. So, it had been Miss Kimble eavesdropping near Dean Maynard's door the other day.

With a sigh, Concordia scooped up the envelope and joined David in her office.

He turned on the desk lamp. "What happened? I heard the footsteps."

"You're not going to believe this," she said, after taking a few slow breaths to quiet her racing pulse. "It was Miss Kimble."

"What!" He abruptly sat down in the other chair, his face a mix of confusion and disbelief. "I don't understand. Did Miss Smedley tell her about the envelope?"

"That's what I assume. Miss Kimble must have offered to check."

David shook his head. "There has to be another explanation. Perhaps she overheard you talking, and was curious?"

Concordia pursed her lips. "She *was* nearby at the time, helping Miss Jenkins rearrange chairs."

"Well then, that explains it," he said. "I have noticed the lady takes an interest in all the goings-on here. Eavesdropping and sneaking around may not be model behavior, but it's not criminal."

Concordia flushed. She too had eavesdropped upon a conversation and done a significant amount of sneaking around this evening, so she could hardly find fault with the woman on that account.

"Perhaps you're right. After she opened the envelope, she put it back."

"Well then, nothing to worry about."

Concordia pursed her lips. Unless Miss Kimble had expected something else to be in the envelope. Something that would implicate her? And when she saw that was not the case, she knew it was safe to return it.

David frowned. "You are not convinced."

"Why didn't Miss Smedley come? The reason must be that Miss Kimble came in her place."

He shook his head skeptically. "We are talking about a student prank. Why are you clinging to the idea that Miss Kimble, one of our *administrators*, tried to harm Maynard?"

She sighed. "I do not *want* to believe it. But you've seen the rancor between them." Perhaps the ill feeling stretched beyond the last two months. Had they known one another before the semester started? *It was long ago…. We would bring ignominy upon the school,* Maynard had said. And what of Mrs. Sanbourne's caricature of Maynard and Charlotte, with Miss Kimble peeking over Maynard's shoulder…in jealousy, perhaps? Had Mrs. Sanbourne noticed something the rest of them had missed?

One thing was certain: if the dean and bursar of Hartford Women's College shared a sordid past, the scandal would be inescapable. She must tread very, very carefully.

David leaned forward. "You suspect Miss Kimble and Miss Smedley of working together?"

Concordia grimaced. "I don't know…Miss Smedley has the motivation, but not the technical ability." Did Miss Kimble possess both? She remembered something…. Yes. Miss Kimble was the granddaughter of a clockmaker. Miss Lovelace had mentioned that. Yes, it was possible.

He shook his head. "What are we going to do now?"

She narrowed her eyes. "*We?*"

He grinned. "'Till death do us part,' you know."

She smiled back. It felt good to have an ally. "Our next step is to talk to Charlotte Crandall."

He frowned. "Why Miss Crandall?"

She hesitated. She could not tell him, not yet. She knew so little. "I'll explain later."

"Remember, we need to speak with Lieutenant Capshaw about who might have been following Guryev on campus," he said. "Now that we know for sure the poor man is dead, it is more important than ever."

Mercy, so many problems at once. The prospect was exhausting. She stood and covered a yawn. "I'll send a note in the morning."

He looked out the window. A pre-dawn glow touched the horizon. "It *is* morning

Chapter 21

Concordia made no progress in speaking with either Capshaw or Charlotte over the next few days. She had sent a note to the Kinsley Street Station, but had not yet received a response. She was feeling distinctly snubbed. Perhaps Capshaw considered it *meddling* and was ignoring her. Should she talk to Sophia? She had not wanted to presume upon their friendship, but she would do what was necessary. The issue was time. Her schedule this week made a trip into town impossible.

Speaking with Charlotte should have been simpler, as they shared a residence, but the young lady had taken advantage of a gap in her assignments to visit her aunt, Lady Dunwick, at her Hartford townhouse.

The one bright spot to the week was the fact that Maisie Lovelace was finally cleared of guilt in the gun prank and her restriction lifted.

The meeting consisted of Concordia, Miss Lovelace, Mr. Lovelace, Miss Pomeroy, Mr. Maynard, and Mr. Langdon, in his office.

Miss Lovelace's uncle took charge of the meeting. He handed the girl a length of fresh wire and a pair of pliers, then held a piece of wood against the wall, just above her head. Three new screws were embedded in it. "Now then m'dear, go on and secure the wire to the screws. Leave a little length, as if ye were attaching something to the other end of each."

With a shrug, Miss Lovelace set to work with practiced ease. Concordia watched her carefully, noting that the young lady was indeed left-handed. The job was done in moments. Miss Lovelace handed back the pliers, re-seated herself, primly folded her hands in her lap, and waited.

Mr. Lovelace brought over the board for them to examine. He gestured to the envelope in Langdon's hands. "We'll compare them."

Langdon dumped the contents upon his desk. "These came from the stable door frame?"

Lovelace nodded. "Ye see the differences in handiwork? Here—" he pointed to twisted-off ends "—and here." He pointed to the wire wrapped around the heads of the screws.

Langdon's frown cleared. He turned to Miss Lovelace. "We owe you a profound apology, my dear."

She flushed and glanced at Maynard. He sat, arms crossed, his expression unreadable.

"We *all* owe you an apology," Langdon said pointedly. "Isn't that right, Randolph?"

"It would seem so," was the curt reply.

Concordia grimaced. That was about as good as they were going to get from the man.

The tension in Miss Lovelace's shoulders eased. "I know that my behavior of last semester is part of why you did not have confidence in my innocence. I promise, sir, I would not pull such a reckless and dangerous stunt. Someone—" she glanced at Concordia "—is trying to get me in trouble."

Langdon leaned forward. "Who is that, Miss Lovelace?"

"We are inquiring into the matter," Concordia interrupted. She shot the girl a warning look. "But we do not have any proof yet. We have already seen how disastrous it is to proceed without evidence."

"On the other hand," Maynard said, glancing at Langdon, "we do know who is responsible for releasing dozens of birds in Sycamore Hall and wreaking havoc upon the Halloween festivities."

Langdon's lips twitched in a suppressed smile. "I was fortunate to miss that."

"Though not the aftermath," Maynard reminded him. "We are still finding feathers and droppings in the first floor rooms."

Concordia sighed. She wished she had discovered the scheme sooner. Before the hampers were opened.

Miss Pomeroy stirred herself and chimed in, pushing her spectacles up her nose for emphasis. "The young ladies are returning today to clean up the places they missed. I have put them on restriction until Thanksgiving. There will be no more mischief."

Concordia shook her head. She truly hoped Miss Pomeroy was right. Otherwise, the cycle of pranks and punishment might never end. She and Miss Pomeroy had spoken to the miscreants, all friends of Miss Lovelace. The students' original intention was to release the birds in Maynard's side parlor study, as revenge for him refusing to allow Maisie to attend the Halloween ball. Perhaps now that Maisie's restriction was lifted, the antics would end.

There was one problem with that line of reasoning. *Bitterness of that sort does not subside*, Charlotte had said. Concordia glanced at Dean Maynard, who stared out the window. Who felt bitterness toward him?

She thought she knew. Miss Kimble. If Concordia had confronted her in the act of rifling through the phony envelope of evidence, would that have prompted a confession? Would she have explained why she had wanted to harm Maynard, and what had happened between them long ago?

Concordia could kick herself for not seizing the opportunity. What if the woman tried again? They needed answers, quickly.

It was pointless to try to extract information from the close-mouthed dean. However, Charlotte was due back tonight. No matter how late, they would have a talk.

"Well! I believe we are finished here," President Langdon said, pushing back his chair and shifting his bulky frame away from the desk. He clasped George Lovelace's hand. "Thank you for bringing this to our attention. How are you getting on with Sanbourne, by the way?"

Everyone else headed for the door. Concordia fussed with re-positioning her chair in the corner, curious to hear the answer.

The cap twitched in Lovelace's hands, as if he were anxious to put it back on. "We're getting on well enough, though he don' let me do much 'round his laboratory. Real secretive, he is. But I s'pose I have plenty o'work helping the students with their projects."

Langdon nodded. "These geniuses are a touchy bunch, I hear. We appreciate your help."

Maynard held the door open. "Coming, Miss Wells?"

She checked her watch. *Mercy!* She would be late for class if she didn't hurry.

Maisie Lovelace waited for her in the stairwell. "Thank you for believing in me all along."

Concordia smiled. "We will get to the bottom of this, don't you worry."

Miss Lovelace gritted her teeth. "*Ooh*, that Alison Smedley! How could she be so awful?"

Concordia hesitated. She had not told Miss Lovelace about the bursar's possible involvement. It was still a puzzle. Why would Miss Kimble implicate Maisie Lovelace? Unless Alison Smedley had acted on her own in that regard, placing the toolkit in the stables later?

This whole business was giving her a headache. "It may be more...complicated, dear. We must learn more."

"I know enough," the girl retorted. "Alison should be punished for what she has done."

Concordia lowered her brows in a stern frown. "We will wait. Do you understand?"

Maisie turned away, her shoulders stiff with anger. "I will not wait long," she muttered under her breath.

Chapter 22

We should be real first, and ornamental afterwards.
                                    ~Mrs. John Sherwood

Week 7, Instructor Calendar
November 1898

That night, Concordia perched in the plush wingback chair in her sitting room, her favorite reading spot. The cottage had settled down hours ago. She struggled to keep her eyes open, despite the windowpanes rattling from the heavy winds. There would be a storm soon.

Where was Charlotte? She usually returned before curfew, also known as the "ten o'clock rule," when students were required to turn out their lights and go to bed. Of course Charlotte was a faculty member now and not bound by the rule, but the lady was a creature of habit. She had not sent word of a delay in her plans.

She could hear Ruby's heavy tread past her door, pacing between the kitchen and front hall. The house matron was worried, too.

The wind, the rhythmic steps, the ticking of the mantel clock, and the lateness of the hour were finally too much for her. Her head slumped against the chair and she slept.

Ruby heard the key turn and hurried to open the door to a weary, wind-blown Charlotte Crandall. "Thank goodness! We were worried about you," she whispered.

Charlotte's cheeks were pale and pinched with the chill. "I am so sorry. I stopped at the office first…to find some papers. It took longer than I anticipated."

"Well, come on in and—" Ruby paused. Was that a noise in the shrubbery outside? Probably the wind, but she stuck her head out of the door, just the same.

Clouds scuttled across the moon, alternately casting shadow and light across the paths. All the buildings were dark, except for a glow on the second floor of Founder's Hall. Ruby gestured in that direction. "Did you leave your light on, miss?"

Charlotte glanced back. "No, my office is in the other wing. That must be Miss Kimble."

Ruby shook her head. "The ten o'clock rule wouldn't be a bad idea for the staff."

Charlotte shivered and closed the door with a quiet click. "Mr. Sanbourne is up late as well. When I came through the gate, I noticed the lights were still on in his laboratory." She hung up her jacket and turned toward the stairs.

"Afore you go to bed, Miss Wells wanted a word," Ruby said.

Charlotte raised an eyebrow. "At this hour?"

"That's what she said."

Charlotte tapped on Concordia's door. No response.

Ruby shrugged. "Ah well, she must a' fallen asleep. Tomorrow will do, I'm sure."

Charlotte nodded. "Good night, Ruby."

"G'night."

Concordia had the strangest dream. She was roaming through a corridor lined on both sides with horse stalls, some occupied, some empty. For some reason, she was compelled to stop and examine every stall, though she had no idea what she was searching for. Sometimes a person rather than a horse would be standing in the stall: Mr. Langdon, Miss Pomeroy, Miss Kimble, Miss Banning. In one stall was a canvas propped on an easel. It was the caricature of Charlotte, Maynard, and Miss Kimble that she had seen at the Halloween ball. At the far end of the corridor, Peter Sanbourne was working a forge, which produced a great deal of smoke. It was getting harder and harder to see. Concordia was obliged to grope her way along, squinting in the haze.

She awoke, coughing, to a smoky room.

This was no dream.

She sprung out of her chair. "F-fire!" She cracked open her door. Smoke billowed in.

She snatched up a shawl and put it to her nose and mouth and made a run for the stairs. The smoke was thicker up here, and in the darkness she could barely make out a glow at the end of the hall.

"Girls, girls, wake up!" she yelled, flinging open doors and hauling bodies out of beds. She heard Ruby run up the stairs behind her and roust the students on the other side of the corridor.

With a collective shriek, the students jumped out of bed, grabbing at belongings.

"No! There is no time—just get out!" She struggled to voice the words between fits of coughing.

Ruby waved the girls down the stairs and started counting heads. "We're missing...five!" she screamed.

There were three doors at the end of the hall, two on the left and one on the right, where the heat was most intense. Concordia and Ruby grabbed ewers from the rooms and threw all the water they had at the fire. It created more smoke without making any difference.

In the distance came the frantic clanging of the fire bell from Engine Company Seven, half a mile away at Main and Capen Streets. She heard Edward Langdon's voice outside. "Concordia! Ruby! You have to get out!"

Concordia pushed open a window and stuck her head out, inhaling blessed, cool air. The wind was as brisk as ever. "We have five more, at the far end of the hall!" she called.

Langdon, in bathrobe and slippers with a nightcap still clapped to his head, cupped his hands around his mouth to be heard over the roar of flames, wind, and alarm bells. "We're getting a ladder for them! You must come down!"

"He's right, miss, we have to go," Ruby said, rubbing her eyes. "The fire's right in front of their doors! We'll never get past."

"Ruby, you go. After all, someone has to keep the girls outside from succumbing to hysterics."

Ruby gave a wan smile. "I think that ship has sailed already. Don't wait too long." She gave Concordia's hand a squeeze and hurried down the stairs.

Concordia stuck her head back out the window. "The others must be unconscious from the smoke," she called to Langdon. "I will try to rouse them." If she had voice enough. Her throat was raw already. "Do you have a second ladder? Miss Crandall's room is on the other side."

"No!" Langdon called back. "We'll have to wait for the firemen to get her!"

Concordia's stomach lurched. It might be too late. But if they rescued Charlotte first, there would be no time to save the four girls in the two rooms on the other side of the corridor. One, or four?

She refused to accept either choice.

Taking one last breath of clean air, she dropped to the floor and crawled to the room next to Charlotte's, not yet blocked by the fire but uncomfortably warm and filled with smoke. She banged on the wall. "Charlotte! Charlotte!"

She heard coughing, but nothing else. At least she was still alive.

Dropping to her knees again, she scrabbled across the corridor to the room adjacent to Miss Smedley and her roommate and banged on that wall. "Alison! Alison!"

"We're here, Miss Wells!" came Miss Smedley's panicked, coughing voice through the wall. "We're trapped!"

Concordia stopped to breathe into her shawl. Her eyes were stinging.

Then she noticed a hole in the wall, near the baseboard, and remembered. *Yes, of course.*

She groped the surface of the tables for something heavy. The pewter candlestick holder would have to do. She swung it with a strength she did not know she had.

"The wall is thin, help me break it down!" she called. She kept at it, striking the wall again and again.

The girls on the other side tore at the bits she had loosened.

After several tries, the thin plaster and paper came down with a crash and a cloud of plaster dust mingling with the smoke. She never imagined she'd be so grateful for the cheap remodeling of the upstairs bedrooms, where one large room had been divided into three.

She climbed through the debris, and the two sobbing girls collapsed into her arms.

"We have to do the same with the next wall, and get to Anna and Mary." Concordia passed Alison Smedley the candlestick, then picked up a silver urn.

"That's my mother's!" Alison cried.

Concordia ignored her and banged on the wall. "Mary, Anna, can you hear me?" She prayed they were still alive. She wheezed into her shawl, struggling to catch her breath. It felt as if an iron band was squeezing her chest.

Having the advantage of practice, they quickly broke through the last wall and roused Mary and Anna.

As the students crawled through the debris to reach the staircase, Concordia opened their window and waved away the ladder that had come into view. "We're coming out! Get Charlotte!"

Before she followed the girls down the stairs and outside to safety, she took one last look at the flames climbing up Charlotte Crandall's door. She could only pray the ladder had reached her in time.

Chapter 23

The lighting of rooms by means of lamps and candles is giving hostesses a great annoyance. There is scarcely a dinner-party but the candles set fire to their fringed shades, and a conflagration ensues.
~Mrs. John Sherwood

Week 7, Instructor Calendar
November 1898

Ruby was keeping the girls at a distance as the firemen worked, pulling out axes and unwinding the hose of their steam-driven pumper truck.

"Is Charlotte out?" Concordia asked anxiously.

Ruby pointed. Randolph Maynard was gently laying the inert form of Charlotte Crandall on the grass. Miss Jenkins and Miss Pomeroy crouched over her.

Stumbling upon shaking legs, Concordia hurried to them.

Miss Jenkins lifted her head from Charlotte's chest. ""She's alive, but she needs more than I can do."

"Has an ambulance been sent for?" Concordia knelt beside them.

Miss Jenkins nodded.

"Miss Kimble is rousing the other teachers, in case they are needed." Miss Pomeroy pushed her braid over her shoulder and self-consciously tightened the sash of her robe. She turned back to Miss Jenkins. "Do you want the Willow Cottage girls to head over to the infirmary, so you can check them when you're finished here?"

Concordia stared. The lady principal could be surprisingly focused when the occasion called for it. Perhaps it took something as extreme as a burning building to rouse her.

A pale-faced Maynard, clad in pajamas and robe, his dark hair tousled, ignored them all. He gently chafed Charlotte's hands and wrists and murmured to her.

"Does anyone know what happened?" Miss Jenkins asked.

Concordia shook her head. "We awoke to the cottage on fire. It was already well underway." She looked over at Willow Cottage, her heart a tight ball in her chest. The roof was now ablaze. Smoke billowed from the windows. Everything was gone.

The fire chief approached them. "Who is in charge here?"

Miss Pomeroy pointed to Edward Langdon.

"Keep everyone farther back," the chief told Langdon. He frowned at the swaying tree line in the distance. "We must evacuate the nearby cottages. I don't like the look of the wind. We may not be able to keep it from spreading."

Fear prickled along Concordia's spine. Langdon ran for the nearest cottage as quickly as his portly frame would allow.

The teachers soon had their charges from the other four cottages swarming out of doors, clutching a few necessities.

"Take them to the gymnasium for now," Langdon called.

The crowd quickly dispersed, the chill air an excellent motivator. Concordia lingered, glancing down anxiously at Charlotte Crandall. She had not regained consciousness.

"Will she...be all right?" Concordia turned aside in a fit of coughing.

Miss Jenkins bit her lip. "I am sorry to say I do not know. But I want you to go to the infirmary, Concordia. You need tending to." She gestured to the burns along her forearm. Dazed, Concordia lifted her arm. How had *that* happened?

"Come, dear." Miss Pomeroy settled a shawl around Concordia's shivering form. "There is nothing more you can do. The ambulance will arrive soon, I'm sure."

Hot tears prickling her eyes, she allowed Miss Pomeroy to draw her away.

Chapter 24

The affections are too sacred for such outward showing,
and the lookers-on are in a very disagreeable position.
~Mrs. John Sherwood

Week 7, Instructor Calendar
November 1898

A light pattering upon glass woke her later that morning. Concordia opened her eyes. Mercy, this was the second time she had been in the infirmary in the past three weeks. At least she had walked in under her own power this time.

The day was off to a dreary start. Rain streaked the windows, and only a pearl-gray light penetrated the gloom.

Miss Jenkins was turning up the lamps and noticed her stir. "How do you feel?"

Concordia grimaced. "My throat hurts," she croaked. She glanced in dismay at her soot-stained skirt and shirtwaist. She had fallen asleep fully dressed in her reading chair last night, waiting for Charlotte's return.

"I have clean clothes for you. You can wash up over there." Miss Jenkins pointed to a sink, where a curtain was partially drawn. "It will have to do for now. Don't get that bandage wet," she added, nodding at Concordia's forearm.

Concordia stood and stretched, glancing around the room. There were only ten beds in the infirmary. The girls were sleeping two to a bed, with a few more curled up on blankets on the floor. "Are they all right?"

"They will be, though the last four who came out with you breathed in much more smoke than is good for them. They will need longer to recover." Miss Jenkins fixed her with a stern look. "Including you."

"I cannot argue with that," Concordia said wearily. She still felt as if someone was sitting upon her chest. "Any word about Charlotte?"

Miss Jenkins shook her head. "But Lieutenant Capshaw is waiting in my office to speak with you."

Concordia nodded in resignation. She expected Capshaw would be assigned the case. She cleaned up as best as she could, changed her clothes, and hurried to join him.

He rose, unfolding his tall, gaunt frame from the chair. She gripped the doorjamb as she waited for a spasm of violent coughing to subside. His brow furrowed. "If you are not well enough for questions, miss, I can come back later."

She shook her head. He came over and helped her gently into a chair.

She fought to suppress a sob. Capshaw's non-customary tenderness threatened to undermine her self-control. Despite their long association and the fact that he had married her best friend Sophia, neither of them felt comfortable enough to address the other familiarly. Instead of Aaron and Concordia, they would forever be Lieutenant Capshaw and Miss Wells.

Capshaw sat and smoothed his shaggy red mustache as he waited for her to regain her composure. The moment passed. Concordia squared her shoulders.

"Now then." He extracted his pencil stub and folded wad of paper. "I understand that the house was awoken by the fire around two this morning. Is that what you recollect?"

She shrugged. "I did not observe the clock. I know I had been asleep for a while."

"What time did you retire, miss?"

She hesitated. "I did not exactly *retire*. I waited up for someone and fell asleep in my chair. When I awoke, the cottage was on fire."

"What is the latest time you remember?"

"Around eleven. Ruby was up as well."

"Who were you waiting for? I thought all of your students were bound by the ten o'clock rule."

She smiled briefly. Capshaw had become quite familiar with the ways of the *college people* he once professed he would never understand. "Miss Crandall is a substitute teacher, and not bound by the rule."

Capshaw scribbled a note. "Why were you awaiting Miss Crandall's return?"

She hesitated. "It is a school matter, and can have no bearing here."

He raised a skeptical brow. "You know from previous experience that we cannot assume that, but we'll let it go for the moment. Would Ruby know what time Miss Crandall returned?"

"I do not know." She watched him fiddle with his pencil. "Lieutenant, do you know how the fire started?"

He shook his head. "It's still too hot to go through. And we'll have to be extremely careful when we do. The second floor buckled and partially collapsed into the kitchen. Most of the roof is gone. The fire chief thinks we can conduct a preliminary examination later today. Perhaps the ladies can even recover a few belongings. *If* the structure is safe enough to enter."

Dread gripped Concordia's abdomen at the thought of losing her home and nearly all of her earthly possessions. "Were the other residences damaged?"

He consulted his notes. "The nearest cottage, Hemlock, has a partially burned roof. It is reparable, I hear. The other cottages were spared. The firemen worked tirelessly through the night."

She felt a wave of gratitude for the strangers who had saved them.

"Tell me about the night-time routine," he said, folding back a fresh slip of paper. "Does anyone customarily leave a candle or lantern burning in the window of the corridor overnight?"

"No, nothing of the sort," she said. "We have them for emergencies, but the cottage was converted to electric lights years ago. We never leave anything burning."

"I see. And the fire was concentrated in the corridor, farthest from the stairs?"

She nodded. "It was blocking the doors of the three rooms at that end of the hallway."

"It was not coming from within a room, but outside, in the hall?"

"As far as I could tell. It was difficult to see through the smoke."

"Who lives in those rooms?"

"Misses Connor and Jackson are in the room nearest the end of the corridor on the left, and Misses Smedley and Tate are on the same side, in the room next door. Miss Crandall's room is directly across, on the right side of the corridor."

"Does anyone have a grudge against one of these individuals?" Capshaw asked.

Concordia started. "A grudge? Enough to set a fire in front of her door and try to kill her? That is ridiculous."

As ridiculous as it was, her mind raced through the possibilities. Could Miss Smedley have been the target? No, no, that would point to Miss Lovelace. Impossible. She swallowed, remembering the girl's anger and impatience to have Miss Smedley punished.

Capshaw's eyes narrowed. "For a minute there, you were considering it."

"How is Miss Crandall?" she asked, in a change of subject.

He grimaced. "Still unconscious. I am anxious to speak with her. She may have been the last person to retire for the night. It's possible she noticed something."

"When may I visit her?"

"I will ask, and send word."

She stood, as did he. "Thank you. What will you do next?"

"After going through the remnants of Willow Cottage with the fire chief, I will begin an investigation of each of the young ladies who were put directly in harm's way."

She caught her breath. "Including Miss Crandall?"

He gave her a sharp look. "Of course. What is it, Miss Wells?"

She hesitated. "Miss Crandall and Mr. Maynard have become good friends, spending much of their free time together. Oh, nothing unseemly," she added hastily, at the policeman's melancholy expression. "I am only telling you so that you will exercise discretion in that regard."

His frown deepened. "I am always discreet."

There was a knock on the door and David entered. His face lit up in relief. "I stayed at my parents' house last night, I only just heard." He bundled her in his arms. She buried her face in the lapels of his jacket. "My dear," he murmured into her hair. "Thank heaven you are safe."

Capshaw diplomatically cleared his throat, and they jumped apart.

"Sorry, lieutenant," David said. "Has she told you what we have figured out about Guryev?"

Capshaw shook his head. "We were discussing the fire. What about Guryev?"

"Did you not receive my note?" Concordia asked.

David escorted her back to her chair and pulled up another.

"I have been at the riverfront these last few days."

Concordia nodded. Capshaw had not ignored her, after all. "The riverfront?"

"Interviewing people who work at the pier and the warehouses, in case someone had seen Guryev or anyone dumping…something in the river."

Such as a body. She swallowed.

"Have you made progress?" David asked.

"After four weeks, the trail has gone cold." He scowled. "Everyone thought Guryev had fled to Russia long ago."

"Except you," she said.

He raised a surprised eyebrow. "How did—? Ah, Sophia."

Concordia nodded. "David and I have some information that may help in that regard."

Capshaw leaned forward. "Go on."

She described what she had seen of Guryev's nervous behavior the night of the alarm clock prank, and what her students had noticed the days before his disappearance. "It strikes me that he felt he was being watched, even here on campus."

Capshaw waved a dismissive hand. "He was. There were two debt collectors trailing Guryev—each with a nasty reputation, I might add. They work for different gambling establishments. Frankly, I am surprised there weren't more after him, but perhaps the others he owed money to didn't want to join the fight."

Concordia frowned. Mercy, what a sordid mess Guryev had gotten himself into.

"I doubt when you saw Guryev gazing out his window that night," Capshaw went on, "it was anything but nerves. Strange men skulking around a women's college in the wee hours would be much too conspicuous."

She bit back her disappointment. Her discovery had not been useful, after all. "Have you located the men following Guryev?"

Capshaw shrugged. "I've talked to one. Barney Johns. He admits to making threats against Guryev and his mother, but of course claims he had not yet resorted to physical violence. However, his whereabouts that night are not entirely accounted for. He's still a suspect."

"What of the other?" David asked.

"Ike Coutts. I'm still trying to find him."

"Is it possible Guryev killed Oster and then drowned himself in the river?" David asked.

Capshaw sighed. "If that were the case, where is the blueprint? We thoroughly searched the campus, his mother's hotel room, and the Armstrong farmhouse."

"So one or the other of the debt collectors is your best suspect right now," David said, "killing both Oster and Guryev and taking the money and the plans."

Concordia rubbed distractedly at her stinging arm. "I do not understand why the murderer would leave Oster's body to be discovered and dump poor Mr. Guryev in the river."

"If we are talking about Johns or Coutts being the murderer," Capshaw said. "Guryev could have escaped when Oster was killed. Then the murderer caught up to him later, killed him and dumped his body in the river."

"So this Mr. Johns is your best suspect for Oster's murder," David said.

"In terms of a motive, yes," Capshaw said. "But how did he know Oster and Guryev would be at the farmhouse? Johns could not set foot on campus grounds to track Guryev's movements. Even if he waited just outside the gate, the sheep tracks leading up Rook's Hill are not visible from that vantage point."

Concordia leaned forward in excitement. "Unless he was disguised as a Trinity student."

Capshaw started. "Hartford Women's College has begun permitting college boys on campus?"

"They attend the new engineering program," Concordia said. "It is only twice per week, and the young men are required to leave campus before dark. Though I suppose it would be possible to conceal oneself and continue to watch Guryev after the Trinity students had left for the day."

Capshaw was madly scribbling upon his notepad. "I had no idea," he murmured. "How many young men are we talking about?"

"You'll have to ask President Langdon for precise numbers, but my students tell me as many as two dozen. The girls know only a few of them by sight."

Capshaw hesitated, lost in thought. "There is one problem with that. Barney Johns is a rough-looking fellow. Big and burly, unkempt, missing teeth. Smells bad, too. Hardly collegiate material." He flipped through his notes, his face brightening. "Ah. The description I have of Coutts, on the other hand—tall, lean, youthful face—it's possible." He straightened. "Now I just have to find him."

Chapter 25

It is the privilege of the bride to name the wedding day.
~Mrs. John Sherwood

Week 7, Instructor Calendar
November 1898

Concordia and David helped the rest of the staff set up cots and curtained dressing areas for the students from Willow and Hemlock Cottages, nearly four dozen of them in all, except for the four young ladies who remained in the infirmary. Word of the college's misfortune had spread, and donations of pillows, blankets, and clothing had been brisk.

It was certainly a boost to the spirits after the dismal experience of picking through her charred, sodden belongings earlier in the day. She had lost all of her skirts and shirtwaists, and the books from her sitting room were a pulpy mess.

But she would miss her bicycle most of all. The adjoining shed it had been stored in was now a pile of rubble.

With a guilty pang, she wished the etiquette book Drusilla had lent her had perished as well, but it and her other books were safe in the office, as was Mrs. Bradley's aquamarine brooch that she had shoved in her desk drawer.

She blew out a breath. "Hand me a pillow, would you?"

David put a coverslip on it and passed it over. "Why doesn't Langdon simply close the school and send the girls home?"

She fluffed the pillow and set it on the cot. "The seniors need to complete their coursework in order to graduate on time. Besides, three out of the five cottages were spared. And then there are the students who live off-campus and ride the streetcar to school. Why penalize all of them?"

"The girls cannot stay in the gymnasium indefinitely," he said. "Can't the remaining cottages accommodate them?"

She shook her head. "Miss Pomeroy and Miss Jenkins surveyed the bedrooms and said each cottage could only hold five more students. Otherwise, they would be crammed together even worse than here."

He pursed his lips thoughtfully. "That leaves thirty-five."

She sat wearily on a cot. Thirty-five young ladies, most without any possessions to call their own. "I do not know what else we can do." If only a place nearby could house them. It would have to be a large residence.

She took a breath. A large house, nearby.

She glanced at David. What had he said? *The entire place has been cleaned out. No debris. Scoured top to bottom. We would need to do very little to get it ready.*

She felt a tingle of excitement, her previous reservations fading. *This is why we found the Armstrong property. This is what we must do.*

David's brown eyes narrowed with curiosity. "You have an idea."

Concordia hesitated. Would he agree to such an outrageous proposition?

She motioned to a chair. "You had better sit down. We have much to talk about."

"So, are we in agreement?" Concordia asked.

David chuckled. "Housing nearly three dozen high-spirited young ladies in our future home is certainly not what I originally had in mind, but there is no denying the place is large enough. And it's the right thing to do."

"You are sure there are ten bedrooms? We did not have the opportunity to tour the entire house before...." Her voice trailed off. How would the parents of the young ladies feel about their daughters staying in a place where a murder occurred? The matter must be handled delicately.

He nodded. "Ten, along with the housekeeper's quarters on the ground floor. You and Ruby would have to share that."

"That would be no problem. If we had three students to a room, we would only need to find other places for five girls," she said. "Perhaps they could stay with the students who board locally?"

He blew out a breath. "I just thought of something. How long will they need the house?"

"I don't know. Months, probably, for Willow Cottage to be rebuilt. Winter weather could slow that down, too. We will have to speak with Mr. Langdon—oh!" Comprehension dawned at last. She gave him a worried look. "The wedding."

"Exactly. We cannot be married and live with the young ladies, you know." He gave her a wink.

She blushed. "No, that would not do at all."

They were quiet for a while. She stole a glance at his face, trying to gauge his feelings on the subject. Was he coming to the same conclusion as she? His faraway air told her nothing.

Finally, she had to say something. "Would you mind terribly...if we...postponed the wedding? Just until the spring semester was over."

He sighed and met her eyes. "I have waited this long, my dear. I can wait a few months more." He gave her an impish grin. "I take it your mother will have the elaborate June wedding for her daughter that she had long despaired of."

Concordia grimaced. "Ah well, nothing is without its price."

Chapter 26

There is something exquisitely poetical in the idea of a June wedding.
~Mrs. John Sherwood

Week 8, Instructor Calendar
November 1898

President Langdon was understandably reluctant at first, but after a tour of the Armstrong property, he quickly warmed to the idea.

Within a week, it was arranged. The money was paid, the papers signed, and the house preparations begun. After a long, closed-door meeting with the mayor of Hartford, Langdon established the college's first Gown and Town Day, dedicated to the special bond between the college and the citizens of Hartford. The *Courant* ran the story. This year, Hartford Women's College was to be the beneficiary, and the plea went out for help. Matrons, shopkeepers, and farmers—many of them long-time friends of the Armstrong family—arrived the following Saturday morning to turn the old farmhouse into comfortable living quarters for the students. They brought tools, furniture, and dry goods. Students and faculty pitched in. Miss Lovelace, her uncle, and the other engineering students set to work hanging curtains and securing wobbly banisters.

One of the farming families apparently thought the introduction of chickens to the homestead was crucial to the young ladies' comfort as well. They set to repairing the dilapidated coop in the barnyard and gallantly presented half a dozen live chickens to Concordia, as the lady of the house.

While she privately cringed at the thought of waking daily to the sounds of a rooster crowing, she graciously accepted the gift.

Mrs. Sanbourne brought a gift as well, a beautifully framed pastel sketch of the farmhouse.

"How lovely! That is most kind of you," Concordia said, examining it closely. Mrs. Sanbourne had created a sunset scene, making liberal use of pinks and oranges. "We will be sure to find a suitable place." She hesitated. "I wish to apologize for distressing you with my questions a few weeks ago."

Mrs. Sanbourne smiled, and the gray feather of her mulberry felt hat swished as she nodded. "Not at all, dear. All is forgiven." She leaned in more closely. "Though you may wish to curb that inquisitive nature of yours. If you will permit a bit of friendly advice from a married woman of ten years, a man does not appreciate a nosy wife."

Concordia flushed and changed the subject. "We'll be setting out the tea things soon. Can you stay?"

"Regretfully, no. Peter and I have a luncheon to attend. But he extends his congratulations as well." With a wave, she was off.

Concordia's mother, accompanied by Sarah and Gracie, arrived soon after. Ten-year-old Sarah ran up and put her arms around Concordia's waist. "It has been ages since I've seen you."

Concordia returned the embrace and smoothed a shiny red braid, very much like her own unfortunate hair color, over the girl's pinafore. "And I've missed you, dear. How are you getting along in school?"

The girl grimaced. "I don't mind the regular subjects like mathematics and Latin, but I hate having to do *needlepoint*."

Letitia Wells gave a disapproving frown. "A lady does not say she *hates* something. You *dislike* needlepoint."

Sarah looked up with innocent eyes. "If you know I *dislike* it, why must I learn it?"

Concordia's eyes watered from the effort of holding in a laugh.

Four-year-old Gracie, thumb firmly in her mouth, tugged on Concordia's skirt and pointed toward the tree swing. "Can you pusth me?" she lisped.

Concordia inclined her head toward Sarah. "I think Sissy can push you much higher. I'm a bit out of practice."

Sarah grinned and grabbed her sister's hand. "All right then, let's go!"

"Not too high!" Mrs. Wells called after them.

The girls nearly collided with the Bradleys, who were climbing out of their carriage. Both men hefted sizable hampers of food. "Whoa. Steady there, young ladies," John Bradley said, lifting his basket high. David handed his mother and Aunt Drusilla out of the vehicle, Bandit jumping out and trotting at their heels.

"Concordia, dear," Mrs. Bradley said breathlessly, coming over to embrace her. "We were so worried when we heard about the fire. I am glad you are safe."

"I appreciate your concern," Concordia said. "It has been a trying time."

"Be sure not to overtax yourself. You sound a bit hoarse."

Concordia pressed her hand. "I promise."

Drusilla's mouth puckered as she took in the view. "I cannot believe you two decided to live *here*, of all places—"

"Now, Drusilla," John Bradley interjected, "we talked about this on the way here. The decision has been made and it is not productive to discuss it further."

Drusilla had just drawn breath for a retort when Bandit started barking. A terrified rabbit leaped from behind a broken fence post and tore across the field. The dog gave chase.

"Bandit! Come back here at once!" Drusilla yelled. The dog paid no attention and was soon out of sight.

"I'm sure he'll return," Concordia said. "If not, we'll send one of the boys after him."

Georgeanna Bradley shook her head. "The mutt definitely has some hound in him. Always sniffing out something."

"I was about to show Mother the house. Mrs. Bradley, would you and Aunt Drusilla care to join us?"

On their tour, Concordia took care to avoid the back porch where Oster was found. She did not want to revive that particular conversation.

"It requires a bit of imagination," she said apologetically, as they surveyed the upper floor, "but once the new wallpaper is hung and the windows have been cleaned, the place will be quite charming."

Aunt Drusilla sniffed as she ran a gloved finger along a dusty windowsill. "So many bedrooms! How *many* children do you and David plan to have?"

Both Concordia's mother and Georgeanna Bradley regarded the bride-to-be with a glint in their eyes.

Concordia flushed. "Let us leave that to Providence, shall we? Come, you haven't seen the kitchen yet. It's enormous."

After coming upon a mice nest in the pantry and enduring Drusilla's gloomy prognostications about drafty rooms, the primitive cook stove, and the ancient state of the pipes, they escaped back outside into the bright sunshine.

More volunteers had arrived, including the Capshaws. Sophia, her blonde hair tucked neatly beneath a charming beribboned leghorn, leaned on her husband's arm to catch her breath as they crested the hill. Aaron Capshaw carried a large wicker hamper on his other arm.

Concordia smiled. *Mercy*, they would have enough food to feed the entire town at this rate.

Today, instead of his police uniform, Capshaw wore a red flannel shirt and denim overalls that emphasized his tall, lanky frame. Concordia blinked, mentally shifting from the accustomed image of Capshaw as policeman to that of Capshaw as country farmer. All he needed was a ragged straw hat and his resemblance to a redheaded scarecrow would be complete. She stifled a chuckle as they approached.

Sophia gave her a hug and whispered, "Can you tell he comes from a farming family?"

Concordia grinned. The less said within earshot of Capshaw, the better. "I'm so glad you came."

Capshaw glanced around at the work in progress. "It's good to see you transforming the place. I know Oster's death gave you pause, but I believe you've made the right decision."

Concordia's mother leaned in closer. "I read about the discovery of poor Mr. Guryev. Any news in that regard?"

"We have a lead, thanks to your daughter."

Concordia quickly checked over her shoulder, breathing a sigh of relief that Mrs. Bradley and Drusilla Fenmore had moved off to chat with President Langdon.

Mrs. Wells' eyes narrowed as she glanced at her daughter. "Indeed? I sincerely hope that is the extent of her contribution."

Concordia laughed. "Don't worry, Mother, I will be too busy feeding chickens."

Eli, the Capshaws' adopted son, caught up with them.

"My goodness, how you've grown! I hardly recognized you," Concordia said.

Life with his new family certainly agreed with the thirteen-year-old. Gone was the thin child with the pale, pinched face, dirty knickers, and skittish manner. Although she could see the remnants of childhood in the hairless cheeks and the curly black hair ever in need of a cut, he was sturdily built now and tall enough to look her in the eye.

He gave her a radiant smile. "I grew four inches this summer."

"Hardly a surprise," Capshaw said with a grin. "The lad eats anything that isn't nailed to the floor." He passed him a hammer. "Speaking of nailing, let's help with the porch steps."

"But—" Concordia sputtered, as Capshaw and Eli walked away. *Drat*, she wanted to know if Capshaw had found out anything about the fire.

Concordia's mother embraced Sophia. "You are blooming, Sophia dear. I hear there is a baby on the way, is that right?"

Sophia blushed. "That is the rumor."

"Oh!" Concordia exclaimed. "I am so happy for you." At second glance, she could see that Sophia's angular form had softened and become more rounded.

"How are you feeling?" Mrs. Wells asked.

"I'm fine. A bit tired." Sophia made a face. "And my dresses are getting tight."

Concordia's glance wandered to the porch, as Capshaw and Eli joined the others working on the steps.

Sophia caught her look. "I know you are eager for news of the fire. He wants to wait until it is quieter."

Mrs. Wells raised an eyebrow. "Indeed."

"You cannot tell us what he has learned?" Concordia asked.

But Sophia was already heading to the trestle tables set out on the front lawn, where Ruby and Miss Kimble were laying tablecloths. "Shall I help you unpack the hampers, Ruby?" she called.

Concordia sighed. She knew she would not get another word out of Sophia, but it was exasperating to wait. Patience was not one of her virtues.

She squared her shoulders. Ah well. In the meantime, there was work to be done.

The college provided a generous feast for the volunteers at the midday break. As the November day was fine and unusually warm, the meal took on a picnic-like quality, with chairs brought outside and large blankets spread upon the ground. They ate cold ham, chicken salad, apples, and fresh-baked rolls slathered with raspberry jam. Large jugs of cold-pressed cider were passed around. Concordia was grateful for a chance to sit down and catch her breath, with David beside her. They had been so busy that she had not seen him all morning.

As the assemblage lounged and chatted, Mr. Langdon made his way to the porch and cleared his throat for attention.

The crowd quieted.

"Thank you all, for the contributions of your time and goods," he began, hooking his thumbs comfortably into the armholes of his pinstripe vest. "We could not have done this without you. As you no doubt heard, or read in the newspaper, our campus has suffered a major setback. Fortunately, it is only a matter of property and not of human lives, but it is still a blow."

Concordia thought of her visit to Charlotte Crandall at the hospital yesterday. Lady Dunwick and Randolph Maynard were there by her bedside. She later learned from Miss Kimble—at last taking on her full duties without interference—that Maynard visited Charlotte as often as the family and propriety would permit. Not that Charlotte was aware of it. The young woman lay in her hospital bed, eyes open and blinking, yet not responding to questions. Carbon monoxide poisoning, the doctors said. We can only give her time. Concordia brushed her hand over her wet cheeks. David moved closer and handed her his kerchief.

"Yet we are resilient," Langdon continued. "We have begun this tradition of Gown and Town Day so that in the years to come we can be of help to each other. We will dedicate this day to serving the needs of the people of Hartford, and vice versa. Whoever needs us. You see, we are inseparably intertwined. Our recent trials have reminded us of that."

Smiling broadly, he gestured toward Concordia and David. "Speaking of inseparable, I want to extend my deepest thanks to Miss Wells and Mr. Bradley. We cannot tell you how grateful we are. To open your new home to the school, and postpone your wedding plans until we have rebuilt the cottages! We are indebted to you both. We wish you every happiness in your future together." He raised his mug of cider in salute.

Concordia blushed profusely and David grinned during the general applause and cheers.

"*Mercy*," she whispered under her breath.

Her mother sat down beside them, eyes gleaming. "I am eagerly awaiting a June wedding."

Dusk gathered as the group packed up the last of the tools and neatly stacked the spare lumber in the barn. Most of the volunteers had gone home, except for Lieutenant Capshaw, who was helping David complete repairs to the back porch screens, and Miss Lovelace, who had just finished hanging wallpaper in the housekeeper's quarters.

Miss Lovelace came out to sit beside Concordia on the porch swing. She pulled her shawl closer. "This will be a lovely view in the spring," she said, gesturing to the gray-brown sweep of woods to the right and the grounds of the college below.

Concordia nodded. "It is a shame that it took the destruction of Willow Cottage before we realized this should be our home." She paused. "Have you called upon Miss Smedley and the other girls still in the infirmary?"

Miss Lovelace plucked at her skirt and did not meet Concordia's eye. "No."

"No matter what your personal differences, or what she may have done in the past, it would be the charitable thing to do. Everyone else has been to visit."

"She would not want me to come, anyway."

"The day after tomorrow her parents will be taking her home to finish recuperating. Can you not put aside your personal animosity and see her just once, before she leaves?"

Miss Lovelace looked up in astonishment. "After what she has done to me, you want me to sit by her bedside and hold her hand?"

"The hand-holding is optional," Concordia snapped. "She has been through a tremendous ordeal. Besides, we do not know exactly what she has done. Suspecting and knowing are two very different things."

"Indeed they are." Lieutenant Capshaw stood in the doorway. He pulled over a chair and sat across from them. David came out of the house and sat on a step.

"Is this a good time to talk about your investigation of the fire?" Concordia asked.

Capshaw nodded and glanced over at Miss Lovelace.

"Do you wish me to leave?" Miss Lovelace said, getting up from her seat.

Capshaw waved her back. "Actually, I have some questions for you as well."

She frowned. "For me?"

"Yes, miss. The fire chief has determined that the fire was deliberate. His best estimate is two o'clock that morning. The arsonist chose the corridor immediately outside of two bedroom doors: the room occupied by Miss Crandall, and the room shared by Miss Smedley and Miss Tate. I have made inquiries, and I understand that you and Miss Smedley have a history of ill-feeling toward one another." He turned toward Concordia. "Something about a prank that had gone awry."

Concordia stiffened. "Miss Lovelace would not be so depraved as to set fire to Willow Cottage in order to settle a grudge against Miss Smedley. She lives there herself. That is absurd." Nevertheless, she had a sinking feeling in the pit of her stomach. *I will not wait long*, Maisie had said. She gave her an uneasy glance.

"I wish that were the case, but when we went through the rubble we found a half-empty box of kitchen matches, along with a rag shoved under a bed in what had been Miss Lovelace's room. The cloth still smelled of accelerant."

Miss Lovelace shifted in her seat. "The matches are certainly mine—we are required to light the gas burners in the laboratory, and the matches were always getting misplaced. I kept them in my room for safekeeping. But any rags you may have found are *not* mine, sir. Someone must have put them there to blame me."

Capshaw raised a skeptical brow. "There seems to be a great deal of that happening to you, Miss Lovelace. I've heard about the gun prank that resulted in the death of one of the school's horses. Mr. Maynard found your pouch of tools in the stable. You were held accountable for that?"

"But she was eventually cleared of blame," Concordia interjected.

Capshaw pulled out his wadded notepad and flipped through several pages. "Yes, so I see. And who was the responsible party, then?"

"Alison Smedley, I'm sure of it," Miss Lovelace said promptly, before Concordia could stop her.

Capshaw sat back in satisfaction. "But you have not yet been able to prove it, have you?"

Miss Lovelace shot an exasperated look in Concordia's direction. "Not yet."

Concordia groaned inwardly. Miss Lovelace was playing right into Capshaw's hands.

"I would imagine there to be a great deal of resentment toward Miss Smedley. Understandable, of course. It would not be so far-fetched for you to want revenge upon her, is that not correct?"

All too late, Miss Lovelace realized the trap. "I would not do such a thing! I promise you, I had nothing to do with the fire."

Capshaw stood, brushing off the knees of his trousers. "Time will tell, Miss Lovelace. I will have more questions for you later, I'm sure."

Chapter 27

The first joy of convalescence is of gratitude,
and the second that we have created an interest
and a compassion among our friends.
~Mrs. John Sherwood

Week 8, Instructor Calendar
November 1898

Concordia finally coaxed Miss Lovelace to visit Miss Smedley in the infirmary the morning before she was due to leave. "I will accompany you."

Miss Jenkins had just finished helping Alison change into a borrowed traveling dress and had settled her in a chair. The girl had lost weight during her ordeal. Her brown eyes were glassy above sunken cheekbones, her pale hair dull, her thin hands resting limply atop the blanket laid over her lap. She barely acknowledged Concordia's greeting.

Miss Lovelace was nearly as pale as Miss Smedley. She perched awkwardly on the bed. "How are you feeling, Alison?"

She shrugged. "I am improving, I suppose. How is everyone settling into the new house?"

"Oh, we are comfortable enough, but the big place takes a bit of getting used to," Miss Lovelace said.

The awkward silence that followed was punctuated by a ticking clock and Miss Jenkins's footsteps in her office.

At least they were not shrieking at each other.

Concordia elbowed Miss Lovelace.

The girl blew out a breath. "I...I am sorry you were so injured in the fire. Heaven knows we've had our differences, but

I would never wish you any harm. I hope that we can…mend our fences?"

Miss Smedley stared at her for so long that Concordia wondered if she was having some sort of fit. Finally, she spoke. "There is a rumor that *you* set the fire."

Miss Lovelace started to speak, but Alison Smedley held up a hand. "But I know you did not."

Concordia's eyes widened. "How do you know that, Miss Smedley?"

Tears streaked down Alison Smedley's cheeks. She made no move to wipe them away.

"Do you know who is responsible for the fire?"

Miss Smedley gave a slow nod. "But I'm…afraid," she whispered.

"Afraid? Of what? Or of whom?" Concordia persisted.

Miss Smedley stared at some distant point beyond them, absorbed in her own thoughts. "I did not mean for the horse to die."

Concordia gently clasped the girl's hands. "Alison, what if I were to tell you that I had set up a false envelope of evidence in the lady principal's office the night of the Halloween ball?"

Miss Smedley started.

"I am sorry to play such a trick on you, dear, but I wanted proof that you were involved. I waited for you to come for it. You did not. Do you know who I saw instead?"

Miss Smedley whispered, "Mrs. Sanbourne."

Miss Lovelace covered her mouth in a suppressed shriek.

Concordia sat back, gaping. *Mrs. Sanbourne?*

She had been sure Miss Smedley would name Miss Kimble as her co-conspirator. What other reason would the bursar have for snooping through Miss Pomeroy's desk?

She would have to leave that question for the moment. The bigger question now was, why *Mrs. Sanbourne?*

"I told her what you had said at the ball," Miss Smedley went on. "She promised to take care of it."

Mercy, how many people had trooped through Miss Pomeroy's office that night? It must have been after she and David had left.

"She said there was no envelope, that you must have been bluffing," Miss Smedley added. "But you say there was?"

Concordia shook her head. "Never mind that now. Why did you tell Mrs. Sanbourne about the envelope?"

"Because she helped me…set up the gun mechanism." Alison's tears were falling fast now, dropping upon her hands that still clasped Concordia's.

"Why would she do that?" Miss Lovelace said impatiently. "Why would she be involved in such an underhanded, malicious prank?"

Miss Smedley flinched.

Concordia shot Miss Lovelace a warning frown before turning back to the quivering girl. "How did Mrs. Sanbourne come to be involved?" She pulled a clean handkerchief from her sleeve and passed it over.

Miss Smedley wiped her eyes. "I spent a lot of time in her studio, and she said I had real talent. We became friends. I confided in her." She looked over at Miss Lovelace. "I admit I was jealous of you, Maisie. You seemed able to do as you please and get exactly what you wanted. Mrs. Sanbourne knew how I felt. She came up with the idea of the prank, to blame you. I took your tools and hid them in the stable. She showed me how to wire everything into place."

"How would Mrs. Sanbourne possess such knowledge?" Concordia asked.

Miss Smedley shrugged. "I don't know."

"She helps her husband in the laboratory when he's short-handed," Miss Lovelace said. "It's possible." She glared at Miss Smedley. "But why would you do something so—so cruel, and dangerous?"

"I didn't realize how cruel and dangerous it was…until after." Her voice dropped to a whisper. "I wasn't thinking about how the horses would react. I'm sorry." She turned to Concordia. "Please believe me. Yes, I wanted to get Maisie in trouble, but she was never in trouble for very long. I thought this time would be no different. I wanted to do something as daring as her buggy stunt last year."

Maisie Lovelace winced.

"How could you believe it wasn't dangerous? A live bullet had fired," Concordia said.

Miss Smedley clenched her hands. "I put a blank in the gun, not a bullet."

"Then how did a bullet get in there?" Miss Lovelace asked.

"Mrs. Sanbourne must have gone back and replaced it. I don't understand it, but she was the only other person who knew it was there."

"Did you ask her?" Concordia asked.

Miss Smedley nodded. "She laughed and said it was her business and to keep my mouth shut."

Her business. Business with whom? Charlotte, or Maynard? Concordia remembered how Maynard froze when he first caught sight of the Sanbournes at the reception. Was it Mrs. Sanbourne he was shocked to see?

And at the Halloween ball, he had abruptly left the table in response to something the woman had said.

Betrayal can come from anywhere, even one's own doorstep.

What had he done? Had he courted her years ago, then jilted her? To hold such a bitter grudge after all these years...it had to be something more.

Jealousy? The unflattering caricature of Charlotte and Maynard came to mind. Concordia shook her head. Miss Kimble had been in the sketch as well. It was all so confusing.

Miss Smedley shivered. "Her expression...was frightening."

"Do you think Mrs. Sanbourne capable of setting fire to the corridor in front of your bedroom to keep you from revealing what you knew?" Concordia asked.

"I...I don't know."

Miss Lovelace's eyes were wide. "What do we do?"

Chapter 28

The person who can write a graceful note is always spoken of with phrases of commendation.

~Mrs. John Sherwood

Week 8, Instructor Calendar
November 1898

It was time to talk to Maynard about this woman from his past, someone who obviously had no intention of remaining there. What deep-seated grudge did Rachel Sanbourne carry? Why risk all she had—marriage to a successful inventor, financial security, the freedom to follow her own pursuits, and the esteem of Hartford society—in order to harm Maynard? If it was revenge for some unknown wrong, why had there been no further attempts? She visited campus nearly every day, painting in her studio or out on the grounds. Opportunities abounded.

During her brisk walk from the infirmary to the Hall and up to the stairs, Concordia realized she hadn't fully recovered from the effects of the fire. She wheezed as she reached the second floor.

Drat. Maynard's light was out, his door closed. He must have gone to the hospital to visit Charlotte.

Visit Charlotte.

If Mrs. Sanbourne were indeed responsible for the fire in Willow Cottage, Miss Smedley as a target barely made sense. Who would believe the girl's account?

Maynard wasn't a target, either—at least, not directly.

Only one person had been harmed in each incident. An unconscious woman who might never regain her senses. A woman beloved by Maynard. *Charlotte.*

Had Mrs. Sanbourne achieved her objective? Was that why nothing more had happened?

As she leaned against the bannister to rest for a moment, she heard the high-pitched tones of Gertrude Pomeroy and the lower timbre of Frances Kimble. Concordia very much wanted to speak with the bursar.

Miss Pomeroy had her hand on the knob of Miss Kimble's door as Concordia came around the corner. "Concordia! How are you feeling, dear?" She frowned and cocked her head, listening. "I do not like that rasp. You should not over-exert yourself. Miss Jenkins says your lungs need time to heal."

The woman's ear for languages served her well in more ways than one. Concordia grimaced. "I will try."

Miss Pomeroy patted her hand. "Do keep that in mind. Well, I must be going."

Miss Kimble came to the door. She was dressed simply in a café au lait-colored skirt and violet-sprigged shirtwaist that made her deep-brown eyes appear bottomless. "Miss Wells, a pleasure. Did you wish to see me?" She opened the door wide and gestured toward a chair.

"Yes. There is something I wanted to ask you." Concordia closed the door behind her and hesitated. What was she accusing the bursar of, anyway? Eavesdropping in the hallway? Creeping into an unlocked office and peeking into an envelope? There was nothing nefarious about excessive curiosity overriding good manners. She had done so herself upon occasion.

Now that she knew Mrs. Sanbourne, not Miss Kimble, was responsible for the gun prank and probably the fire, she was tempted to leave Miss Kimble be. On the other hand, nothing tainted a close-knit community worse than suspicion. It would be best to clear the air.

"Of course, Miss Wells. I am entirely at your disposal." Miss Kimble squinted at her in concern. "You seem unwell. Can I get you some water?" She reached for the carafe and a glass. "What is your question?"

Concordia sat and smoothed her skirt. "Why have you been spying upon Randolph Maynard?" she blurted out.

Miss Kimble's hands stilled for a moment before she passed the glass. "Spying? What on earth do you mean?"

"The night before the Halloween Ball," Concordia said, clutching the tumbler with both hands, "Mr. Maynard and I had a heated discussion in his office. As I was leaving, I heard light footsteps hastily retreat down the stairwell. It was you, Miss Kimble. You had been eavesdropping."

Miss Kimble's face reddened as she fiddled with a pencil. She did not meet Concordia's eye. "A great many people use those stairs."

"I am not here to reprove you. I merely want to understand why you are so preoccupied with monitoring the dean. If I were at odds with the man as the two of you have been, I should not wish to spend any more time than is necessary thinking of him, let alone poking into his affairs."

Frances Kimble spoke through gritted teeth. "You have no idea."

"Then why don't you tell me? While you are at it, explain why you went through Miss Pomeroy's desk, in search of evidence from the gun prank."

The bursar froze, eyes wide. "*You* were behind that?" she whispered.

Concordia nodded. "I had hoped to catch Alison Smedley. Imagine my surprise when you appeared."

In the silence that followed, Concordia added, "Please, tell me *why*. That's all I want to know."

Miss Kimble sighed. "You don't ask for much, do you?" She was quiet for a moment. "Very well. It was thanks to another conversation you and I had—remember when I helped you clean up the kitchen after your aborted attempt to make an apple pie?"

Concordia grimaced. She was not likely to forget that.

"It was then that I decided to learn as much as I could about the dean. I hoped to find a chink in his armor, so to speak. He appears so sanctimonious, so...so perfect. But beneath it all, he is...afraid."

"Afraid?"

"He has a secret. And an enemy. Now I know what those are."

Concordia frowned in confusion. "You learned his secret from the envelope in Miss Pomeroy's desk?"

Miss Kimble waved an impatient hand. "Of course not. The envelope was useless. I found it out later."

"When? How were you planning to make use of the information?"

Miss Kimble shook her head, a small smile on her lips.

Concordia sat back and folded her arms. "You were prepared to blackmail Maynard, weren't you?"

The bursar's smile faded. She cleared her throat. "I...I am not proud of it. I was tired of fighting for permission to do my own job." She met Concordia's eye and tossed her head in defiance. "Yes, I was prepared to use it against him. Fortunately, circumstances intervened."

"The circumstances themselves are most *un*fortunate," Concordia said tartly. Anger constricted her chest. "*You* did not lose your home and nearly all of your possessions, Miss Kimble. *You* were not grievously injured, lying unconscious in a hospital bed."

Miss Kimble flushed. "I apologize."

When Concordia had taken a few breaths and recovered her temper, she asked, "What is it you discovered about Mr. Maynard? Did you learn who is behind the gun prank and the fire?" She was reluctant to offer Rachel Sanbourne's name. The bursar might *think* she knew Maynard's secret. She could be wrong.

Miss Kimble took a breath, then hesitated. "I think it best that I keep my discovery to myself."

Concordia stood to leave. "There may be a time when you will be required to reveal it." *Such as a police inquiry.*

Miss Kimble's lips twitched in a small smile. "Today is not that time."

Concordia checked her watch as she left Founder's Hall. Nearly time to dress for dinner. Perhaps Mr. Maynard had returned to change by now. She could at least check on her way to the farmhouse. She hurried down the path and rang the bell of Sycamore House. After some delay, the maid answered.

"Is Mr. Maynard in?"

She shook her head. "I'm sorry, Miss Wells."

"Will he return for dinner?"

The girl pursed her lips. "He didn't say. He was in an awful hurry to leave."

"I see." Concordia hesitated. What should she do now? Did she dare talk to Mrs. Sanbourne alone? No, perhaps she should tell someone. But who? President Langdon? Capshaw?

Echoing in her mind was the anguished voice of Randolph Maynard. *Newspapermen, peering into my private life? Writing about it in the scandal sheets? We would bring ignominy upon the school.... The college has had enough of that.*

He was right. There would be plenty of ignominy to go around, she had no doubt of that. The dean of Hartford Women's College, hiding a dark secret involving the wife of the man in charge of the new engineering department? A woman bent on revenge, no matter who else suffered in the process?

"Are you all right, miss?" the maid asked, brows drawn in a puzzled frown.

Concordia realized she had been standing in the doorway all this time. "I beg your pardon. May I leave a note?"

"Of course." The girl stepped aside and pointed to the side parlor door. "You'll find stationery and pens in the writing desk. Would you excuse me? The housekeeper needs my help."

Concordia sat at the small writing desk and pulled out pen and paper. After collecting her thoughts—how does one broach such a subject?—she decided to keep it brief and cryptic. It would not do if it were mislaid.

> *Mr. Maynard,*
> *It is urgent that I speak with you about a certain person of your past acquaintance. Kindly send me a message as soon as you have returned this evening.*
> *Yours,*
> *Concordia Wells*

That should do it. She sealed the envelope and wrote his name across it. She glanced at the large oak desk beside the French doors. Miss Jenkins had said Maynard used this room as his study. That must be his desk. He'd be more likely to come upon the note if she put it there.

She approached the desk and laid the envelope on its surface, bare of anything beyond a blotter and letter opener. Her hand strayed, almost of its own accord, toward the center drawer. She froze, straightening. *No.* One does not search a man's desk! Such snooping was beneath reproach. It was probably locked, anyway.

Well, she could give it a little tug, to make sure.

The drawer slid out easily. The dean must have forgotten to lock it in his haste. She released a breath and crouched to look inside.

With an ear for steps in the hall, she quickly scanned bundles of correspondence—bank statements, department store bills, letters from a brother in Albany.

The deep bottom drawer was dedicated to file folders, sorted by years. What an exceedingly methodical man. She skimmed to the tab marked 1888, deciding to work backward from there. Whatever had happened occurred more than ten years ago, likely before the Sanbournes were married.

Farther along, in the section marked 1883, Concordia noticed a folder slightly out of place, as if someone had recently pulled it out and then hastily pushed it back again. With trembling fingers, she slid it out and opened it.

The first page that met her eyes had her groping the chair back for support.

Mrs. Rachel Maynard
CERTIFICATE OF COMMITMENT

Concordia took a breath. The woman was Maynard's *wife?* And…she was mad. Bigamous *and* insane? Oh no, this could not be good for anyone.

Concordia scanned the page, glancing past the names of the admitting doctors and the address of the asylum in Massachusetts. She was searching for a diagnosis.

She finally found it: *post-partum dysplasia, resulting in infanticide.*

She closed her eyes and took deep gulps of air, struggling to quiet her pounding heart.

Footsteps outside sent her into a panic. She shoved the folder back into its slot and pushed the drawer closed. As she heard the knob turn, she ran to the bookshelves and began perusing them. She clenched her hands tightly to keep them from shaking and blew out a long, steadying breath.

It was the maid, a brass scuttle over her arm. She stopped short. "Miss Wells! I thought you'd gone long ago." Her tone was slightly reproachful. Her glance strayed to Maynard's desk.

Concordia jumped, as if startled out of a reverie. "Oh! I beg your pardon. I was admiring your impressive collection of Spenser." Mercy, she'd told a great many falsehoods lately.

The maid gave her a curious look as she moved to the hearth. "It's growing chilly. I must get this fire burning proper."

Concordia headed for the door, breathing a quiet sigh. "I will get out of your way. Good night."

She hurried along the path up Rook's Hill. She did not want to be late for supper. Now that she and the students from Willow Cottage were living at the old Armstrong house, they had to allow ten minutes of additional walking to get to the dining hall on time. She was sure that under the circumstances she, Ruby, and the students would be excused if they were late, but she wanted to show Langdon that they could make it work, without any special accommodations.

The bell tower clock of Memorial Chapel had just struck the hour when they entered the dining hall. The girls eagerly greeted their friends from the other cottages, regaling them with stories of the chicken accidentally trapped in the food pantry and the raccoons in the attic bedroom.

"I was just stepping into my room to change, and a flash of eyes in the dark made me jump in fright!" Miss Gage said with a laugh. "Ruby had to get a broom and shoo it out the window."

Concordia smiled. At least they were taking it in stride. Youth was happily resilient in that regard.

Miss Banning was sitting by herself at a table, scowling at her water glass. Concordia picked up her plate and joined her.

"How are you today? Doing well, I hope?" Concordia asked.

Miss Banning glanced up. "Huh, what? Fine. Any news of Charlotte?"

The old lady tried to make the question sound casual, but the way she curled her fingers around the stem of her glass spoke volumes.

"Well, her eyes are open, but she remains insensible to her surroundings. I am sorry to distress you so," she added, alarmed at Miss Banning's sudden pallor. "Have you been able to visit her in the hospital?"

Miss Banning's lips thinned in an angry line. She shook her head.

"I plan to stop by tomorrow, after my morning classes," Concordia said. "Would you like to accompany me? I will ask Mr. Langdon if we can borrow the buggy."

Miss Banning's face brightened, and she plucked a roll from the basket. "*Hmph*, I suppose that will be all right. I will be in my office when you are ready."

Concordia slept poorly. It was only the third night of living in the farmhouse, and she was unaccustomed to the noises: the soughing of the trees, the wind rattling the shutters, the creaking of old wood. Then, of course, she shared her bedroom— formerly the housekeeper's quarters—with Ruby. A roommate who snored like a lumberjack took some getting used to.

Nonetheless, it was an improvement over camping in the infirmary or gymnasium.

She put on robe and slippers and went to the kitchen for a glass of milk. She shivered as she felt the chill air brush over her ankles. She had to admit, Aunt Drusilla was right about the drafts. They would need heavier curtains before winter set in.

She turned up the hurricane lamp and sat down at the heavy oak table with her glass. More than the noises of the house kept her awake. She did not know what to do about Mrs. Sanbourne. Maynard had not been at dinner, nor had he sent her a message this evening.

She did not honestly think they were in immediate danger from the woman—both Miss Smedley and Charlotte Crandall were away from campus, if either truly was the target—but something had to be done. Alison and Maisie had already promised to say nothing about their conversation. Quite generous on Maisie's part, as Capshaw claimed to suspect her of setting the fire. Concordia hoped the quick-witted policeman would not stick to that theory for very long. At least he had not returned with more questions.

No one else knew about the commitment papers she had found today. Did she dare hope this could be settled quietly? Certainly the gun prank could be swept under the rug. Although Capshaw was aware of the incident, the police had not been officially called in for that.

However, the fire that destroyed Willow Cottage and put Charlotte in the hospital was a different matter entirely. She knew Capshaw would work tirelessly on the case until it was resolved. One could not stuff that genie back in the bottle.

If Mrs. Sanbourne were exposed as the culprit, the rest of the scandal would quickly come to light: her previous asylum commitment and the reason why. Unless there was a divorce decree in Maynard's papers that Concordia had not seen—could one even divorce a madwoman?—Mrs. Sanbourne would also be exposed as a bigamist.

How Maynard kept his composure in Rachel Sanbourne's company was incomprehensible, with such a painful past between them. Mrs. Sanbourne, likewise, seemed to have nerves of steel when presenting a public face to the world. The woman had even sought out Maynard's company on occasion, such as the time Concordia encountered them coming from the garden of Sycamore House. Perhaps she had wanted to extract a promise that he would not reveal her secret. But she must have known he never would. It would pull him down in the mire along with her.

Mrs. Sanbourne did not always present an unruffled façade, of course. There had been her unease at the Halloween dinner, when Maynard had blurted out the news of Langdon's niece losing her baby, and the bitter edge to her voice when she'd spoken of betrayal. Concordia had misunderstood it at the time. It was not Guryev's betrayal, but Maynard's. To the rest of the world, consigning the woman to an asylum would appear a prudent and merciful act, after what she had done. However, an insane person likely wouldn't view it that way.

Concordia shook her head. How could she have thought Miss Kimble was to blame? Although her intention to blackmail Maynard was certainly disturbing, the bursar's antagonism toward Maynard was quick to flare and open for all to see. She had confused things greatly by searching Miss Pomeroy's desk for the envelope and eavesdropping on Concordia's conversation with Maynard. Concordia recalled the caricature of Maynard and Charlotte, with Miss Kimble peeking over his shoulder, shaking money in a clenched fist. Had Mrs. Sanbourne been aware of Miss Kimble's prying?

Concordia set her glass in the sink, using both hands to awkwardly work the pump. The faucet shuddered as she rinsed the glass.

Mrs. Sanbourne. The woman appeared to be everything Miss Kimble was not: cool, serene, amiable. Concordia understood now that pain and anger smoldered unseen, beneath the ashes of a tragedy few knew about. Yet despite the face she presented to the world, the conflagration had come at last. Perhaps literally.

Charlotte suffered the most in the aftermath, though no one at the school would escape the pain of the scandal. Including Peter Sanbourne, upon whom the entire engineering program rested. Did he know? Surely not. What a blow that would be. First a treacherous assistant, then a treacherous wife.

She dried the glass and put it back. She could not see a way out.

Chapter 29

*Command of temper, delicacy of feeling, and elegance of manner—all
these are demanded of the persons who become leaders of society.*
~Mrs. John Sherwood

Week 8, Instructor Calendar
November 1898

At last, Concordia caught up with Maynard after her
morning classes. She tapped on his partly open door.
"I am on my way to retrieve Miss Banning, and visit Miss
Crandall," Concordia began conversationally, as she came in
and closed the door behind her. Miss Banning's office was right
beside the dean's, and she did not wish to be overheard. The old
lady had the ears of a bat.

Maynard waved an impatient hand. "Fine. Give Lady
Dunwick my regards if you see her. Leave the door open on
your way out, if you please. I am expecting a student."

She gritted her teeth. The man could tax the patience of a
saint. "I will leave it closed for now. There is something
confidential I wish to speak to you about. Did you get my
note?"

Resigned, Maynard set down his pen. "Note? No."

She frowned. What had happened to it? The nosy maid,
most likely.

He did not offer her a chair, but she sat down anyway. "It is
about Mrs. Sanbourne. Something must be done."

Maynard's face paled, but he continued with his usual
bluster. "And what, pray, am I to do with Mrs. Sanbourne?
Should that not be *Mr.* Sanbourne's province?"

"Only if you are no longer married to her," she snapped.

Maynard stared, open-mouthed.

She pressed her advantage. "Alison Smedley told me Mrs. Sanbourne helped her rig the pistol mechanism, then switched out the blank cartridge for a live bullet without the girl's knowledge. I believe her. Mrs. Sanbourne was trying to kill you, Mr. Maynard. Or was it Charlotte she hoped to harm?"

The dean dropped his head in his hands. She waited. Finally, he met her eye. "How did you find out?"

"Never mind that now." She was reluctant to admit snooping through his private papers. "The woman is a menace. I am convinced she is also responsible for the fire, which makes it her second attempt upon Charlotte's life, not to mention putting the rest of us in harm's way. She seeks to cause you pain by hurting Charlotte, no matter what the cost. She is not sane."

Maynard's features had taken on an anguished expression. She knew she was causing him distress, but she had no choice. "We must go to the police."

He shook his head. "Not sane...." His eyes narrowed. "What do you know about her sanity, Miss Wells?"

Drat. She bit her lip. "I found the certificate."

Maynard made a choking sound. "You found—"

"—I have not told anyone," she interrupted. "Not yet. But the authorities must be contacted. Besides the fact that she is dangerous, the atmosphere of suspicion and blame on campus is tearing us apart. Even now, Capshaw suspects poor Miss Lovelace of setting the fire as revenge upon Miss Smedley. This cannot be allowed to continue."

"Please." Maynard's voice was thick with emotion. "Let me handle this...privately. If I can convince her to place herself under the care of doctors, somewhere she could...rest, it would be better for everyone."

Concordia's frown made clear her doubt about that.

"When she was discharged fourteen years ago," Maynard hurried on, "the doctors told me the melancholia could recur. I believe that is the problem. The shock of seeing me after all this time must have caused a relapse."

"Then you do believe her mad," Concordia said quietly.

He raised his hands in a gesture of helplessness. "I do not know. But no one here is in immediate danger. She and Sanbourne are already in New York City for the Thanksgiving holiday." His eyes were wide, pleading. "I need more time."

"You should at least tell Mr. Langdon what is going on."

He shook his head. "Langdon is a creature of duty. He would feel compelled to call the police."

She understood his point. A student prank was one thing, but the fire was something else entirely. Still, Maynard's plan had significant flaws. "Are you saying we should leave this case permanently unsolved, with people fearing that an arsonist is on the loose?" She doubted Lieutenant Capshaw would leave it be.

Maynard grimaced. "The talk and the worry will die down in time. It would be absurd for Capshaw to consider Miss Lovelace a suspect for long. And it is my intention to contribute funds to help rebuild the affected cottages."

She hesitated. "If Miss Lovelace is further harassed by the police about the fire, I will tell Capshaw what I know."

"Fair enough. But you'll stay silent if that is *not* the case?"

She didn't want to. However, he had saved her life six months ago. She owed him that. She sighed. "Very well. But only until we have returned from Thanksgiving break."

She closed the door behind her quietly, leaving him staring out the window.

She knocked on the doorjamb of Miss Banning's office. "Shall we go visit Charlotte?" It was an effort to keep her voice bright.

Miss Banning was scowling down at the book in her lap. Whether the reading material met with her disapproval or she was lost in thought, Concordia did not know. She rarely saw Margaret Banning smile, unless the lady had gotten the better of someone in an argument, or Charlotte was in the room.

"Miss Banning?"

"Hmm?" The lady roused herself. "Yes, yes, let us go," she said impatiently. With a grunt, she pushed herself away from the desk and reached for her cane.

President Langdon not only granted the use of his buggy, he offered to drive them to the hospital himself. With his help, Miss Banning was bundled comfortably beneath a carriage blanket, and they were on their way.

"How is she?" Miss Banning asked Concordia.

Concordia shrugged. "When I saw her several days ago, there had been little change. But she is young and strong. She may rally." She prayed that would be the case.

Langdon pulled up in front of Hartford Hospital and helped them alight. "I will be back for you in a little while."

They made their way through a maze of narrow corridors that smelled sharply of bleach and carbolic acid. Lady Dunwick's money and influence had secured her niece a private room and a full-time nurse. Charlotte lay upon a narrow iron bed, asleep. She appeared to be well cared for, her hair neatly brushed, the sheets crisp and smooth. Concordia frowned at the large metal tank and rubber hosing that took up much of the space on the left side of her bed. A nurse sat in a chair on the other side, quietly knitting.

Miss Banning staggered at the sight of the girl's pale, still form. Concordia steadied her and eased her into a chair.

The nurse jumped up and poured a glass of water. "Will you be all right, ma'am?"

Miss Banning waved her cane in Charlotte's direction. "She looks...terrible."

The nurse straightened. "Take heart. She is actually improving. She said a few words earlier today, though she's still disoriented about what happened."

"Do you think she will wake soon? We were hoping to talk with her," Concordia said.

The nurse shook her head. "The doctor gave her something to help her sleep. She was quite agitated. It was as if she had something important to say, but was frustrated that she could not remember it. Poor thing." She clucked her tongue. "However, you are welcome to sit with her for a while. Lady Dunwick just left." She pulled over another chair.

"What is all…that?" Concordia asked, gesturing to the equipment.

"It's an experimental oxygen therapy. They've brought in a lung specialist, Dr. Von Seymour. He only employs it for the most extreme cases, but it seems to be helping." She straightened the covers over her patient, checked her watch, and headed for the door. "You cannot stay long. In fifteen minutes, she is due for another treatment. I'll be just down the hall if you need me."

Miss Banning's color had returned. She gazed steadily at Charlotte, her bottle-glass spectacles getting misty. "She is the daughter I could never have," she whispered. "She must pull through." She didn't look in Concordia's direction. Perhaps she wasn't talking to her at all.

Concordia sat quietly, pretending not to notice the old lady drying her lenses and dabbing her nose with a kerchief.

All too soon, the nurse returned. "Could you wait outside, please?" She pulled out what looked like a mask of black rubber and began turning the valve on top of the tank.

Concordia glanced at her watch. "We should be going. Mr. Langdon will be returning for us soon."

Miss Banning did not resist, but passively allowed Concordia to help her up and make their way to the street.

Chapter 30

Yet we must remember that not all the black sheep are killed yet.
~Mrs. John Sherwood

Week 11, Instructor Calendar
December 1898

Students and staff returned to campus after the Thanksgiving break in brighter spirits, including Alison Smedley, who had made a full recovery.

Concordia had been wondering what to do about a room for the young lady. Would it be better for her to live completely away from her fellows, in one of the other cottages, or stay with her friends—and enemies—in the farmhouse? Both arrangements were cramped for sleeping and privacy, though the common areas of the farmhouse provided more space to relax. She decided to summon Miss Smedley to her office and allow her to decide her own fate.

"Oh, I want to be with you and all of my friends, Miss Wells," was her prompt answer.

"Really? You do realize that the farmhouse does not have the same... amenities as the cottages. And we have the occasional unwelcome visitor." Bats, mice, raccoons, straying chickens…. She grimaced.

Miss Smedley laughed. "The girls have been telling me of their adventures. It sounds rather fun."

Concordia hoped it would remain so, at least for the rest of the semester. The installation of steam heating was scheduled for the winter recess, although electricity would take longer.

"You would be living under the same roof as Miss Lovelace," she warned.

Miss Smedley waved a dismissive hand. "Maisie and I are fast friends now."

Concordia stared. If Alison Smedley had said she was planning to ride the trolley to the moon and be back in time for supper, she could not be more surprised. She realized her mouth had dropped open. She shut it.

Miss Smedley grinned. "No, really. She and I have been corresponding these past two weeks. She offered to copy notes from our European History and Rhetoric classes to send me, so that I would not fall behind. I wrote back, and soon we had a daily correspondence going. She is quite a nice girl."

Concordia shook her head in disbelief.

"I know, we have both admitted that we were being absolutely silly this whole while. Especially me." The young lady straightened. "And I want to go to Mr. Langdon, confess to the prank, and offer a sincere apology." Her tone grew subdued. "I hope I am not expelled."

Concordia pursed her lips. President Langdon, still ignorant of Maynard and Rachel Sanbourne, should not learn about any of this sordid business from a student. The story should come from Maynard himself. She had not seen him or the Sanbournes since her return. Had Maynard been successful in getting Mrs. Sanbourne to retire to a quiet facility for treatment? No, the scuttlebutt would be brisk if the lady was gone.

Alison Smedley looked at her expectantly.

"That is commendable, dear," Concordia said. "I would suggest that you speak with Mr. Maynard, and let him take it from there. It was his favorite horse that died, after all."

The young lady paled.

"I will stay with you the entire time," she added, her voice gentle. "I believe the dean will understand how you were influenced—sabotaged, actually—by Mrs. Sanbourne. That will be a mitigating factor, and I will emphasize that fact."

Miss Smedley's blue eyes widened. "You would do that...for me? You were hurt as well."

Concordia gave a wan smile. "Not seriously."

The girl plucked at her skirt. "I thought you would hate me," she whispered.

"Absolutely not," Concordia declared. "Now then, shall we get you settled in at the farmhouse? I will arrange the meeting with Mr. Maynard, and let you know. And remember—we must keep this confidential in the meantime."

Miss Smedley nodded. "I know. We don't want the college to suffer a scandal."

Concordia sighed. "Let us hope that can be avoided." She had the uneasy feeling that more trouble was to come.

Once Miss Smedley was happily unpacking and chatting with her fellows—Miss Lovelace now, astonishingly, counted among them—Concordia started back down Rook's Hill to search out Maynard in earnest. Really, this arrangement provided her quite a bit of exercise. She still missed her bicycle, of course. Perhaps in the spring she could afford a second-hand one. She paused to catch her breath and admire the sunset. Even in early December, the expanse of pinks and violets that splashed across the sky and reflected off the buildings was breathtaking.

She jumped when a tall, slim figure came out of the gloom behind her. It was Mrs. Sanbourne, awkwardly carrying canvas, easel, and a wooden box.

"Ah, Miss Wells, how propitious." She tapped on her box with a paint-stained finger. "Would you mind?"

Silently, Concordia took the box from her grip. *Be calm. She does not know what I have learned.*

Still, it was difficult to keep her steps steady. She was walking beside a woman who had murdered her own baby and had been shut in an asylum. A woman who had tried to kill Maynard or Charlotte, or both. Who may have set fire to Willow Cottage to finish the job and thrown one of the rags into Miss Lovelace's room to shift the blame.

Concordia gave the woman a covert glance in the growing dusk. What little light there was reflected in the blond wisps that had escaped the confines of her dark wool beret and brushed her gracefully arched brows. The effect was delicate, piquant, and utterly charming. Even with all Concordia knew or could conjecture, her eyes were telling her otherwise.

"I understand we are to have Christmas Revels this evening?" Mrs. Sanbourne asked.

Concordia nodded, not yet trusting herself to speak. Her heart pounded in her chest.

"I look forward to it. I hope to convince Peter to set aside his work for once and accompany me."

The silence stretched awkwardly between them.

Concordia cleared her dry throat. She must keep up the pretense. "Have you had a good painting day? I would think it too cold to work outdoors."

The woman waved a dismissive hand. "I was quite comfortable in the sun, but now—" she shivered "—yes, it grows cold quickly in the evening."

Concordia shifted the case from one hand to the other. "What a heavy box. How did you manage to carry all of this up the hill yourself?"

"Oh my dear," she said with a laugh. "Why do something oneself when one has a man to do it? Randolph carried my supplies today."

"Randolph?" Concordia repeated.

Mrs. Sanbourne gave her a shrewd glance. "Why pretend? He told me you know. We had quite the interesting chat."

Concordia's breath caught. "Oh?" They were approaching the quadrangle. Thank heaven their conversation was taking place outdoors. She would not have felt safe otherwise.

Mrs. Sanbourne gave a pout. "But for you to suspect me of such terrible deeds! I certainly hold no ill will toward Randolph. I must admit, it was quite disconcerting when I first saw him here. He promised to keep our secret." She hesitated. "But if I am to believe that, how did you find out?"

"He did not tell me," Concordia said. "I found the commitment certificate."

Mrs. Sanbourne stopped dead on the path. Her dark eyes narrowed. "So. You know that, too." Her expression cleared and she moved on. "How enterprising of you," she said evenly.

Concordia winced. She had said too much. As there was no going back, she may as well go forward. She took a breath for courage. "The folder it was in looked as if someone had hastily shoved it back in place. As I recall, you sketched caricatures in the side parlor on Halloween night. Was there a lull, giving you a chance to break into Maynard's desk?"

Mrs. Sanbourne shrugged. "The lock was laughable. Yes, I found the commitment paper. That did not worry me. Randolph knows better than to show anyone *that*. But I was never alone long enough to find what I really wanted."

Concordia shook her head in confusion. "What were you looking for, then?"

"The divorce decree. When I learned that Randolph was here at the school, I told Peter. I had never named my first husband when I told him my story. To give him credit, he took it calmly enough. However, he wants to be reassured that our marriage is not a bigamous one."

At least it was a relief that Maynard was no longer married to this troubled woman, particularly since he was courting Charlotte. "He will not give it to you?"

Mrs. Sanbourne's eyes narrowed. "Not unless I leave the school. Which I have no intention of doing. He will come around eventually."

The sight of Founder's Hall and the surrounding buildings gave Concordia the courage to speak her mind at last.

"But you *must* leave, Mrs. Sanbourne. It is not good for any of us if you stay. You say you had nothing to do with rigging the gun to go off, but Miss Smedley says otherwise. She has no reason to lie." Her stomach fluttered. Mrs. Sanbourne had been on the path near the farmhouse just now. "We will be keeping a close eye on the girl from now on. For her safety," she added sharply.

Mrs. Sanbourne gave a small smile that Concordia could barely see in the growing dusk.

Concordia continued. "When the gun prank failed, you started a fire in front of Charlotte's door—conveniently opposite Alison Smedley's room—and threw a soaked rag into Miss Lovelace's room to implicate her."

Mrs. Sanbourne laughed. "You have no proof, my dear."

"Perhaps not. You use solvents in your painting, is that not so? I imagine they are quite…flammable."

Mrs. Sanbourne stiffened. "Yes, one must be extraordinarily careful. There are dangers everywhere." She gestured toward the box Concordia carried. "This case, for example. It is a strange irony of nature that, to create certain colors of paint, the addition of poison is necessary. At this very moment, you are carrying Paris green—also used as a rat poison, arsenic that produces yellow pigment, lead that makes white, and cobalt that makes blue. So you see, if it suited me to do away with someone, I would not require such crude methods as propping guns and setting fires. A simple tea reception would provide ample opportunities."

Her smile made Concordia shiver.

"But it is absurd to even speak of this," she went on. "I have no quarrel with Miss Crandall."

"Perhaps not," Concordia said, "but Maynard is too much on his guard to be vulnerable to you. Charlotte was an easier target. It caused him great pain to see her come to harm. The perfect revenge. And it *is* revenge you are after, is it not? You have never forgiven him for shutting you up in an asylum for killing your child."

Mrs. Sanbourne flinched. "I did *not* kill my baby." Her voice had dropped to a strained whisper.

Concordia hesitated. She did not want to be cruel. The woman was obviously unbalanced. They were at the quadrangle now, just outside Founder's Hall. She set down the box with a *thump*. "I am sorry to say that I have grown fatigued. You will need to find someone else to help you." She turned and left, hurrying past the open windows of the ground floor library. It was not until much later—too late—that she would wonder who might be in there to overhear.

Chapter 31

Far more often does discouragement paralyze than does hope exalt.
~Mrs. John Sherwood

Week 11, Instructor Calendar
December 1898

A short while later, Concordia found Randolph Maynard at the stables. He was uncharacteristically clad in dusty black overalls and a gray plaid flannel shirt with the sleeves rolled back, hard at work giving Chestnut a rubdown by the light of a sputtering lantern. Above the glow, she could see the breath from the horse's nostrils in the chilly air.

With the memories of the place still fresh, she tentatively stepped inside. "Mr. Maynard."

He dropped the brush and whipped around. With a suppressed sigh but no other greeting, he retrieved the brush and went back to work.

The sharp odors of horse and hay made her nose twitch as she stepped closer. "Miss Smedley wishes to confess her role in the gun prank, and ask forgiveness. Have you told Mr. Langdon yet?"

Maynard shook his head, not looking at her. "I have not had the opportunity to first speak with Rachel."

"That is utter falsehood." She did not suppress the sharp edge to her tone. "I talked to her a few minutes ago. She told me you spoke."

She saw Maynard's back stiffen before he turned around.

She stepped closer. "It would seem that your conversation had little effect. We must tell Mr. Langdon, and the police."

Maynard set down the brush and wiped his hands, not immediately meeting her eye. "That would mean ruin. For me, and likely for the school."

"You do not know that." She pulled over a nearby stool and sat. "Tell me, when did you divorce her?"

Maynard upended an empty bucket and sat as well. "After the doctors pronounced her cured and discharged her from the facility." He glanced down at his hands. "I could never love her, not after what she had done. But I did not want to be cruel. She had obviously suffered a temporary madness."

Rachel Sanbourne's agonized whisper came back to her. *I did not kill my baby.* Concordia shivered and wrapped her shawl more closely.

"I gave her money for a new start," Maynard continued. "She went back to using her natal name, and moved to where no one knew her. Contact between us lapsed after that." He gave a bitter laugh. "It was quite a shock to see her here, and married to Sanbourne."

Concordia took a breath. "Are you sure she...killed the baby?" Her heart twisted in pity for the child. *Infanticide.* The law rarely prosecuted a woman for such a crime. The mother was assumed to be insane. But sometimes, inexplicably, babies died for no obvious reason. It was a sad fact of nature, even in today's modern world.

He ran a hand through his hair. "I did not witness it, if that's what you mean. She must have smothered him...in his sleep. I did not hear him cry. He had not been ill. When I found him, he was...blue." He rubbed his face.

"She admitted to this?"

"No. She denied it. Vehemently. But she was already suffering from melancholia, just after the child was born. Lethargy, uncontrollable fits of weeping. Then...this. The doctors confirmed what I suspected."

After watching her own sister die two years ago, Concordia was not as sanguine about medical infallibility. It was one thing to be melancholy and entirely another to commit murder. Had Rachel Sanbourne truly been guilty of killing her child? Or had she been innocent, then driven mad by the grief of loss and the bitterness of being unjustly consigned to an asylum for two years? After leaving behind such a painful past, what had it been like to see Maynard, without warning, after so long? Had her long-held fury been unleashed?

"You say the doctors willingly released her?"

"They were satisfied with her improvement after the treatment. As far as I know, she has not been a danger to anyone since. Until now, that is," he added bitterly. "First my horse, and now Charlotte."

"Do not lose hope for Charlotte."

Maynard stood. "I will try again to convince Rachel to leave."

Concordia shook her head. "I gave you more than enough time to try. It is time to tell Langdon, and call the police." She got up to go.

"No!" Maynard exclaimed, jumping up and grabbing her elbow. "You cannot."

Concordia brought down her booted heel, hard, upon Maynard's foot.

"Ow!" He jumped back.

"You will refrain from touching my person in the future," she said coldly.

Maynard cleared his throat. "I-I beg your pardon."

At the sight of Maynard's anguished expression, Concordia relented. "Since we already have the Christmas entertainments scheduled for this evening and I do not wish the spoil the event for the students, I am willing to wait until morning. You may try once more to convince her to leave, but I doubt you will succeed. No matter what happens, tomorrow morning I will bring Miss Smedley to speak with you and Mr. Langdon. It is not a forgone conclusion that Mr. Langdon will call the police once he learns the truth. My guess is he will."

Maynard expelled a resigned breath and headed out of the stable, limping slightly.

"Oh, and Mr. Maynard, one more thing," Concordia called.

He turned and waited.

"Do not let her serve you tea."

Chapter 32

Week 11, Instructor Calendar
December 1898

Concordia went through supper in a distracted haze as students chattered excitedly around her. They returned to the farmhouse afterward to change for the Christmas Revels and reception. The girls had been practicing their lines and rehearsing their dance steps every night for the past week.

In addition to the Revels, the young ladies were in a frenzy of preparing their homemade Christmas gifts. The fire had destroyed all of the projects they had started, so there was no time to be lost. The common room was a veritable explosion of colored tissue paper, ribbons, scissors, and bright yarns.

The girls dressed carefully in their most festive holiday gowns brought back from home, chatting and pinning up each other's hair.

Concordia took Alison Smedley aside before they left. "Be prepared to give your account of the gun prank to Mr. Maynard and Mr. Langdon tomorrow." At the girl's sigh, she added, "Try not to worry."

David came to the farmhouse to escort them. His admiring glance made her glad she had retrieved her old emerald satin from her mother's house. It was a number of years out of style, with slim sleeves and more of a bustle than was currently fashionable, but it served its purpose.

Concordia, Ruby, and David made sure to extinguish every candle and lantern before they left. It would be a long while before anyone took an open flame for granted.

The auditorium was crowded by the time they got there. The Revels were open to the public and nearly every Hartford dignitary and society matron was in attendance, in addition to the faculty and trustees. Concordia recognized many faces from Gown and Town Day, though this time all were dressed in their finest. Miss Pomeroy and Miss Jenkins talked animatedly with President Langdon in the front row. There was no sign of Miss Banning or Miss Cowles, though given the hour that was hardly surprising. Both elderly ladies tended to retire early. Maynard was absent, as were the Sanbournes. Had Maynard convinced Mrs. Sanbourne to leave? Was she packing even now?

Ruby leaned in and murmured, "Since Miss Crandall in't here to help backstage, I told the girls I'd help." She headed toward the stage curtains.

Concordia's chest tightened. Charlotte had been looking forward to the event, her first Revels as a teacher.

"Concordia!" a familiar voice called. Sophia waved from the fifth row. Eli and Mrs. Wells sat beside her.

"How fortunate that you saved us seats," Concordia said. She surveyed the room. The decorating committee had done a splendid job. The electric light fixtures were garlanded in evergreen and topped with bows of red velvet. Additional ribbon adorned the ends of aisles. Strands of merry electric lights were affixed to the apron of the stage, a cheery effect and welcome at this light-starved time of year. Concordia felt her mood lift a little. Perhaps she could put her worries aside for one evening.

Eli plucked at her sleeve. "I made you a Christmas present."

She pulled apart the wad of tissue paper and ribbon. Inside was a delicately carved figure of a wren. "Eli! It is beautiful." She held it up. "Look, David. Isn't it lovely?"

He nodded and gave Eli a wide smile. "You have impressive skill, my lad." He turned to Sophia. "Where is the lieutenant?"

Sophia grimaced. "Working, unfortunately. Miss Crandall sent for him."

Concordia started. "Charlotte? Her memory has returned?"

"I assume so, but I don't know anything else," Sophia said.

Mrs. Wells put a finger to her lips. "The performance is about to start."

Concordia sat back, her heart considerably lightened.

The Revels were a success, judging by the wide smiles of the red-faced, breathless young ladies.

"I am so glad things went smoothly," Concordia said, as David helped her out of her chair. "The young ladies deserve a bit of revelry."

Mrs. Wells gathered up her jacket. "It was delightful." She smiled at Eli, now nearly of a height with her. "What did you think, young man?"

Eli nodded enthusiastically. "I liked the round dance, though it was kinda funny for them to be all ladies. Couldn't some o' them dress up as fellas?"

"The students portraying 'ladies' wore bows, and the ones portraying 'gentlemen' wore vests," Concordia explained, as they made their way down the aisle. It was a fearful crush to get to the punch bowl and cookies set up in the foyer. "The college does not allow proper young ladies to wear trousers, even for play-acting purposes."

David Bradley gave her a quick glance, a smile twitching at his lips. Concordia wrinkled her nose at him. If he dared to mention the time she was caught out in public in the dean's trousers, she would smack him with her fan.

Wisely, he stayed silent.

"Can't they be *im*proper ladies, just for one night?" Eli asked.

Mrs. Wells smothered a laugh that turned into a cough.

"Mama thinks," Eli went on, "that ladies are proper by how they *act*, not what they wear. Isn't that right?" He looked over at Sophia.

Concordia smiled. How wonderful for the boy to be referring to his adoptive mother as *Mama*, since his own mother had died only ten months before. She knew it meant the world to Sophia.

"What do *you* think?" Sophia said to Eli.

The boy shrugged. "They should be allowed to wear what they please. Where's the harm?"

Sophia smiled and ruffled his hair affectionately. "That's my boy."

They reached the refreshments table at last, where the students were ladling the punch and passing out napkins.

"Miss Smedley, how nice to see you fully recovered," David said.

Alison Smedley blushed and handed him a cup. "I am glad to be back, Mr. Bradley." She leaned toward Concordia and dropped her voice. "I have been considering what I should say to Mr. Maynard about the gun prank."

David frowned and glanced at Concordia, who grimaced. In an abundance of discretion for Maynard—perhaps more than he deserved—she had not told David what she knew about Mrs. Sanbourne's guilt. He had a right to be angry, of course. She had been guilty of keeping discoveries to herself upon other occasions.

David drew her away to a quiet corner. "What did she mean?"

"I cannot talk about it here," Concordia said, dropping her voice. "Come back with us to the house."

Eventually goodnights were exchanged and Concordia, Ruby, David, and the farmhouse students climbed wearily up Rook's Hill. The young ladies went straight to bed.

As Ruby worked on her mending in a comfortable rocking chair nearby—it would not do for Concordia and David to be alone in the common room—Concordia told him the whole story. To do him credit, he listened without interruption, which was more than she could say for Ruby. Judging by the exclamations coming from the far corner, she heard nearly everything. Well, she would have learned of it soon enough.

"Mr. Maynard said he would try, one last time, to convince Mrs. Sanbourne to leave the school quietly, before the police become involved," Concordia finished. "If she agrees, the arson would never be solved in the public eye, but the dean believes it would die down in time. Assuming, of course, President Langdon agrees to that. I honestly do not know what he will do. But making Mrs. Sanbourne's guilt known could cause considerable damage to the school's reputation."

David leaned forward, watching her face intently. "Why did you not tell me sooner?"

She took a breath. "It was not my secret to reveal. I should not be telling you now, but if Maynard's plan fails, it will all come out tomorrow." She reached out and touched David's arm. Ruby bent closer to her needle. "The dean saved my life last May. I owed him this chance, don't you see?"

David was silent for several minutes. Concordia withdrew her hand and waited.

"Do you think Mrs. Sanbourne will agree to leave?" he asked.

Concordia quietly blew out a sigh. They were in this together. "I do not. We must brace ourselves for the worst."

Chapter 33

*Let us make sure of the aesthetic and intellectual, the sympathetic
and the genial, and sift out the pretentious and the impure.*

~Mrs. John Sherwood

Week 11, Instructor Calendar
December 1898

Concordia smothered a succession of yawns during
chapel and breakfast the next morning. Judging by the
shadows under Miss Smedley's eyes, she had not slept well,
either. After breakfast, Concordia motioned to the girl. "Shall
we speak with the dean now?" She hoped Maynard was at his
office. He had not been at chapel or breakfast.

Miss Lovelace got up from the table. "Alison told me what
is happening this morning. I want to come too."

Concordia took a breath to object, then noted Miss
Smedley's grateful expression. "All right, then. Come along."

Dean Maynard sat at his desk, staring out the window at the
steel-gray sky that promised the season's first snow.

Concordia rapped on the lintel. "May we come in?"

He gestured to the chairs set out for them. "I have already
asked Mr. Langdon to join us, to save you from repeating
yourself." He glanced in confusion at Miss Lovelace. "I did not
expect you. We are a chair short."

He started to get up, but Concordia waved him back. "No
need. Miss Lovelace can sit next to Miss Smedley. I will sit
here." She perched on the deep windowsill, leaving a chair free
for Mr. Langdon. Perhaps it was not entirely ladylike, but she
was too nervous to sit properly.

Maynard's pale cheeks and dull eyes bespoke a restless night.

"Did you speak with her?" Concordia asked him in a low voice.

He sighed. "She was nowhere to be found. Have you called Capshaw?"

"No. Mr. Langdon should make the call, once he is apprised of the situation."

Finally, President Langdon came in, brushing crumbs from his vest. His shirt was rumpled already, as if it were the end of the day instead of morning. "My, my, we have quite a group here! My apologies for keeping you waiting." His booming voice seemed out of character for the occasion, but of course he had no idea what he was about to hear.

"Miss Smedley has something to tell you both," Concordia said. She nodded to the young lady.

Sitting up straighter, Alison told them about rigging the gun to go off in the stables, planned for when Mr. Maynard and Miss Crandall were to ride the next morning, and hiding the pouch of Miss Lovelace's tools nearby. She then described the assistance she had received from Mrs. Sanbourne.

Langdon sat back in astonishment. "Mrs. Sanbourne? Why would she do such a thing?"

"Mr. Maynard will explain that in a moment," Concordia said. She was about to prompt Miss Smedley to continue, but Miss Lovelace interrupted.

"Mr. Langdon, do you remember when we were discussing the prank, and you asked me if I had confused a live bullet for a blank?"

He nodded.

"Well, Alison *did* put a blank in the gun. Someone went back before morning and substituted a live bullet."

"And you think that person is—?" Langdon prompted.

"Mrs. Sanbourne," Miss Smedley said miserably.

"You know this?"

Miss Smedley wrung her hands, her chest heaving as she forced out the words between sobs. "I...I asked her. She laughed…she didn't deny it. She was the only…the only one who knew…who knew the gun was there."

"But again, why?" Langdon protested.

Maynard leaned forward. "Could you take the young ladies to your office, Miss Wells? I wish to tell my story in private."

"Of course." Concordia led the girls out and closed the door behind her.

President Langdon came to her office half an hour later, grim-lipped. He gestured at the students. "Do you have classes soon? I may need you again."

Miss Lovelace shook her head, but Miss Smedley stood, shaking. "Am I…expelled?"

"No, no, not at all," Langdon said with a distracted air.

Miss Smedley sank back down in her chair. "What is my punishment to be?"

One glance at Langdon's expression and Concordia knew that disciplining the girl was the last thing on his mind. "Sir, shall I send the students back to the farmhouse to wait until needed?"

Langdon came out of his reverie. "Yes, yes, of course. If you will excuse me, I have to make a telephone call."

Concordia took a deep breath to slow her fluttering pulse. Lieutenant Capshaw would be no end of furious with her when he discovered what she had kept from him.

After Langdon left, Miss Smedley shifted uneasily in her chair. "He's angry, isn't he?"

"I believe it is directed toward someone else entirely," Concordia said. Maynard, most likely.

"That's a relief," Miss Lovelace said. She gestured excited to Miss Smedley. "Let's go back and work on our Christmas gifts, while the others are out."

Concordia watched them leave. At least two souls on this campus were happy.

She walked down the stairs to see how Mr. Maynard was faring. His office was empty.

Miss Banning stood in her office doorway. She waved her cane in the direction of Maynard's door. "He has gone off to search for that Sanbourne woman."

"How do you know?"

The old lady gestured behind her. Concordia peeked over her shoulder at the vent in the wall the offices shared.

"I hear everything through there." Miss Banning chuckled. "Not that I needed it today. Edward was fit to be tied, and quite voluble."

"I do not find this funny," Concordia retorted.

Miss Banning's expression through her owl-eyed spectacles was inscrutable. "'Pride goeth before destruction, and a haughty spirit before a fall.' Proverbs. Maynard needed taking down a peg or two. A sordid past is as good a remedy as any for arrogance."

Concordia blew out a breath. "Since you know so much, can you tell me if anyone is trying to locate Peter Sanbourne?"

Miss Banning nodded vigorously. "Maynard said he was going to Sanbourne's laboratory in case he knew where to find his wife."

"He is breaking the news to Sanbourne now? With no one to accompany him?" Concordia asked in a panic. The two were bound to come to blows.

"That is what I assume. I would not want to be in his shoes, I can tell you—" Miss Banning broke off as Concordia ran out of the office.

She did not bother to retrieve her coat, but rushed down the stairs and out the door, puffs of breath beating against the cold air as she ran past bemused students. As she approached the engineering laboratory, she winced at the sound of breaking glass.

"Stop! Stop it!" She burst through the doors. Sanbourne had Maynard pinned to the floor, hands at his throat.

With unexpected force, she grabbed Sanbourne's collar and pulled him off. The wide-eyed expression on his face suggested that such unladylike behavior had given her the advantage of surprise.

Maynard got to his feet, brushing off his jacket and rubbing his jaw, where a bruise had begun to darken it.

Concordia surveyed the laboratory. What a mess. Broken glass jars littered the floor, along with papers, crumpled sketches, pencils, filing tools and wrenches.

"Where is your wife?" Concordia asked, between breaths. "The police will be here soon."

Sanbourne scowled. "I do not know. I have not seen her since last night."

"What!" Concordia exclaimed.

He pointed to a curtained alcove in the back room. "I was working late, and decided to stay the night. There is a bed and a sink. I keep a spare change of clothes."

"You have no idea where she would be?" Concordia asked.

Sanbourne ignored her, bending down to collect the tools from the floor and returning them to the bench. "It is absolutely absurd to accuse her of wrongdoing. I do not care what has happened in her past." He glared at Maynard, speaking through gritted teeth. "And I do not believe for one moment that she is guilty of what you accuse her, then or now. She paid a dear price for your sordid conclusions back then. I will not have her pay a second time."

Once again, Concordia wondered if Rachel Sanbourne really had killed her child all those years ago. How different their lives would be at this moment if Maynard had assumed her innocent!

However, they did not have that luxury.

"Innocent or guilty, we must find her. Mr. Langdon is calling the police now," Concordia said.

Peter Sanbourne gave a reluctant nod and shrugged on his jacket. "I'll go home. She may still be there."

Concordia turned to Maynard. "We should search the campus, in case she's already here."

Chapter 34

One teaspoonful for each person and one for the pot.
~Mrs. John Sherwood

Week 11, Instructor Calendar
December 1898

"We will separate," Maynard said, after they left the laboratory. "I will start with her studio and Founder's Hall, and you can search the dining hall and infirmary."

"Oh no, I am not leaving you alone again," Concordia said. "Should you be the one to find Mrs. Sanbourne, it will not be pleasant for either of you. Bursar Kimble would have plenty to say about the cost of replacing more broken equipment and furniture."

The dean gave a wan smile. It was as close to an expression of gratitude as she was going to get. "Very well."

"I do agree that her studio should be the first place we go."

They followed the path at a brisk pace. "You say you couldn't find Mrs. Sanbourne last night?" Concordia asked.

Maynard shook his head. "Just after you left, I changed my clothing and went in search of her. I even went to the Sanbourne residence when I failed to find her here. The maid told me she was out."

"Mrs. Sanbourne had said she and her husband would be attending the Revels. I saw neither of them there," Concordia said. "I noticed you weren't in attendance, either."

Maynard shrugged. "I was not in a celebratory mood." He hesitated. "You may as well know, I have submitted my resignation. It is best for the college."

Concordia stopped. "I am sorry to hear that." To her surprise, she actually meant it. Maynard, for all of his curmudgeonly ways, cared deeply for the school and kept things running smoothly. "Are you *sure* that is what's best for the college? It will create more disruption. And for what? You have done nothing wrong. It is not uncommon for a person to have suffered past misfortune."

His lip curled. "That is not how the newspapers will portray it. I want to spare the school further scandal."

"You must realize your departure will not accomplish that. If anything, it will fuel speculation, and appear to be an admission of guilt."

Maynard's hands clenched at his sides. "I *am* guilty. Rachel did these things because of me."

Concordia stood on tiptoe to meet his eye, giving him her sternest lady professor glare. "Did *you* rig the gun? Did *you* set the fire? No. You cannot be responsible for everything and everyone. That woman had free will, and *she* made those choices, horrible as they were. You know that. Your real reason is a cowardly one."

Maynard stared at her, mouth open. Concordia plowed on. "You cannot face us, now that your personal life is about to become public knowledge. So you are running away."

His shoulders slumped. "Think what you wish, Miss Wells." He turned down the path to the studio door, Concordia hurrying to keep up.

The building was unoccupied. Concordia touched the canvases and cleaning rags. All dry. The paint tubes and brushes were neatly arranged on their shelves. "I don't believe she has been here yet today."

With barely a nod, Maynard headed back outside.

They searched the library, the dining hall, even the side garden of Sycamore House, now brown and withered. No sign of her.

Concordia shivered in her skirt and shirtwaist, wishing she had stopped for her coat. "I doubt it is useful to continue the search out of doors. It is too c-c-cold for her to be outside painting landscapes, and her supplies are still in the shed."

"Agreed. Where to next?" Maynard shrugged off his jacket and put it around her shoulders.

Concordia huddled gratefully into its warmth. "The teachers' lounge, perhaps?" Besides, she could do with a cup of tea. She checked her watch. "The police should be here soon."

When they reached the lounge, the door was locked. Concordia let out an exasperated sigh. "I'm surprised the custodian hasn't unlocked it by now."

"He's away this week. Just a moment." Maynard pulled a ring of keys from his pocket, unlocked the door, and pushed the wall switch. Electric light flooded the dim room.

Only just visible behind a skirted table on the far side of the room, a rocking chair and a tray were overturned on the floor. Concordia's heart beat faster. She took a few steps. "Mrs. Sanbourne?"

Maynard brushed past her and crossed the room in rapid strides. "What has happ—?" He froze, staring at the floor. Concordia impatiently stepped around him, then sucked in a sharp breath at the sight of slender, paint-stained fingers, curled around a teacup.

Rachel Sanbourne.

Her face was contorted in a painful grimace, her stare unblinking. Concordia shuddered.

Maynard roughly grabbed her by the shoulders, turning her away. "Get Langdon."

She stumbled on rubbery legs and rushed down the stairs.

When she reached Langdon's office, she was greeted by a welcome sight: Lieutenant Capshaw and one of his men—a sergeant, she seemed to remember. It took every ounce of self-control she had not to collapse into Capshaw's arms and weep from the shock of what she had just seen. She clutched the door handle, trembling.

Capshaw eased her into a chair. "Water, quick."

Langdon reached for the pitcher and tumbler beside his desk.

"I was just about to leave the station to come here when President Langdon called," Capshaw said, handing her the glass. "Easy, now." He helped steady her shaking hands so she could sip it.

When she had caught her breath, Capshaw asked, "Where is Mrs. Sanbourne?"

She swallowed. "The teacher's lounge, the floor above this."

Capshaw nodded to the sergeant, who was already moving toward the door. "Better get up there, Maloney."

"She's...she's dead," Concordia said.

Capshaw's lips thinned in a grim line. "I gathered that."

"Mr. Maynard's with her."

He shook his head. "You left him alone at the scene? He's our prime suspect."

Concordia blinked. "Prime suspect? I don't understand. And why were you coming here *before* Mr. Langdon called?"

"I spoke with Miss Crandall last night. It took a while to collect her statement. She needed to rest frequently. She believes Mrs. Sanbourne was responsible for the fire and the gun prank."

"How does Charlotte know about Rachel Sanbourne?" Concordia bit her lip. Had Charlotte convinced Maynard to tell her the truth? But when would that have been? Charlotte had not been talking coherently since the fire.

Capshaw shook his head. "Later. First, tell me what you know."

After Capshaw had taken down the basics of her account, he tucked his notepad back in his tunic and got up to leave. "Go back to the farmhouse and wait. I will call upon you when I am finished here, but it may be a while." He looked her up and down. "May I suggest that you get some rest in the meantime?"

"What about my afternoon classes?" Concordia protested.

President Langdon shook his head. "I am canceling classes for the rest of the week until we get this sorted out. Now, do as the lieutenant says. Go and rest."

News of Mrs. Sanbourne's death had spread quickly, though Concordia was too exhausted to contemplate how that had come to be. By the time she returned to the farmhouse, Ruby and the girls had already heard. Ruby shooed the hovering students out of the parlor. "Give the poor lady some air! Off with you, now. I'm sure you all have chores, and if you don't, there's plenty that needs doing around here."

Concordia gave Ruby a tired smile as the girls shuffled off. "Thank you. I don't feel like talking about it right now." Not that there was much to say. She'd only had a brief glance at the dead woman, which was more than sufficient. She shuddered.

Ruby tucked the afghan more snugly around her and turned to stoke the fire. "'Course you don't, miss. But when you do, you'll let me know?" Her tone sounded hopeful.

Concordia nodded. "Is Miss Smedley here? Capshaw will want to speak with her."

"She's in Miss Lovelace's bedroom, working on their gifts for the other girls." Ruby shook her head. "Thick as thieves, those two. Who would have believed it?"

Concordia sighed and closed her eyes.

The delectable aromas of vegetable soup and toast woke her. She lifted her head as Ruby set down a tray. "The police are here, talking wi' Miss Smedley right now. I thought you might want a bit o' something before they come to see you."

"Thank you. This is exactly what I need," Concordia said, reaching for the napkin.

"I hope you have an extra bowl, Ruby. It smells divine," a male voice said.

David Bradley stood in the doorway, reassuringly strong and solid and comforting. Without a care for Ruby's sensibilities—who was backing out of the room with alacrity—he gathered Concordia in his arms and let her cry it out.

Fortified by David's presence and Ruby's soup, Concordia was feeling more like herself by the time Capshaw knocked on the parlor door, his hat under his arm.

"Come in, lieutenant," David said, pulling up a chair.

"Would you care for some tea?" Concordia asked, starting to get up.

Capshaw motioned her back. "Mrs. Hitchcock has already given me an ample supply, thank you all the same." He shook his head. "I wish you had told me about Mrs. Sanbourne, miss."

Concordia stared at her hands. "I wanted to."

"So Mr. Maynard says." Capshaw cocked his head. "Though he did not mention how you learned of it."

She felt the hot flush rise to her cheeks. "Um, well, I went through his desk."

Capshaw shook his head. "Your association with Miss Hamilton has rubbed off on you."

David chuckled. "Concordia was searching desks before she took up with a lady Pinkerton, lieutenant."

Concordia's blush deepened, but she did not deny it, as she had searched Miss Hamilton's own desk, years ago.

"How did Mrs. Sanbourne...die?" she asked quietly, in a change of subject. "Mr. Maynard pushed me out of the room very quickly." She hardly dared hope for some natural occurrence, such as a fatal fit or something of the sort. She suspected they would not be so lucky.

"Our theory is she drank poison," Capshaw said, pulling out his well-worn notepad. "The doc will analyze the remnants of the teacup still gripped in her hand as well as the—" he gave a delicate cough "—body, to rule out a natural cause."

"Is it possible that Mrs. Sanbourne committed suicide?" David asked.

Capshaw shrugged. "Not likely. I still think Maynard is our man. Look at the dark history they shared. He was desperate to keep it secret. Who else had such a powerful motive?"

Concordia frowned. She could not imagine Maynard and his former wife sitting down to a cozy tea together. It was ironic that she had warned Maynard against that very thing, in fear that

Mrs. Sanbourne would be the poisoner, not the other way around.

That reminded her of something. "Poison actually came up in my last conversation with Mrs. Sanbourne." She recounted the woman's comments about the common poisons in artists' paints.

Capshaw's eyes brightened in interest, and he scribbled a note. "That could be helpful. If she died by her own hand, a letter has yet to be discovered. Maloney is going through the Sanbourne house now."

"But if Mrs. Sanbourne took her own life," David said, "why would she do so in the teachers' lounge of the school?"

"Perhaps as revenge upon the dean," Concordia said. "She knew he wanted to avoid scandal here at the college."

Capshaw shook his head. "I'm afraid there is no preventing that now."

She leaned forward. "That's why Maynard would *not* have killed Mrs. Sanbourne in the teacher's lounge. It would have brought on the very scandal he has been trying to avert."

Capshaw looked at her pityingly. "Men do not always act prudently."

She did not have an answer to that.

"Now then," Capshaw flipped to a fresh page, "what time yesterday was your conversation with Mrs. Sanbourne?"

"About four o'clock. I was heading to the Hall."

"Did anyone see her after that?" David asked.

"A group of students spoke with her just before supper at six o'clock, but we haven't found anyone who saw her after that." He shook his head in disgust. "It's like the Guryev case all over again. How do people disappear from a crowded campus and no one sees them?"

"Sometimes people do not want to be seen, which was the case with Mr. Guryev," Concordia said. "But as far as last night, we were all busy getting ready for the Christmas Revels. I can tell you, however, that neither of the Sanbournes attended the event." She did not add that Maynard was not there, either. No point in making things worse for the man.

"Speaking of Guryev, how goes the murder investigation?" David asked. "Have you found the other debt collector—what's his name again?"

"Ike Coutts." Capshaw ran a hand through his bright-red hair. "Yes. And his movements are accounted for."

"Are you sure?" Concordia asked.

Capshaw flushed a deep red. "It took me so long to find him because he had been arrested in New Haven for nearly killing another man. He was in jail at the time of the murders and has been there ever since."

"Oh." That was certainly an unbreakable alibi. "And you said it was impossible for the first debt collector—"

"—Barney Johns," Capshaw interjected.

"Mr. Johns could not have gotten on campus unobserved?"

Capshaw shook his head. "It's obvious by looking at him, he has no business at a women's college. We are back to Guryev killing Oster and taking his own life. The problem is, the blueprints were never found."

"You are sure that Guryev's mother didn't return to Russia with them?" Concordia asked.

"We searched her belongings and the steamer thoroughly— her compartment, and anywhere else she had access—before allowing her to depart."

"Maybe Guryev threw them into the river, before jumping in himself," David said.

"Or ruffians assaulted him and tossed him in there," Concordia chimed in, "and the blueprint was lost in the process."

"Perhaps. We may never know." Capshaw stood and retrieved his cap. "Unless there is a break in the case, my focus now must be solving Mrs. Sanbourne's death."

Concordia nodded. She did not envy him the task.

Chapter 35

*This world should be known and served and treated with as much respect
and sincerity as that other world, which is to be our reward.*

~Mrs. John Sherwood

Weeks 12 and 13, Instructor Calendar
December 1898

O ver the final two weeks of the semester, students and staff struggled to maintain the routine of classes and examinations. But with worried mommas scooping up their daughters to withdraw them early, and reporters and police trouping through administrators' offices, normality had flown out the window. Mr. Sanbourne, naturally, canceled his classes for the rest of the semester. After a very private funeral service—to which no one from the school was welcome—Sanbourne spent nearly all of his time in his laboratory. He still had project deadlines to meet. George Lovelace stayed on as his assistant.

The only happy bit of news during this time was that Charlotte had left the hospital and was recovering at her aunt's house. Concordia paid a visit as soon as the young lady was well enough to receive callers.

Concordia waited in the Dunwicks' comfortably appointed parlor, watching the play of firelight reflected in the well-polished cherry wood tables and brass candlestick holders. She rubbed her hands in front of the fire. It had been a chilled streetcar ride.

Lady Dunwick bustled in soon after. "Ah, Miss Wells, so good of you to visit, dear. Charlotte will be down shortly. Would you care for some tea?"

"That would be most welcome, thank you."

Lady Dunwick tugged at the bell pull, then glanced out the window at the dull gray sky. "I fear we will have snow again this evening."

Concordia had little interest in conversing about the weather. "How is Charlotte? We've been so worried."

"Though she tires easily, she is nearly well. I fear I cannot say the same for her spirit." Lady Dunwick lowered herself into a wingback chair. "She has been reading the newspapers, you see."

"About the death of Mrs. Sanbourne?"

"Yes, that—and the speculation that Randolph Maynard will be arrested at any moment. She is quite fond of the gentleman, but I...." Her voice trailed off.

Concordia knew what she did not say. The newspapers had been full of the story of Mrs. Sanbourne's past with Maynard. Lady Dunwick could hardly approve a match between her niece and a divorced man who was once married to a lunatic.

"I imagine the shock of learning about Mrs. Sanbourne's past was difficult for Charlotte."

"Oh, she already knew about that," Lady Dunwick said.

Concordia's cup clattered in the saucer. "I...I beg your pardon? Did Mr. Maynard tell her?"

"No, more's the pity. That would have raised him a bit in my estimation. Instead he lied to her, saying he had jilted Mrs. Sanbourne long ago and the woman must be holding a grudge. When Charlotte last stayed with us, she was making inquiries about the woman. Without my knowledge." Her jaw clenched. "Sir Anthony used his court connections to help her, though he did not tell me of it until it all came out in the papers." Lady Dunwick shook her head. "I would never have permitted Mr. Maynard to visit her in the hospital had I known."

"What did Charlotte do when she learned the truth? Did she confront Mr. Maynard or Mrs. Sanbourne?" Concordia asked.

"Sir Anthony said she planned to, but…." Lady Dunwick's voice faltered.

Concordia grimaced. "Yes, I see. Charlotte returned quite late that evening. And then we had the fire. She had no opportunity."

"Actually, I did speak to her." Charlotte stood in the parlor doorway, pale-faced and swaying slightly as she clutched the doorframe.

Concordia hurried over to put an arm around her shoulders and lead her to the settee. "You spoke to her? When?"

"The night I returned, quite late. I went to Randolph's office to talk to him first about what I learned. He wasn't there, but I discovered Mrs. Sanbourne, crouched at his door. She was trying to break into his office."

"Break into his office? Why?" Lady Dunwick asked.

"She refused to say." Charlotte sat back against the cushions. Exhaustion shadowed her eyes.

"She was probably searching for the divorce decree," Concordia said. "Maynard would not give her the paper unless she promised to leave the college."

Charlotte sighed. "I knew she was after something. At the Halloween Ball, Randolph found his desk had been broken into. He knew she was responsible."

Ah, so that was why Maynard's desk had opened easily when she'd tried it. Mrs. Sanbourne had broken the lock. "What happened when you caught Mrs. Sanbourne in front of Maynard's office?"

"I am sorry to say I lost my composure." Charlotte looked down at her hands, self-consciously unclenching them and flexing her fingers. "I told her I knew everything. About her marriage to Randolph, about what she had done to her baby, about the asylum. It just came spilling out."

Lady Dunwick shifted in her seat. "Oh dear."

Charlotte sniffed and wiped at her damp cheeks. "I had not planned to do that. I was only going to tell Randolph what I had learned, talk with him about what we should do. I feared she would try to hurt him again."

Lady Dunwick leaned forward and patted her hand. "You were under tremendous strain."

Charlotte grimaced. "But don't you see? My outburst prompted her to the desperate, reckless act of setting fire to the cottage. She felt she had nothing to lose."

"So this is what you told Capshaw, just before we found Mrs. Sanbourne in the teachers' lounge?" Concordia asked.

"My mind had finally begun to clear. It all came rushing back."

Concordia pursed her lips, struck by a sudden thought. "Was anyone else working in The Hall that night?"

"I noticed Miss Kimble's office light was on." Charlotte sucked in a breath. "Do you suppose she overheard?"

Concordia waved a dismissive hand. "It doesn't matter now." Thank goodness Miss Kimble's blackmail scheme had never come to fruition. They had enough of a mess on their hands.

Lady Dunwick passed Charlotte a handkerchief. "You cannot blame yourself, my dear. Rachel Sanbourne was obviously unstable to begin with. Anything could have provoked her."

They were interrupted by a polite cough from the parlor maid. "Ma'am? There's a Lieutenant Cap…Capshin?—at the door."

Charlotte and Concordia exchanged a glance.

Lady Dunwick calmly plucked a speck of lint from her sleeve and smoothed her skirt over her knees. "Show him in."

Capshaw entered soon after, cap clutched respectfully, red hair tousled from raking a hand over it. His brows settled into their usual gloomy furrow as he bowed. "I fear I have bad news. Randolph Maynard has been arrested."

Chapter 36

There are instincts in the humblest understanding which will tell us where to draw the line.

~Mrs. John Sherwood

Week 13, Instructor Calendar
December 1898

Charlotte clasped her hands so hard the knuckles were white. "Arrested?" she choked.

"Sit down, lieutenant," Lady Dunwick said, motioning to a chair.

Capshaw awkwardly folded his lanky legs as he perched on an antique rocker, which creaked in protest. "I wanted to tell you myself, Miss Crandall, before you read it in the newspapers."

Dread pooled in Concordia's stomach. How would the school recover from such a disgrace? "There was no way to have avoided this?"

"We had no choice. He is the only one with a motive."

"And what exactly do you judge the motive to be, Lieutenant?" Lady Dunwick asked.

"Revenge. Protection. Either will suffice. Rachel Sanbourne had twice tried to kill Miss Crandall, and nearly succeeded the second time. We have found combustible paint thinner in her studio, and a gown hidden away behind her canvases. The hem smells strongly of the stuff. Between that and Miss Crandall's account of confronting the lady mere hours before the fire, I have no doubt Mrs. Sanbourne was responsible."

Concordia was about to point out that Randolph Maynard would not have known of such evidence, until she remembered that she had convinced him of the woman's guilt. "You have ruled out suicide?" she asked instead.

Capshaw nodded. "No note in the Sanbourne home, or her studio, or anywhere near or upon her person. Our doc checked with a colleague of his, a chemist at Yale. He says there was definitely poison in both the tea and the victim's stomach."

Charlotte leaned forward. "Do you know what kind of poison?"

"Atropine."

Concordia frowned. "Atropine? What is that?"

Capshaw pulled out his notepad. "It is used to treat a slow heart rate…*bradycardia*, the doc called it. The stuff's also used for bronchial congestion. Doc says it can be fatal in large enough doses, causing the heart to go into—" he glanced down at his notes "—fibrillation. Without medical help, death soon follows."

"And Mrs. Sanbourne was not prescribed this…atropine?" Concordia asked.

"No."

"What about Mr. Maynard?"

Capshaw shifted in his chair, generating more creaks. "No, he doesn't take it, either. But Langdon does. The living quarters for the dean and president are on the same floor in Sycamore House. Langdon admits that he does not customarily lock his door, and regrettably has no idea if the amount of liquid in his bottle—there was very little left—is correct. He was prescribed the medicine for an episode of breathing trouble last winter, and he has not needed to take it in some time. If the bottle was full enough to begin with, Maynard could have easily extracted a lethal amount without Langdon's knowledge."

"So why isn't Mr. Langdon under suspicion?" Charlotte asked.

Capshaw shook his head. "He has no motive. He only learned the truth about Mrs. Sanbourne after she was dead."

Concordia grimaced. That was true enough. "Does anyone else on campus take this medicine?"

"I was still checking on that when I was ordered to arrest Maynard."

"Do you intend to continue the inquiry?" Charlotte asked in a quavering voice.

Capshaw rose. "I will have a few details to pursue, but I doubt if it will prove Maynard innocent. I am sorry. If you'll excuse me, Lady Dunwick, I will see myself out."

After he left, Charlotte turned to Concordia. "We must do something. We cannot allow Randolph to be hanged for a crime he did not commit."

Concordia did not answer right away. Her heart ached for Charlotte, watching the man she loved pilloried by the press as he sat helpless in jail. But what could be done?

She straightened. Last spring, Maynard had done the impossible for her. He had saved her life. It did not matter how daunting the task of clearing him might be. "How do you suggest we start?"

Charlotte's shoulders sagged in relief. "We should learn who else is on this medication. We must act quickly, before the newspapers broadcast the details and the murderer disposes of it."

"It would be reckless of someone to dispose of needed medicine," Lady Dunwick objected.

Charlotte waved a dismissive hand. "Hide it, then."

Lady Dunwick raised a skeptical brow. "It seems unwise in the first place, to use one's own medicine to commit murder."

Concordia remembered Capshaw's words: *Men do not always act prudently.* "It could have been a last-minute decision, and the medicine was ready to hand."

"I suppose so," Lady Dunwick said.

"We cannot conduct a search of everyone's rooms on campus looking for it," Concordia said. "So where do we begin? We have no idea of motive. Who besides Mr. Maynard would have wanted to kill Mrs. Sanbourne?"

"I read once, in a penny-dreadful crime story," Lady Dunwick said, "that the husband is the most likely person to do away with the wife."

Charlotte gaped in astonishment. "Aunt Susan, *you* read penny-dreadfuls? Do not let Mamma hear you say that."

Lady Dunwick cleared her throat. "It was only the once. The train had been terribly delayed, and there was a rack of them at the station. I had not a scrap of anything to read." The corners of her lips twitched. "It was actually quite engaging."

"I don't believe questioning a grief-stricken husband will get us anywhere," Concordia said. "No doubt Capshaw has already done so."

"But we could search his belongings for the medicine," Charlotte said.

Concordia shook her head. "Given the man's trim form and boundless energy, I very much doubt he needs medication for a slow heart."

"We won't know until we look."

"How would we get into his house?" Concordia asked. "Are we to be sneak thieves now?"

Lady Dunwick grimaced. No doubt the lady wished she were anywhere else at the moment.

"We'll worry about his house later, and concentrate our efforts on his workshop," Charlotte said. "He essentially lives on campus since his wife died. If he needs heart drops every day, the bottle is probably in a jacket pocket."

Concordia remembered the partitioned alcove beyond the laboratory, where Sanbourne said he often slept. Yes, it would be feasible to conduct a search there.

Mercy, more snooping. "Very well, on two conditions," Concordia said.

Charlotte narrowed her eyes. "Which are?"

"One, we ask Mr. Bradley to accompany us in case of trouble. He can be counted upon for his discretion." He would not be thrilled by the request, she was sure.

Charlotte nodded. "And the other?"

"If we find something, we take it straight to Capshaw, and *not* confront Sanbourne." If she had learned any lessons from her impromptu experiences as a *lady sleuth*, it was that one.

Charlotte clasped her hands together in excitement. "Agreed."

Chapter 37

Education is always a power.
~Mrs. John Sherwood

Concordia was grateful for Lady Dunwick's offer of the carriage to take her and Charlotte back to campus.

Once Charlotte had packed an overnight bag, they were on their way. The long-anticipated snow had started to fall, quickly coating the freezing streets and sidewalks. They huddled under the lap rug.

Progress was agonizingly slow along the slick streets, amid the crush of Christmas shopping traffic in the downtown district. The vehicle continually stopped for pedestrians darting across, expressmen unloading deliveries, and passenger-laden streetcars. Storefronts sported jaunty red bows and fresh boughs of greenery across their doorways, now dusted in sparkling snow. Tinkling shop bells, the call of street vendors, and the strains of an accordion-player grinding out Christmas carols rung in the air. If Concordia had been in a more congenial mood, she would have welcomed the sights and sounds of the season. As it was, she felt as if she were passing through another world.

She opened her jacket to peek at her watch. Nearly three. Once they were clear of downtown, they would make better time, but David still had another half an hour of class, anyway.

"I have an idea," she said to Charlotte. "We should talk to Miss Jenkins first. She may know who on campus besides Mr.

Langdon takes atropine. I would imagine it is not a long list. We can also inquire as to whether she keeps such medicine on hand."

Charlotte nodded mutely, staring down at her gloved hands.

"You love him very much, do you not?"

Charlotte blushed. "I could not have imagined it when I first met him."

Concordia chuckled. "Your imagination is wilder than mine. He does not give a favorable first—or second—impression."

The carriage deposited them in front of the farmhouse, and Charlotte had her first view of the place. She gave an approving nod. "I remember this as a ramshackle old homestead. The grounds still need tending, but you've done wonders with the house."

Concordia looked around. The fresh coating of snow softened the landscape and made it quite pretty. The grounds would come in time. "We could never have made the necessary repairs without the town's help. You heard about Gown and Town Day?"

"I missed quite a lot in the hospital."

Concordia squeezed her hand. "Let's get your bag inside and show you where you'll be sleeping. The accommodations are a bit tight, I have to warn you."

Once Charlotte had deposited her valise upon a folding cot in Miss Smedley's room, they put on warm boots and headed for the infirmary. It was still snowing, but very finely now.

"This is a healthy walk," Charlotte puffed.

"I hope it is not over-taxing."

"I'm fine."

Fortunately, Miss Jenkins was in her office writing reports. Concordia explained their errand.

Hannah Jenkins nodded. "I am, of course, acquainted with the basic medical condition of each staff member. But you must know that information is confidential." She sat back and tucked her pencil through the topknot of her thinning white hair.

"Under normal circumstances, we would not presume to ask you to breach patient confidentiality," Concordia said. "But

Mr. Maynard's future is at stake. The police will require you to reveal the same information to them, anyway. We already know that Mr. Langdon takes this medicine. Capshaw told us."

The infirmarian raised a skeptical brow. "If Maynard has been arrested, why would the police make further inquiries?"

Charlotte spoke up. "Lieutenant Capshaw promised me he would pursue all leads, in case Mr. Maynard is innocent. He did not want to arrest him yet. He was instructed by his superior to do so."

Miss Jenkins shook her head. "I will wait for the police to make the request. I cannot help you."

Concordia stayed Charlotte's protest, putting a hand to her arm. "Tell us one thing, at least. Do you have this drug in the infirmary?"

"I do not. The infirmary's primary function is to serve the medical needs of the students. No one of that age suffers from bradycardia."

Concordia stood, as did Charlotte. "Thank you."

Miss Jenkins nodded, her deeply lined face creased in regret. "I wish I could have helped you."

"That got us nowhere," Charlotte said miserably, as they left the building.

"At least we know it could not have been taken from the infirmary," Concordia said. "That's something." She stopped.

"What is it?" Charlotte asked.

"Wait here for me. I have one more question for Miss Jenkins." Concordia ran back inside.

"Yes, Concordia?" Miss Jenkins called out impatiently.

"I have a general question that could help us know where to look, without violating patient confidentiality."

Miss Jenkins gave a sigh. "I'm listening."

"What characteristics would a person have if he or she needed this...atropine? I assume it would be an older person, but what else?"

Miss Jenkins studied her for a long moment before answering. "You certainly are persistent. All right, then. One use is for chronic bronchial congestion. It dries up the secretions. Mr. Langdon took it when he suffered from the lingering effects of pneumonia last year. Someone with a breathing problem may take it. Its primary use, however, is treating bradycardia. Many factors can create that condition: a heart weakened by old age, a heart blockage, rheumatic fever, or a sedentary lifestyle."

Concordia bit back her disappointment. By that description, every sedentary academic with health problems could be a candidate. "Is it only men who have this condition?"

Miss Jenkins shook her head. "It is more common in men, but there are women who have it, too. Doctors think that we inherit a predisposition for it. The risk increases with age."

Concordia was silent, thinking. It was looking more and more unlikely that Sanbourne had such a condition.

"Does that help?" Miss Jenkins asked.

"I don't know," Concordia said.

Charlotte anxiously waited outside.

Concordia checked her watch. "Mr. Bradley should be in the Chemistry laboratory."

Chapter 38

Love without trust is without respect, and if a lover has not respected his fiancée, he will never respect his wife.

~Mrs. John Sherwood

Week 13, Instructor Calendar
December 1898

"I'm sorry, Miss Wells, but Mr. Bradley has already gone," a student said. She was drying the last of the glass beakers beside the sink. "With so few of us left attending class, we finished up early. I volunteered to clean up."

"How kind of you," Concordia said. "Do you know where he has gone?"

The girl shrugged and gestured to the newspaper flung on his desk. "He was reading that—the boy just brought in the mail—and suddenly said he had to leave."

Concordia picked up the paper. Her stomach clenched.

Dean of Women's College Arrested for Sanbourne Murder

Wordlessly, she passed it over.

"We are too late," Charlotte whispered.

Concordia blew out a breath. "They must have printed a special edition." Was this the death knell for the college? "David must be looking for me in order to break the news. We'll try the farmhouse."

They huffed back up the snow-covered cart tracks of Rook's Hill.

They were just in time. David was stepping off the porch, pulling up the collar of his dark-gray woolen overcoat.

Concordia felt the knots in her stomach loosen at the sight of him.

A short *yip* brought her attention to the dog jumping beside him, trying to catch snowflakes.

"Bandit? What's he doing here?" Concordia asked. David dropped the leash and the dog bounded towards them.

"I volunteered to take him off my mother's hands for the day. They are preparing for a dinner party." Worry clouded David's deep brown eyes. "I thought I'd missed you. I have news."

Charlotte crouched down to rub Bandit's belly. "We know. One of your students showed us the newspaper."

"Bad news travels fast."

Concordia shivered. "Let's go inside."

They settled in the kitchen, closing the door to the students in the common room. Bandit curled up on the rag rug in front of the stove as Concordia got the kettle going. Soon they had hot, fragrant tea in front of them.

She warmed her chilled fingers around her cup.

"So you already knew about the arrest," David said. "I did not need to come rushing up here." He refilled his cup. "Good tea." He winked at Concordia, who wrinkled her nose at him. Making tea was not *cooking*.

"We were looking for you, in fact," Charlotte said. "We need your help."

David sat back. "I am at your disposal, ladies. What can I do?"

As outwardly composed as Charlotte appeared at first glance, Concordia saw the rigidity of her jaw and the lines of worry creasing her forehead. She put a reassuring hand on the girl's forearm. "I'll tell him." Turning to David, she said, "You're not going to like this, but we believe it is our only recourse." She explained their scheme to search Sanbourne's laboratory.

David's dark brows nearly met his hairline. "You're right. I do not like it at all. You wish to *break in* to Sanbourne's laboratory? Are you mad?"

Concordia crossed her arms and glared. "I am quite in possession of my faculties. If you do not want to help...well then, never mind."

"I am certainly not going to leave you to do this alone." His jaw tightened.

"The problem is *when* could we do it?" Charlotte asked.

"Good point," David said. "Since the death of his wife, the man practically lives in his laboratory."

"Actually, he is going out this evening," a voice broke in.

Miss Lovelace stood in the kitchen doorway, Miss Smedley close behind. The dog lifted his head at the newcomers, then settled back with a sigh.

Concordia smothered a groan. Of all students to walk in on them now. "This is not for your ears, ladies."

Maisie Lovelace shook her head. "Too late." She regarded the group with narrowed eyes. "Why do you want to search Mr. Sanbourne's workshop?" She gestured for Miss Smedley to close the door. They both stood in front of it.

Concordia, David, and Charlotte exchanged glances. David shrugged. "You had better tell them."

Concordia waved them into chairs. "This must stay confidential. Do you promise?"

The girls nodded. She proceeded to explain the dean's arrest and the evidence against him. When she got to the point of describing the search for another suspect, Miss Lovelace shook her head vigorously. "No. Not Mr. Sanbourne. How can you think that? He has lost his assistant and his wife, the two people he was closest to in...in...the world." Her voice trembled.

"We merely want to look in his alcove, where he would most likely keep medicine, if he has any," Concordia said gently. "We will be very careful not to disturb a thing. If we find nothing, then we will know he is innocent of his wife's death. We can eliminate him and move on." Although who they would consider next was beyond her.

Alison put her arm around her friend's shoulders. "If you're sure he is innocent, then where is the harm?"

Maisie sniffed.

"You said Mr. Sanbourne is out tonight," Concordia said. "Where is he going?"

"Uncle George said they have a meeting at the Plaza Hotel. Assistant Secretary Allen is in town to get a report on the progress of the project. Given the recent...circumstances, Mr. Sanbourne will be requesting an extension."

"Tonight sounds as good a time as any, then," Charlotte said.

"But how are we to get in?" David asked.

Maisie dabbed at her eyes with Alison's handkerchief. "I recently discovered a way. I'll show you, *if* you bring me along." In the stunned silence that followed, she added, "I promise, I won't give you away. I just want to see for myself what is going on."

"I suppose that is fair," Charlotte said.

Concordia rolled her eyes. "Four of us, sneaking around Mr. Sanbourne's laboratory? Oh no, that will not attract attention in the least."

"Not four, Miss Wells," Miss Smedley said, leaning forward. "Five. I am coming, too."

Maisie Lovelace clasped Alison's hand, her eyes shining in gratitude.

Concordia sighed. "Why not?"

Chapter 39

In America a woman can go anywhere and do almost anything
without fear of insult.

~Mrs. John Sherwood

Week 13, Instructor Calendar
December 1898

Concordia firmly suppressed a sudden urge to giggle as she crept close behind Miss Lovelace, who held the partly shuttered lantern. The five of them—plus the dog, which was David's idea—circled to the back of the building, hunched low in the shadows, like some parody of a gang of burglars. It had stopped snowing at last, leaving a crunchy few inches underfoot. The wind was picking up. She pulled her dark hood closer to her neck and ears.

Miss Lovelace passed her the lantern. "Hold it up to the latch," she whispered. Concordia did so as Miss Lovelace felt in her pocket for the file.

David leaned closer to look. "What are you doing?" He kept his voice low.

"I noticed the latch had become misaligned with the strike-plate," Miss Lovelace whispered back. "Wood settling, I expect. Unless one firmly pushes it closed, it won't completely lock. If I can just lift it a little—" They heard a slight scrape. With a sigh of satisfaction, the girl slowly eased it open. They slipped inside.

"Leave the electric lights off," Concordia warned. "They'll be visible from the gatehouse."

"How are we to see?" Miss Smedley protested.

Concordia looked up at the high windows, out of reach. "I think we can safely use lanterns, if we keep them low." She set her light on the floor and fully opened the shutter. "There must be another lamp in here." She groped around Sanbourne's alcove.

Charlotte was searching the laboratory. "Found one! On a nail beside the door." She hurried back with it, crashing into a cart.

They froze.

Bandit started barking. David quieted him down.

"Sorry," Charlotte said in a subdued voice.

Concordia cracked open the door and peeked out. No one coming out of the gatehouse, barely visible on the slope. "Perhaps we are too far away to be heard." She looked around the tiny living space, equipped with sink, dresser, cot, and a coat rack. "We cannot *all* search. Miss Lovelace, hold onto Bandit and listen here by the back door. Alert us if someone comes. Miss Smedley, you do the same at the front door of the laboratory. Miss Crandall, Mr. Bradley, and I will search."

David grinned. "One would think you'd done this before, Madam Ringleader."

She ignored him.

The three of them pulled out every drawer, groped under the cot, went through the pockets of Sanbourne's laboratory coat and the spare jacket hanging on the coat rack, and even checked the waste bin. They found receipts, scraps of notes and reminders, toiletries, a tin of throat lozenges. No medicine bottles or vials of liquid. Prospects for clearing Mr. Maynard were looking bleaker by the minute, as was the expression on Charlotte's face, visible in the dim light.

"Well, Miss Lovelace," Concordia began, swinging the lantern in her direction as David and Charlotte made sure everything was back in place before they left, "you see? Mr. Sanbourne is innocent—" She broke off when she noticed Miss Lovelace on her knees by the door lintel with the dog crouched beside her, his nose quivering. "What on earth are you doing?"

"Miss Wells, there's something here!" Miss Lovelace's voice was high-pitched with the excitement of the hunt. "Bandit started sniffing and pawing at this spot."

"A medicine bottle?" Concordia asked, bringing the lantern closer. The trim had pulled away from the wall. Miss Lovelace had her fingers in the gap.

"No. It feels like…paper." The young lady grunted, stretching her reach further. "Ah." She gently slid it out between two fingers.

Charlotte and David joined them, frowning over the long, tightly rolled paper. "It's in poor shape," he said.

Concordia had to agree. One end was rumpled and the entire back was scuffed. David cleared a space on the floor and helped Miss Lovelace unroll it. The girl sucked in a sharp breath.

"What is it?" Concordia leaned closer.

David sat back on his heels, expression grim. "You recognize this?" he asked Miss Lovelace.

The girl swallowed. "The missing blueprint."

Chapter 40

*The rogues, the pretenders, the adventurers who push
into the penetralia of our social circles are many.*
~Mrs. John Sherwood

Week 13, Instructor Calendar
December 1898

"Blueprint!" Concordia exclaimed. "For the *Blue Arrow* project? But Guryev made off with it. Poor Mr. Sanbourne has been working for weeks, reconstructing the plans from his notes."

David pointed to the left edge of the paper. "Shine the light here."

Concordia did so, and leaned in for a closer look. The edges were crumpled and torn. Ink spots spattered that side.

Wait…not ink spots.

Concordia's heart beat wildly.

Blood. That must have been what the dog had detected.

Miss Lovelace swayed. "I cannot believe…."

Charlotte pulled the girl over to the cot and sat her down. "Breathe. Slowly."

Concordia's quivering lantern cast erratic shadows on the wall.

"I need more light," David said impatiently, pushing Bandit's head out of the way. She brought it closer, her thoughts in a whirl. They were here to search for proof that Sanbourne might have murdered his wife. Instead, they had found…she struggled to make the mental shift, feeling as if she had set out to play lawn tennis equipped with a bicycle instead of a racquet.

She took a breath. "*Sanbourne* murdered Oster?"

He nodded. "The conclusion is unavoidable, I am afraid."

"And then he took back the blueprint but pretended it was missing."

David reached for the lantern and anchored a curling edge with it. "No doubt Sanbourne didn't realize at the time that a ripped scrap remained in Oster's hand. And with blood on the paper, he would have to keep it hidden anyway."

"What about Guryev? Did Sanbourne kill him as well?"

"I don't know."

She shuddered. Scandal upon scandal was being heaped upon the school, and they were nowhere closer to clearing Maynard of blame in Mrs. Sanbourne's death.

Unless...had Rachel Sanbourne learned her husband's secret? Was he forced to kill her to keep her quiet?

Charlotte left Miss Lovelace on the cot and crouched next to them on the floor. "What do we do now?" she asked quietly.

Miss Lovelace let out a strangled sob.

"First, we should get her home," Concordia said.

David carefully rolled up the paper. "Good idea. You all go on ahead. I want to find a cylinder to keep this in."

Charlotte helped an unsteady Maisie Lovelace to her feet while Concordia stepped into the laboratory. "Miss Smedley," she called, "it is time to go."

Alison Smedley hurried over. "Did you find anything?"

"Miss Crandall will explain." Concordia turned to Charlotte and passed her the leash. "Wait for us at the farmhouse. Get Miss Lovelace to bed. Mr. Bradley and I will finish here in a moment. We'll go to Sycamore House and telephone for the police from there."

The young ladies left, along with the dog. Concordia carefully made her way in the dim light back to David, who held the lantern over a worktable. "No tube?"

He straightened. "Sorry, I became distracted." He pointed to a large sheet of tracing paper spread across the table.

"Sanbourne has nearly finished re-copying the blueprint. For the sake of appearances, I suppose. He certainly would not want anyone laying eyes upon the other." He shook his head. "The design is quite clever. What a shame such a talent became corrupted."

Concordia was about to reply, then stiffened. Was that a sound outside?

Her stomach fluttered with unease. "I don't think we should stay much longer."

"You're right." He rolled the paper more tightly. "We shall have to make do without a tube. Let's go."

No sooner were the words spoken when they heard the crunch of footsteps in the snow.

David quickly extinguished the lantern.

They stayed motionless. She hardly dared to breathe. Perhaps the person would move on. It could not be Sanbourne. Only an hour had passed since he had left for town.

Unless the appointment had been postponed.

If it was Sanbourne...Concordia's heart sank when she remembered the snow. He would know someone—several people and a dog—had been in here. They had left any number of footprints to give them away.

The sounds stopped at the front door of the building. They heard the key in the lock. She glanced at David, who nodded grimly and set the blueprint aside, freeing his hands. He crept over to the door.

She felt a rush of gratitude that he was here. No matter what may come, they were in this together.

Chapter 41

A woman is allowed much less freedom of posture than a man.
~Mrs. John Sherwood

Week 13, Instructor Calendar
December 1898

D avid jumped Sanbourne as soon as he entered. The struggle seemed to take forever, the pair painfully colliding with a tool-laden workbench, a utility sink, and a table rigged with pointed knobs that gave a faint hiss in protest. Concordia scrambled in the dark for some implement that would help. Finally, she gave up on ladylike propriety and launched herself like a banshee upon Sanbourne's back, knocking them all to the floor. David subdued him with a twist of an arm and a chokehold around his neck.

She got to her feet and pushed the wall switch. Harsh electric light flooded the room and dazzled her dark-adjusted eyes. Sanbourne stopped struggling and stared in astonishment. "Miss...Wells! What is the meaning of this?" He twisted to look at the man who kept him in a painful grip. "And...Bradley? How dare you!"

David said nothing, but pushed him toward a chair. "Sit down. And stay there, or I shall have Miss Wells tackle you again." His lips twitched.

Open-mouthed, Sanbourne sat.

David pointed to the blueprint roll on the workbench. "That proves you killed Oster. And presumably Guryev. What happened that night?"

Sanbourne looked desperately around the room.

"There is no escape," David said.

Sanbourne brushed the dark hair from his eyes. "I am not telling you a thing."

David glanced at Concordia. "I'll hold him here. You go for Capshaw."

Concordia leaned toward David and whispered, "I don't want to leave you alone. You saw how difficult it was to subdue—" She stopped at the sound of light footsteps outside.

Charlotte Crandall opened the door. "I sent Maisie, Alison, and the dog along to the farmhouse and thought I would come back here—oh!" Her eyes widened at the sight of Sanbourne. David tightened his grip on Sanbourne's shoulder as he tried to rise.

"Charlotte, thank goodness," Concordia said. "Call Capshaw and have him come right away. And stop at the gatehouse on your way. Tell Clyde to come." She wasn't taking any chances. The burly gatekeeper would keep Sanbourne in line until Capshaw arrived.

With an uneasy look at the inventor, Charlotte hastily left.

"So now we wait," David said.

Concordia decided to try one more time. With the knowledge that Capshaw was on his way, perhaps Sanbourne would be more talkative. "How did you come to be at the farmhouse the night Oster died? You were at a social function, were you not?"

Sanbourne folded his arms and glared.

Concordia had had *enough*. She picked up the blueprint, hands shaking. She could not remember the last time she had felt this furious, at anyone or anything. And she was *tired*. Tired of searching for answers and finding resistance at every turn. Tired of seeing those she cared about suffer. Tired of anxious, sleepless nights trying to untangle the puzzle. Tired of uncertainty.

Starting at one corner, she slowly began to rip.

David gaped in disbelief but he did not intervene, keeping a firm hand on the squirming inventor.

"All right, all right, stop!" Sanbourne shouted. "I'll tell you."

She set it aside and took a deep, calming breath. "How did you come to be at the farmhouse the night Oster died?"

He shifted in his seat. "It was at my wife's urging. She came separately to the Dunwick party—a painting lesson had delayed her. On her way out of the college gate, she saw Ivan holding a cylinder, hurrying along the path to the old abandoned farmhouse. She was suspicious."

"How could she know Guryev was up to no good?" David asked. He released his grip and sat across from Sanbourne.

"Rachel, rest her soul, had been suspicious of Ivan for quite some time." He brushed at his dusty trousers. "She believed that the destruction of our Baltimore laboratory was the work of debt collectors who were after Ivan. I knew about his gambling, and yet I did not believe her."

David raised a skeptical brow. "So you left the Dunwick party? Did you not worry that you would be missed?"

"It was a crush of people. Rachel said she would make a suitable excuse should anyone inquire."

"What happened when you arrived at the farmhouse?" Concordia asked.

"There was no sign of him at first. I thought she was mistaken." He hesitated. "I wish she had been."

"Then you found him." David said. "The back porch?"

Sanbourne's hooded eyes took on a faraway look. "I saw the glow of a lantern. Ivan and Oster were leaning over a worktable." His jaw clenched. "My blueprint was spread out upon it."

"Did you kill them both then?" David asked.

Sanbourne shook his head. "I knew I could not overpower them together. I waited. Oster passed an envelope to Ivan, who left quickly. Oster turned back to the drawing. I realized if I did not act then, Reeve would be in possession of my secrets, my years of hard work. I grabbed something, I don't remember what—"

"A poker," Concordia interjected. David gave her a sharp look.

"I suppose." Sanbourne shrugged. "All sorts of debris lay about. In my anger, I struck him harder than I thought. I was horrified to find that he...was dead." He looked up at Concordia with pleading eyes. "I only wanted to knock him out, to take back my blueprint. I did not mean to kill him."

She said nothing. Mr. Oster was no less dead because of Sanbourne's intentions.

"So you took the blueprint and fled," David said.

"Yes. I yanked it out of his hand and ran out the back door," Sanbourne went on. "I did not even stop to find the tube to put it in."

"What happened then?" David asked.

"I returned to the lab to conceal it until I could figure out what to do. It was fortunate that I did not turn on a light. A student came by and knocked on the door." He shook his head. "The young ladies here are certainly...persistent."

Concordia glanced at David. "Miss Lovelace." The girl had been correct about someone being inside the laboratory that evening.

Sanbourne nodded. "I heard her call to Ivan."

"Then what?" Concordia asked.

"I waited until she had gone. Then I secreted the paper and returned to the Dunwick party."

"Did you know that a piece had torn away and remained in Oster's hand, or that blood had stained the paper?" David asked.

Sanbourne shook his head. "My first chance to get a good look was the next morning. Fortunately, I had time to hide it in a better place before you discovered Oster's body. The police conducted a surprisingly thorough search of my laboratory, twice. I had no idea your Hartford Police were so diligent."

"Did you tell your wife what happened?" Concordia asked.

Sanbourne looked surprised. "Of course."

The man's casual tone sent a chill along her spine, along with a ripple of disappointment that Sanbourne had no motive for murdering his wife. "How did she respond?"

"Rachel was exceedingly distressed. She feared that suspicion would quickly point to me, once Oster's body was found. Something needed to be done about Ivan before the police located him."

"I see," David said. "With Oster dead, the police would double their efforts to find Guryev. Once they questioned him, he would admit to stealing your blueprint to sell to Oster but deny killing the man. After all, what motive would he have? He had the money. The blueprint was no longer in his possession. The authorities would then revisit your account of your whereabouts that night."

Sanbourne nodded. "The police had questioned Lady Dunwick as a matter of course, but did not inquire extensively among the guests, one of whom had wondered about my absence just before I returned to the party. Rachel made an excuse, but it was bound to look suspicious upon closer scrutiny. We had to be sure that Ivan was out of reach of the police, one way or another."

One way or another. Concordia and David exchanged a look.

"So you just went along with your wife's proposal to kill your assistant?" David said sarcastically.

"As Rachel pointed out, Ivan had been deceiving me for a long time. I would not have been in my present predicament if I had heeded her before."

Talk of deception reminded Concordia of what had brought them here in the first place. "What of your *wife's* deception? It must have been a blow to find out about her marriage to Maynard. Is that why you poisoned her?" It was a wild shot in the dark.

Sanbourne's eyes widened in surprise. "Of course not! I would never harm her."

"But to learn she had been married to Maynard, and put in an asylum for smothering her own child. To me, that is a worse deceit than Ivan Guryev's."

Sanbourne shook his head vehemently. He had grown pale, or was that Concordia's imagination? "Before our marriage, she told me of her past. She did not name the man, and I did not ask. Learning it was Maynard was indeed awkward, but it changed nothing of my feelings for her. I only wanted to be assured that our marriage was a legal one." He looked at Concordia and David with narrowed eyes. "It is obvious your dean is guilty of the deliberate, premeditated murder of my poor Rachel. Whatever happens to me, he will not escape the consequences of that."

"I am sure the police will explore the matter further," David said grimly, with a glance at Concordia, who discreetly checked her watch—*Where was Capshaw?* "You already have a number of things to answer for. How did you kill Guryev?"

Sanbourne shifted restlessly. "Must we do this? You said yourself—I will be in police custody soon. It is so tedious to have to repeat oneself."

"I am sure it will be of equal fascination the second time around," Concordia said dryly.

He blew out a breath. "I left early the next morning to intercept Ivan. I was correct in my assumption that he would book passage for himself and his mother as soon as possible, and that he would use the same agent as he had in the past. The ticket office is at the foot of State Street. I took care that Ivan did not see me, but I could hear his conversation through the window." He hesitated.

Concordia checked her watch again. She could understand Capshaw being delayed, but what of Clyde? He should be here by now.

"What then?" David prompted.

"You must understand, even then I felt conflicted about killing Ivan, despite what Rachel wanted." Sanbourne gripped the sides of the chair until his knuckles were white. "I hoped he could secure passage and be gone before the police found him."

David folded his arms and sat back. "You really expect us to believe you would simply let him escape?"

Sanbourne sighed. "What happened in the ticket office decided Ivan's fate."

"Go on," David said.

"He had a heated discussion with the ticket agent. He wanted passage aboard the *Edam*, sailing for Amsterdam from New York the next morning, but it was already overbooked. The best he could do was the *Teutonic*, sailing for Liverpool the following Wednesday. I knew I could not risk the police finding him in the meanwhile."

"What did you do?" Concordia asked quietly.

"I intercepted Ivan after he left the ticket office. The panicked look on his face made clear he wanted to run, but I pointed out that I could have his mother arrested as a co-conspirator. It was to my advantage that he knew nothing about Oster yet. I allowed him to assume that I had simply discovered the blueprints were missing and had realized he was responsible. With a bottle of chloroform in my pocket, we walked along the docks and talked for a while. I tried to put him at his ease, proposing ways we could get the blueprints back from Oster and offering to lend him money to leave afterwards. Once he had relaxed his guard, and I had found a secluded spot...." His jaw tightened.

Concordia shuddered. The riverfront docks adjoining that end of State Street were seamed with warehouses and loading areas, with endless rows of shipping crates stacked high above one's head. Even with dockhands about, there were undoubtedly places to overpower a man and hide his body until it was dark enough to push him into the river. As she had learned from the Inner Circle killings last spring, chloroform could kill as well as incapacitate. Weight the body in the river to delay discovery—yes, it was possible.

Sanbourne looked at her closely and gave a nod. "I see you have put it together."

She felt peculiarly light-headed. Was it all this talk of murder? She was made of sterner stuff than this.

"It was all for nothing, Sanbourne," David said brusquely.

Sanbourne had grown pale. Sweat beaded his forehead. "All I wanted was my blueprint. I had no wish to kill anyone."

"Your blueprint will do you little good now," David said. "The Navy will no doubt pull out of the project."

Sanbourne shrugged. "I have other offers. Rival countries, willing to pay even more for my device."

"There will be no laboratory in prison to finish your work, or to entertain foreign dignitaries," Concordia said tartly. The arrogance of the man was astonishing. The flickering light from the single lantern made his eyes appear hooded, inscrutable. She frowned at the sputtering lamp. The fuel was running low.

David had noticed it, too. "We cannot wait any longer." He stood. "All right, Sanbourne. You're coming with us to Sycamore House. No point in fighting it, now that the truth is out."

Sanbourne wearily started to rise, David gripping his elbow. Abruptly, he sagged. David lost his balance, gashing his temple upon the corner of the chair.

"David!" Concordia gasped.

Sanbourne pushed the limp body out of his way and snatched the blueprint from the table. She clutched at his arm in an effort to restrain him. He backhanded her in the face with a force that made her ears ring and lights spark behind her eyes.

By the time she had caught a shuddering breath, he had fled the building.

She let him go, scrambling toward David's unconscious form. Was he breathing?

"David, David." She laid him flat on the floor and put her head to his chest, her breath quickening in gratitude when she heard the steady beating of his heart and felt his chest rise. *Thank heaven.* She used her skirt hem to dab at the blood trickling down the side of his pale face.

She must get help. It would mean leaving him here alone. She pulled herself up to stand on wobbling legs. Her head ached, and she felt nauseous. Surely, Sanbourne had not hit her that hard.

Then, in the silence, she heard it. The hissing. It had been going on all along, since they had first struggled to subdue Sanbourne.

Gas.

Chapter 42

Concordia groped toward the nozzle and finally located the metal wheel that controlled the cut-off valve.

Drat, it was bent. She couldn't turn it.

She crawled back over to David.

Carrying him was out of the question. She clutched his collar and tried dragging him along the floor. Her limbs felt so heavy. Dizziness came in waves.

She collapsed against him, chafing his wrists, shaking his shoulders. "David!" she shouted in his ear.

His eyes fluttered, then closed. He sighed.

"Oh, David," she sobbed against his cheek, making it wet with her tears. "Please, please...." She kissed him.

He stirred, and put his arms around her languidly. "M'dear...." He opened his eyes.

She gulped down relieved sobs and helped him sit up. "I can't...turn off...the gas. We must...get out."

He gave a weak nod. She helped him stand, trying to keep herself steady as the floor tipped beneath her feet. She pulled his arm over her shoulder and gripped his waist. They lurched through the room, clutching tables, racks, stools...anything sturdy enough to keep them upright and moving toward the promise of fresh air.

After what seemed an eternity, they made it through the door and collapsed into the snow. Concordia rolled onto her back. The cold wetness seeped through her jacket, but she was happy to breathe deep lungfuls of air.

David leaned over, eyes wide. He clasped her hand. "Was I dreaming, or did you kiss me?"

Concordia blushed.

David grinned. "You see? I was right. Anywhere I am stuck with you is heaven."

They heard running footsteps crunching in the snow, the sounds growing closer. Concordia propped herself up on her elbows as Lieutenant Capshaw came into view. Clyde, huffing for breath, followed close behind with a lantern. He stopped short at the sight of Mr. Bradley and Miss Wells sprawled in the snow. "Lordy!"

Capshaw's shaggy mustache twitched as he helped Concordia to her feet. "I inevitably find you in the most curious of positions, Miss Wells."

Chapter 43

The voice is a treacherous servant; it deserts us,
trembles, often when we need its help.

~Mrs. John Sherwood

December 22, 1898
Christmas Recess

Ruby tapped on Concordia's open door. "Sorry to interrupt your packing, miss, but that policeman's here, and he's brought a visitor."

"Oh? Who is it?" Concordia secured the strap of her valise. Since the fire, packing did not take her long. Besides, she would only be at her mother's house for winter recess.

Ruby's lips quirked in a mischievous smile. "It's a surprise."

"I will be right down." She hoped Capshaw came with news of Sanbourne's arrest. The police departments in Hartford, New Haven, New York, and Boston had watches set in all of the major train stations and ports in the area, but after a week, there was no sign of him.

She resettled the pins in her hair with a sigh. With Sanbourne at liberty, Maynard still in prison, and the newspapers airing the woes of Hartford Women's College across the nation, it was difficult to know what would happen next. Certainly the engineering program had been a disaster for the school and would close. Concordia's heart ached for Maisie Lovelace and her fellows. She hoped that Langdon's recent meeting with the presidents of Yale and Trinity Colleges about setting up independent study for the young ladies had been productive.

She shook her head. Would there even be a school when all was said and done?

Capshaw and the gentleman beside him stood politely as Concordia entered the parlor. She stopped short. "Mr. Maynard!"

Randolph Maynard's mouth barely turned upward in a smile, his lips stretched thin and pale against a shadowed face and stubbled jaw.

"Does this mean he has been cleared?" she asked Capshaw, settling herself upon the tufted ottoman across from Maynard.

Capshaw stretched his bare hands toward the glowing hearth. "Sanbourne's flight and his implication in the other two murders have raised doubts about Mr. Maynard's guilt. The prosecutor has decided there is insufficient evidence to bring a case against the dean."

"That is good news," Concordia said. "Any news about Sanbourne or the blueprint?"

"I'm afraid not." He passed a weary hand through his hair. "Two ships departed before a watch was in place: the *Rosefield*, bound for Hamburg, and the *Dona Maria*, for Lisbon. We have cabled the authorities in both cities, but he has likely eluded us."

That was disappointing. "At least you have been released, Mr. Maynard. Does Charlotte know?"

Maynard grimaced. "We called upon Lady Dunwick, who informed us that Charlotte was out Christmas shopping. It was quite a chilly reception. The lady forbade me to resume an acquaintance with her niece." He shook his head. "I cannot say I blame her."

"I am sure she will come around eventually," Concordia said.

Capshaw shifted in his seat. "The problem is that Mr. Maynard has not been definitively cleared of Mrs. Sanbourne's death. Suspicion remains."

"But Mr. Sanbourne killed two other people, by his own admission," Concordia said. "Who knows what could have set him against his wife?" Even as she said it, the doubts whispered.

"Based upon what you and Mr. Bradley told me, there was no motive for him to kill her," Capshaw said.

Maynard gave a reluctant nod. "By all appearances, Peter Sanbourne was exceedingly fond of his wife. He was certainly prepared to defend her to anyone who suggested otherwise." He grimaced and rubbed his jaw.

"Then who is responsible?" Concordia asked. "No one on campus carried a grudge against her that I know of. She had a pleasant disposition and was popular with the young ladies, especially her art students. The faculty admired her talent. We all appreciated her willingness to spend her free time teaching the girls." She gestured to Maynard. "Very few people knew of her past, or that she was responsible for the fire—" She stopped short.

Capshaw leaned forward. "What is it?"

"Miss Smedley suspected Mrs. Sanbourne of starting the fire. She told us so, when Miss Lovelace and I visited her in the infirmary. Perhaps—"

"Surely you do not believe Miss Smedley or Miss Lovelace is responsible?" Maynard interrupted incredulously.

"No, no, that is not my point. What if someone *else* on campus knew or suspected the fire was started by Mrs. Sanbourne?"

Capshaw frowned. "Murder seems a drastic form of retribution. Why not simply turn her in to the authorities?"

"Much harm had been done, especially to Charlotte," Concordia said.

"Which brings suspicion right back upon my head," Maynard said caustically. "That line of thought gets us nowhere."

She sucked in a breath. Another person on campus was exceedingly fond of Charlotte Crandall.

She is the daughter I could never have.

Even as Concordia experienced the familiar twinge of satisfaction at seeing the puzzle pieces align themselves, her heart recoiled at the path her mind was forcing her to take.

That path led to Margaret Banning.

Miss Banning's office adjoined that of Maynard. *I hear everything through there,* she had said, pointing to the wall vent. Concordia had not realized it at the time, but that meant the old lady must have heard her and Maynard discussing Mrs. Sanbourne's guilt. Miss Banning had certainly appeared distracted just after that conversation, when Concordia had come to take her to the hospital.

Perhaps Miss Banning had heard even more than that. Concordia recalled the open window in the library of Founder's Hall, the evening she and Mrs. Sanbourne were out on the quadrangle. Mrs. Sanbourne had tauntingly elaborated upon the ways in which she could do away with someone. *A simple tea reception would provide ample opportunities,* she had boasted. Could Margaret Banning have been in the library and overheard her words? Had she feared that her beloved Charlotte remained in danger? The irony of using Mrs. Sanbourne's own words against her might have appealed to the old lady. The Shakespearean phrase *hoist with his own petard* would have sprung to mind.

Then there was the poison. Miss Banning's health had been poor for quite some time. Did she have a heart condition that required atropine? Capshaw could determine that.

Assuming that atropine was at the ready, Margaret Banning would have had little difficulty coaxing Mrs. Sanbourne into joining her for a cup of tea in the teacher's lounge. Who would be wary of a frail old woman? Everyone else was at the Revels.

Concordia's heart clenched in her chest. She desperately wanted to be wrong. As acid-tongued and cranky as the history teacher was, she had a sharp wit, a wealth of knowledge, and a passion for her teaching. She had dedicated her life to instructing young ladies, during a time when few gave a thought for a woman's intellect or dreams. She had been a pioneer.

But the persistent dread that roiled her stomach and made her heart pound told her she was not wrong.

"Miss Wells," Maynard said sharply. "We have been talking all this while. You are paying no attention at all."

Concordia shuddered and looked at Capshaw, not troubling to mask her anguish.

Capshaw's eyes widened. He sat beside her. "You know," he murmured.

She nodded, closing her eyes as the tears trickled down her cheeks.

Chapter 44

It is not easy to speak the unvarnished, uncorrupted truth.
~Mrs. John Sherwood

December 3o, 1898
Christmas Recess

Capshaw and Concordia took a hansom cab from her mother's house to pay a call upon Miss Banning. She wished they could have done this a week ago.

The local newspapers—taking only a brief Christmas respite to publish accounts of how the wealthy and famous spent their holiday—had not relented in their conjecture over Maynard's guilt. Maynard had respected Lady Dunwick's wish that he keep his distance from Charlotte. Despite Langdon's protests, he had moved out of Sycamore House and into lodgings off campus. No doubt it had been a sad Christmas for them both.

Capshaw had needed the time to be sure of his facts, for course. Finding people during the holiday season had slowed his progress.

Both Miss Banning's physician and the neighborhood chemist confirmed she had been taking atropine drops these past few months. Capshaw had determined that conversations in Maynard's office could indeed be heard through the vent in Miss Banning's office.

Piling on evidence of Miss Banning's guilt was the librarian's account of the lady's presence in the library the afternoon preceding the Revels, at her favorite spot by the window that provided the best natural light. She had complained of the chill and had asked that the sash be closed, but the request had been overlooked. When Miss Banning grew agitated and abruptly left, the librarian had assumed she was annoyed at the oversight.

Capshaw pointed out that none of this was proof. It was merely the means by which to attain proof. A confession.

Concordia leaned back against the carriage cushions. Suppose Miss Banning confessed to the murder? What then? A public trial? She shuddered.

Capshaw passed over another carriage blanket. "Are you sure you want to talk with her alone?"

She met his eyes, adopting an air of confidence she did not quite feel. "It will be best. Don't worry—I will be perfectly safe." She had likewise reassured David and Charlotte. She could not have a crowd trailing in her wake.

"I'll be waiting outside, ready to come in whenever you say."

"What will you do with her?" That question had kept her awake until the wee hours.

"She will have to come to the station to sign a confession and be formally charged, but given her age and the state of her health, I'm sure she will be permitted to remain at home until the hearing. She is not at risk of fleeing."

Concordia looked out the window of the cab. How would Miss Banning endure a public airing of her crime? Concordia could not help but pity her, despite what she had done.

Miss Banning's house was a modest brownstone along the quieter eastern end of Capitol Avenue. As she rang the bell, she blew out a breath and settled her spectacles more firmly upon her nose.

The same middle-aged parlor maid she remembered from her visit years ago answered the door. Though hardly a maid in the etymological sense of *maiden,* she gave a creaky curtsy, took Concordia's coat and scarf, and went to announce her.

The parlor was much as Concordia remembered it, too: a jumble of décor and collectibles in the old Victorian style of excess, from the ornately worked Turkish carpet to the litter of china figures, alabaster vases, embroidered pillows, and dried flowers. The fire burned brightly in the stifling room. A plump ginger tabby dozed on the hearth. There had been ten felines the last time she was here. Perhaps the others had succumbed to old age or over-indulgence.

Miss Banning sat close to the fire, in her favorite padded armchair, upholstered in a faded shade of olive that had lost its sheen some twenty years ago. The crocheted lace doilies spread over the arms could not halt the inevitable passage of time, or keep the stuffing from bursting through whatever breach it could find.

As Concordia approached, Miss Banning watched her closely through bottle-glass spectacles but did not try to rise. She waved her cane with thin-skinned, knobby hands. "Sit down." There was a labored wheeze in her voice.

Mercifully, the chair indicated was farther from the hearth. Concordia sat and smoothed her skirts.

Miss Banning turned her head toward the door. "You did not bring Charlotte with you?"

Concordia winced, recalling her earlier conversation with Charlotte. The young lady had taken the news of her respected mentor committing murder for her sake with a dry-eyed, white-lipped dignity.

"Charlotte, umm—conveys her regards."

Miss Banning sighed. "I have not seen her in a week."

"She wanted to come. I told her I wished to speak with you alone. You know why, do you not?"

"*Hmph.*" Miss Banning gazed steadily at the fire, the light reflecting in her glasses and making her expression unreadable. Concordia waited. Did the old woman understand? Surely, she must have expected someone to put it together. What now? By the look of her, Miss Banning was not about to unburden herself. Concordia balked at rehashing the details.

She decided upon a different approach. "It has been almost two years since the last time I visited. Do you remember?"

The lady rapped her cane on the leg of the table, causing the cat to twitch its ears. "Of course I do," she snapped. "I am not dispossessed of my faculties, missy. You came to consult me about how to stage the senior play. The students were performing *Macbeth*."

"That's right. You and I spoke of the play's themes, and how to help the young ladies understand character motivation." Concordia clasped her hands tightly in her lap. "I still remember a point you made about Macbeth's character."

Margaret Banning leaned forward. "Go on."

"You said," Concordia closed her eyes to bring back the exact words, "*He is human, like the rest of us. No matter how kind, well-intentioned, or amiable we may be, we are each equally capable of malice, under the right circumstances.*" She opened her eyes. Miss Banning had both hands on her cane, leaning heavily. "That applies to you as well, does it not?"

Time and again, Concordia had seen it. Most of them—the guilty ones—were not wicked criminals. Under normal circumstances, they were upstanding citizens, even kindly souls. Many were talented, vivacious, personable. Yet, when the crisis had come, they had made a desperate, ghastly choice. There was no going back.

Miss Banning shifted in her seat, wincing. "You *are* a sharp one. It doesn't surprise me that you figured it out. I suppose your friend the policeman is waiting outside for me?"

"He wants you to sign a confession."

The old lady let out a bark of laughter. "Does he, now? If I do sign anything, it will not be a remorse-ridden plea for leniency. I cannot say I am sorry for what I have done. 'When a man is compelled to choose one of two evils, no one will choose the greater when he might have the less.' Plato. I could not allow Charlotte to be harmed again."

Concordia shook her head. "Charlotte continues to suffer. The man she cares for is accused of the crime."

Miss Banning's face registered surprise. "*Hmph.* May-Not. He isn't good enough for her. She will get over him eventually."

"No, she won't. She will always love him. 'Love is an ever-fixed mark, that looks on tempests, and is never shaken.'" One could always rely upon Shakespeare to make one's point.

Miss Banning frowned.

"Charlotte is miserable," Concordia went on, "because public doubt about Maynard's innocence is keeping them apart."

Miss Banning looked down at her hands, still gripping the cane in front of her. She was quiet for so long, Concordia wondered if she had dozed off.

Finally, she stirred. "Does Charlotte know?"

"That you killed Mrs. Sanbourne?" Concordia asked quietly. "Yes."

"I want to talk to her."

"I do not know if that is possible. Lieutenant Capshaw wants you to accompany him to the station."

Miss Banning paid no attention. She waved her cane toward the bookcases. "Bring over my writing desk. Tell your lieutenant that I am writing out my confession. He can come back for it in the morning."

Concordia fetched the desk, laying out pen and paper. "Do you wish me to accompany Capshaw when he returns tomorrow?"

Miss Banning's frown softened. She laid a bony hand on Concordia's sleeve. "I can manage on my own. You have already shown me more kindness than I deserve. It is time to leave behind this sordid business."

Chapter 45

Truth is a virtue more palpable and less shadowy than we think.
~Mrs. John Sherwood

Christmas Recess, 1898

Concordia waited anxiously in the library at her mother's house for Capshaw to bring word of Margaret Banning. David and her mother waited with her.

During her formative years, the family library was one of Concordia's favorite rooms. She had always loved the smell—redolent of old paper, crumbling spines, and faded ink. A hint of pipe tobacco lingered in the comfortably worn leather chairs. She had spent many happy hours in this room, poring over Papa's illustrated Greek mythologies.

But Concordia felt no peace in this room today. As she paced, Mrs. Wells sat with her knitting, and David perused the shelves.

After a time, her mother looked up. "Concordia, dear, you will wear out my best Turkish carpet. Do sit down."

So she sat and stared out the window at the gray-brown bones of the dormant trees against a dull slate sky. The vista looked as dreary as she felt. She wished she had gone with Capshaw, despite Miss Banning's refusal. At least she would know something by now.

The doorbell rang. Concordia jumped up, but her mother waved her back. "Mrs. Houston will answer it."

The visitor was not Lieutenant Capshaw, but Randolph Maynard. Although he was immaculately attired in a finely pressed, wool pinstripe suit, his face was pale and he crushed the brim of his derby between his hands as if it were a lifeline.

"Forgive the intrusion," he said in a gruff voice. "I had hoped the lieutenant would be here. The man at the station was uncertain of his whereabouts."

Concordia shifted over on the sofa. "We are expecting him. You are welcome to wait."

"Are you here to learn the status of Capshaw's investigation?" David asked. "He is—"

"—I want to stop it," Maynard interrupted impatiently.

"It may be too late to stop it," David pointed out. "Capshaw was to call upon Miss Banning and bring her to the station this morning. She must have been formally charged by now."

Concordia frowned. "Mr. Maynard, why do you want to stop it? Surely you wish to be cleared of suspicion in Mrs. Sanbourne's death?"

Maynard stared at the fire, its light reflecting in the brass andirons. "The cost is too high. I have given this a great deal of thought. To reveal that the college's oldest and most respected professor is guilty of murder would irrevocably damage Hartford Women's College, now and in the future. Even if I am not officially cleared of the crime, I am not at risk of being arrested again."

"But what of the stain upon your name?" Mrs. Wells asked.

"Public speculation will die out in time. Those closest to me know the truth." Maynard turned to Concordia. "I have you to thank for that. And I have decided to stay on as dean. Edward never wanted to accept my resignation. He said the same thing you did."

"What was that?" Concordia asked.

"That I was running away from the scandal, instead of facing it." He hesitated. "I owe you a great deal, Miss Wells."

Concordia flushed. "It was my debt to repay." She glanced at the mantel clock yet again. One o'clock. What was taking Capshaw so long?

The doorbell rang again. Concordia felt her spirits lift. *At last.*

But it was Charlotte Crandall this time, who stopped short as she encountered a chorus of suppressed sighs. "Have I come at an inopportune time?" She caught sight of Maynard, who stood as she entered. "Randolph! I…I did not expect you here."

The strain of the past few weeks was evident in her pale lips and the smudged hollows beneath her eyes. "Although I am glad you are here. I have news."

"What is it?" Mrs. Wells asked.

"Miss Banning sent for me last evening. She wanted to tell me in person what she had done and her reasons for it." She nodded toward Concordia. "It happened much as you said. Then she gave me this." She held up a sealed envelope, scrawled with the name *Randolph Maynard*. "She said it would allow me to go on with my life and be happy."

"But she promised to write her confession to Capshaw, not Mr. Maynard," Concordia said.

"It surprised me as well," Charlotte said. She walked over to Maynard, holding it out. "She told me it is for you to do with as you wish."

Maynard broke the seal and pulled out a sheet covered on both sides in spidery writing. After a few minutes, he tucked it back in the envelope without a word.

"But that isn't all of it," Charlotte said with a shiver.

"Come, sit by the fire," David said, escorting her to a rocking chair nearest the hearth. "What else did she say?"

Charlotte bit her lip. "She asked me to come back for Caesar. Naturally I agreed, though Aunt Susan cannot abide cats."

Concordia, not over-fond of cats either, made a dismissive gesture. "Don't worry, he can stay with us. We have a large barn where he can hunt mice to his heart's content." Not that Caesar was likely to *stay* in the barn. The idea of the spoiled, indolent cat hunting for its supper defied the imagination. The beast would undoubtedly be running the place in no time.

David frowned. "Does Miss Banning expect to be *kept* in jail? Surely that is not Capshaw's intent."

Concordia shook her head. "He told me she would be allowed to return home after signing her statement." She glanced over at Charlotte's stricken face. All at once, she realized what the young lady feared. Her stomach twisted. "Where is Miss Banning now? At the station?"

"I hoped you would know." Charlotte said.

Concordia stood. "I think we've waited long enough. We should telephone the station."

The doorbell rang again.

This time, finally, it was Capshaw who stepped into the library, hat tucked under his arm.

"At last, lieutenant," Mrs. Wells said. "We are all eager to hear how Miss Banning is doing."

Maynard quietly slipped the envelope in his jacket pocket.

Although Mrs. Wells gestured toward a chair, Capshaw remained standing. He tugged at his tunic and cleared his throat. "I am sorry to say that Miss Banning is dead. Her maid found her this morning."

No one spoke.

David was the one who broke the silence and asked the question on their minds. "By her own hand or from natural causes?"

"The coroner will try to determine that. It may be difficult to tell, given her age and ailments." Capshaw peered closely at Concordia. "You told me yesterday she was writing her confession when you left. I found no such document."

Concordia avoided glancing at Charlotte or Maynard. "That is what she said." She sighed, her heart heavy. "It cannot matter now."

Margaret Banning had resigned at last. This time, the decision was irrevocable.

Epilogue

"It is quite possible for the lady to be fond of her husband without committing the slightest offence against good taste."
~Mrs. John Sherwood

Memorial Chapel, Hartford Women's College
June 1899

Concordia tried not to fidget as Mrs. Wells and Charlotte adjusted the circlet of orange blossoms in her hair and settled the tulle veil over her shoulders.

"There." Mrs. Wells stepped back to assess the result. "You make a lovely bride, my dear."

Concordia turned to the small mirror behind the door of the vesting room, and examined the ivory satin gown from the few angles she could manage. She had chosen a simpler design than Mother had wished, but both were pleased with the result. The fitted bodice crossed in elegant Grecian folds, flattering the bosom and waist. Mother had prevailed in the choice of a full petticoat and a sizeable train, but Concordia had to admit the skirt's soft chiffon draping and point lace trim made for a becoming effect.

Although there had been a number of lemon tarts since the final fitting, the months of trudging back and forth between farmhouse and classes had ensured the dress still fit.

She adjusted the aquamarine brooch at her shoulder. Mother had managed to soften the look of the horrid thing with a pretty lace rosette that partly obscured it. One could still see the sparkle of the water-blue gems. The compromise satisfied

David's mother, though Concordia would have to take care not to impale any congratulatory guests after the ceremony.

The thought of guests reminded her of something. "Has Penelope Hamilton arrived yet?"

Charlotte nodded. "I saw her on my way to the vestry."

"Wonderful! I wasn't sure she could come."

"She was surrounded by teachers and students. I don't recall her being so popular when she was lady principal."

Concordia laughed. "Lady principals are rarely a popular breed." Particularly the strict ones, as Miss Hamilton had been.

"Her popularity might have increased if they had known she was working a case for the Pinkerton Agency at the time," Concordia's mother said, a mischievous glint in her eye.

Concordia smiled. Penelope had tried on several occasions to recruit her for Pinkerton work. Their joint assignment last summer in San Francisco was enough adventure for a lifetime.

"Let me help you with your train," Charlotte said, shaking out the folds.

Concordia eyed Charlotte's gown, a high-cut satin duchesse. "I'm glad we decided on the peach tint. It's most becoming."

Since Sophia was in no condition to serve as Concordia's Lady of Honor—the baby was due any day now—Charlotte had agreed to fill the role.

With a twinkle, Concordia added, "Mr. Maynard is sure to like it."

Charlotte blushed and self-consciously smoothed the skirt.

Randolph Maynard had remained true to his resolve, only once making use of Miss Banning's confession: to convince Lady Dunwick of his innocence. According to Charlotte, his discretion and selflessness had impressed her aunt, who permitted their courtship to resume, discreetly. If Lieutenant Capshaw knew Maynard had possession of Miss Banning's confession, he gave no indication. Mrs. Sanbourne's death remained officially unsolved.

The whole affair was briefly revived when Peter Sanbourne's body was discovered in a back alley in Hamburg. There was no sign of the blueprint. By that time, the college had turned over Sanbourne's notes to the Navy, dismantled the engineering laboratory, donated the equipment to Boston Tech, and washed its hands of the program for good.

Public opinion alternately sneered and sympathized with the college's attempt to offer women such a progressive course of study, but most considered the incidents confined to the unsavory Sanbournes and the now-defunct program rather than the school as a whole.

Eventually the newspapers moved on to fresher news, including the latest in the Philippine-American War. It was certainly a relief to the faculty and staff of Hartford Women's College. They wanted to get back to the business of educating young women for the challenges of a new century.

Mrs. Wells turned toward the window. "What is that *noise?*"

A rhythmic pounding in the distance echoed against the stone walls of the chapel.

"Ah." Charlotte cocked her head to listen. "Hammers, I expect."

"They are re-building Willow Cottage," Concordia added, noting her mother's puzzled frown.

The lady's frown deepened. "Why *today*, of all days?"

"They must take advantage of the good weather. It's only two months before the students return," Concordia said.

Mrs. Wells nodded toward Charlotte. "I hear you will be taking my daughter's place as teacher-in-residence. Congratulations."

Charlotte smiled. "I am looking forward to it."

Concordia was silent. Despite all of the daily aggravations that came with living among two-dozen lively young ladies, she would miss it. The farmhouse would be quiet without them.

Mrs. Wells gave Concordia a quick glance and pursed her lips. "Miss Crandall, would you tell Mr. Langdon to expect us in a few minutes?"

Once Charlotte had left on her errand, Mrs. Wells sat down on the bench and patted the seat beside her. Concordia sighed. They had already had a private talk about what a woman should expect on her honeymoon. She did not think another speech was in order.

Her mother had something else in mind. "You know I am thrilled about you marrying David, but…are *you* happy?"

Concordia smiled, clasping her mother's delicate, blue-veined hands. "There are new adventures ahead. I am happy."

Mrs. Wells nodded. "With the right man, marriage can be delightful."

Concordia's eyes crinkled mischievously. "There is that, of course, but I was referring to something else. Mr. Langdon has offered me a position."

Her mother's eyes widened. "A…a position? Surely you have not accepted it?"

Concordia laughed. "Of course I have. Don't worry. David knows all about it."

"Indeed," her mother said faintly. "I thought the college would not permit a married woman to teach."

Concordia nodded. "This is something else. I am to be a lecturing fellow for the literature department. The college has never had one, although the position is not unheard of at other schools. My duties will include overseeing the seniors' independent study projects and conducting monthly seminars." She felt a rush of gratitude for Miss Kimble's creative appropriation of funds and President Langdon's equally creative job designation, which had circumvented the need for board approval. Her duties would ease the workload of the short-staffed English department. Not even Maynard had protested.

She smiled to herself, remembering what a lady on last summer's cross-country train trip had told her: *You must be the exception, rather than the rule.* She had been right. Perhaps, over time, such a circumstance would become the rule rather than the exception.

Mrs. Wells frowned. "That is quite a lot to be responsible for, in addition to being a wife."

"No more burdensome than those charity projects you took up when Papa was alive. The duties are light in comparison to what I did before." She grinned. "I am wondering what I shall do with all of my leisure time."

Mrs. Wells raised an eyebrow. "Should you find time on your hands, you may always visit your poor, neglected mother. But keep in mind, running one's own household is more time-consuming than it might seem."

"At least I will not have to cook." Their savings from the lower price of the Armstrong house had enabled them to hire someone.

Mrs. Wells rolled her eyes. "Do not remind me of how remiss I had been in not teaching you that skill. It was difficult to extricate you from the library when you were growing up. How long will you be a...a—"

"—lecturing fellow," Concordia said. "The appointment is renewable yearly. It will depend upon the needs of the college."

"Or a change in your own circumstances, such as children?" Mrs. Wells asked with a twinkle.

Concordia blushed. Children. *Land sakes.* Four chickens and Miss Banning's moody cat were sufficient for now.

Charlotte tapped on the door and stuck her head in. "Whenever you are ready. Everyone is in place."

Concordia took a breath. "Ready."

Charlotte passed her the bouquet of peach roses and white orange blossoms, trimmed in pale green satin ribbon. Concordia's mother arranged the veil over her face. "Shall we remove your spectacles, dear?"

Concordia shook her head. "I want to do this with my eyes wide open."

They left through the outside door of the vesting room, following the stone-paved path around to the chapel's front doors. With a final squeeze of Concordia's hand, Mrs. Wells slipped into the chapel to be escorted to her seat.

President Langdon waited for Concordia just outside the doors. She put a hand to her sun-dazzled eyes for a better look at the man who would accompany her down the aisle. Instead of his usual rumpled jacket, ill-fitting trousers and dusty shoes, Langdon was attired in grand style for the occasion, sporting light gray pleated trousers, white foulard cravat, and a dapper Prince Albert coat. The effect was only slightly undermined by the strained buttons at his middle.

He gave her a wide smile and held out his arm. "You look absolutely lovely, my dear. That Bradley fellow is a lucky man."

She gripped his arm, suddenly taken with a fit of nerves. *She was going to do this. She was going to be married.* If only Papa were here.

It was as if she had said it aloud. Langdon patted her hand in reassurance. "Your father would have been pleased to see the woman you have become. I am a poor substitute, but we must make do, mustn't we?"

Concordia smiled. During her years at the college, Langdon had been her staunch ally, very nearly like a father to her. "It will be more than 'making do,' sir."

The ushers pulled the doors wide. Langdon tugged at his jacket and assumed his most dignified expression. "Shall we?"

Sarah and Gracie, combed and scrubbed within an inch of their lives, waited eagerly with Charlotte in the vestibule. Concordia bent down and gave her young cousins a hug. "What beautiful young ladies I have to accompany me," she murmured. Their faces glowed with excitement beneath their charming white chip bonnets, trimmed in pale green ribbon and white lace. Gracie swished the full skirts of her dotted muslin. Her older sister put a hand on her arm to keep her still.

"Remember now," Charlotte Crandall whispered to the girls, "just as we practiced." She gave them a gentle prod as the organist played the first notes of Mendelssohn's wedding march from *A Midsummer Night's Dream.* The congregation stood and turned as one to face the back of the church.

"*Mercy,*" Concordia muttered under her breath. She had not had so many eyes upon her at chapel since her first day of teaching here, when she and her charges had been late to morning service.

Walking side by side, the girls proceeded at a dignified pace up the center aisle toward the chancel, followed by Charlotte, then Concordia and Langdon.

Concordia was grateful for the veil that obscured her flushed cheeks and misting eyes. She clung to Langdon's arm to steady her steps. Every pew she passed held smiling associates, friends, and loved ones: Miss Pomeroy, Miss Jenkins, Miss Kimble, Mr. Maynard...so many. Ruby Hitchcock was already wiping her eyes. Alison Smedley and Maisie Lovelace had returned for the occasion, and fluttered their handkerchiefs as she passed. And there was Penelope Hamilton, too, eyes shining with happiness—and perhaps a tear or two. She inclined her head in greeting as Concordia passed by. The lady seemed as reserved as ever, though she *did* surreptitiously pull her handkerchief from her sleeve.

Concordia stopped heeding them all as she approached David, waiting in front of the sanctuary steps, his father as best man standing beside him. Her heart leapt in her throat. David looked quite handsome today, dressed in a finely tailored, dark frock coat and light-gray pinstripe trousers. His hair curled at the collar in a manner that made her want to smooth it aside. His eyes held the promise of love and longing that she recognized within herself, and something more. She could not look away. A thrill ran through her at the many aspects of the man she would come to know.

The moment felt strangely private between them. Langdon stepped aside with a light squeeze of her hand and the organ music ceased. The minister cleared his throat. Startled, Concordia and David came out of themselves to commence the business of getting married properly.

The ceremony itself was a blur of bible readings, vows, kneeling, ring, and pronouncements. It was only when David tenderly lifted her veil away from her face and pressed his lips to hers that Concordia came back to herself. His kiss was warm and pledged more than could be expressed in present company. Concordia returned it with a full heart.

They drew apart amidst cheers, applause, and mothers sniffling in the front pews.

"Mercy," she murmured, sniffling a bit herself.

David grinned and handed her his kerchief. "I hope your nose does not run every time I kiss you, Mrs. Bradley," he teased, "for I plan to do so with great regularity."

She let out a contented sigh as they led the recessional down the aisle and out the chapel doors. "I suppose we must take that chance."

He drew her hand through the crook of his arm as they turned to greet their well-wishers.

THE END

Afterword

It's a great time to be a historical author, with the wealth of digitized historical material available on the internet. For anyone interested in the background research that went into the writing of this book (including a link to the full text of Mrs. John Sherwood's *Manners and Social Usages*), I've shared some wonderful primary and secondary sources on my website, kbowenmysteries(dot)com. I'd love to see you there.

I hope you enjoyed the novel. Should you feel so inclined, please consider leaving a review on your favorite online book venue. Word of mouth is essential to help readers find books they will love, particularly those written by independently published authors. Thank you!

To order other books in the Concordia Wells series, please visit kbowenmysteries(dot)com and click on the "Books" tab. Purchase links to all of the online venues are provided.

Also by K.B. Owen

From The Concordia Wells Mysteries:

Dangerous and Unseemly (book 1)

Unseemly Pursuits (book 2)

Unseemly Ambition (book 3)

Unseemly Haste (book 4)

From The Chronicles of a Lady Detective:

Never Sleep

Acknowledgments

Many people have had a hand in bringing this book into the world, and I want to express my sincerest thanks to them here. Among those who helped were several experts and scholars. Any errors found are solely mine, not theirs.

To Pamela Mack, Ph.D., at Clemson State University, who generously provided information about women engineers in the late-nineteenth century.

To firefighter Andrew Camp, for his expertise, and to writer Laura Feigin, for facilitating my query.

To Luci Zahray, the "Poison Lady," who helped with a crucial question.

To Carla Marcinek, RN, who helped with medical information.

To Debora Lewis for her formatting of the print version. You truly make these words a thing of beauty.

To artist Melinda VanLone, who never fails to create such wonderful covers. I am grateful for her time and talents. Melinda can be reached at BookCoverCorner(dot)com.

To Kristen Lamb, Piper Bayard, and the generous community of fellow writers known as WANAs, for their advice and support. We are truly not alone.

To Vinnie Hansen, for her wonderfully helpful edits, and Kirsten Weiss, for proofing and formatting the ebook editions.

To my parents-in-law, Steve and Lyn, and the extended Owen clan. Thanks for cheering me on!

To my dad, Steve Belin, who passed away during the writing of this book. I miss you.

To my mom, Agnes Belin, who enthusiastically supports my writing career and instilled an abiding love of reading.

To my sons, Patrick, Liam, and Corey, who encourage me and make me laugh.

To Paul Owen, my husband and my love. I waited to dedicate this particular book to you. May Concordia be as happy as we are.

K.B. Owen
November 2016